"Here's the real lowd
everybody—the mc
swinging novel abc
business in twenty y⊞⊓⊔⊐.
Claude Thornhill

"In *Angel's Flight*, Lou Cameron
created a be-bop jive jazz noir novel
that sings loud and true with terrific
characters…an underrated and
unacknowledged noir masterpiece."
Gary Lovisi, *Paperback Parade*

ANGEL'S FLIGHT
Lou Cameron

Black Gat Books • Eureka California

ANGEL'S FLIGHT

Published by Black Gat Books
A division of Stark House Press
1315 H Street
Eureka, CA 95501, USA
griffinskye3@sbcglobal.net
www.starkhousepress.com

ANGEL'S FLIGHT
Originally published in paperback by Gold Medal
Books, Greenwich, and copyright © 1960 by Fawcett
Publications, Inc.

"Angel's Flight: Cool Jazz & Hot Murder" copyright
© 2016 by Gary Lovisi. All rights reserved.

ISBN: 978-1-944520-18-2

Book design by Mark Shepard, SHEPGRAPHICS.COM
Cover art by Mitchell Hooks

First Black Gat Edition: February 2017

First Edition

Angel's Flight:
Cool Jazz & Hot Murder
by Gary Lovisi

It is *soooo* good.

Soooo perfect!

Can a novel be so good you could say it was perfect? The answer is yes.

I can promise you that this book you are about to read will give you a jolting experience you will not soon forget. *Angel's Flight* is a classic crime masterpiece of darkness and doom set to a jazz and a be-bop beat. It's not noir despair — because it goes even lower than noir — it delves into what you might almost call — anti-life! It's that dark, dismal, and it's that good a read!

Angel's Flight was crime and thriller novelist Lou Cameron's first novel. It was originally published in 1960 as a Gold Medal Books paperback original, (#S1047), with stunning sexy gal cover art by Mitchell Hooks. As far as I know this book has never been reprinted. In 2015, in my book collector magazine *Paperback Parade* (#90), I wrote an article in praise of this book. As a result, Greg Shepard the keen-eyed publisher of Stark House Press read the book and knew it deserved to be reprinted for a new generation of readers and fans. So this new Stark House Press, special Black Gat edition — after over half a century — is now available, well overdue, and most welcome for crime noir aficionados and collectors.

The story begins in the Depression Era jazz world. What was called the Dirty Thirties, then moves to 1939 when Germany invaded Poland, then 1940 when FDR sends help to Churchill and England during The Battle of Britain and on to the close of World War Two, and later into the Korean War. However, this is not a war novel at all. Cameron only mentions these then current events through his narrator Ben Parker, to put this decades long saga of the music business into historical perspective. Cameron is telling a grand story, an epic of sorts — a noir horror tale set to a hot jazz beat.

This is Ben Parker's story. Ben's a decent bass who is one of only three white boys in Daddy Holloway and his Hot Babies jazz band. Daddy is a three-hundred pound black piano player and most of the band is African-American of various shades of black, but Ben fits in because he's a good musician and a real friend to Daddy whom he has known for many years and has great respect. Daddy's a cool cat, a leader and a talented musician — he coulda been a contender if not for his race. These are jim crow days, and worse. Daddy plays those piano keys hard and true as he travels the country with his band, with his gorgeous mixed race daughter, Blanche, in tow. Daddy has a lot of demons that cause him to pound those piano keys like a demon himself. He's made his band a jazz legend during the Depression and in him Cameron has created a terrific and fascinating character. But Daddy's not the only character who will ring true, or tug at your heart in this fine novel. In fact, the entire book is crammed with cool cats, fascinating guys and gals of all types, and a lot of really interesting jazz and jive talk of the era that makes it a compelling read. The language Cameron has Parker use to tell his story is vibrant and rich and it rings bold and true like the music itself. Cameron uses that language like a master craftsman as he builds this compelling tale of music, life, betrayal, and much worse.

Ben Parker's life takes so many twists and turns you could get whiplash from reading this book. Those around Ben are shown effected by the times, by the changes in jazz and the prejudices of those times which Cameron chronicles so well; the pain, the anger, the deep hurt of betrayal. The chief betrayer of them all is a young punk name of Johnny Angel. He shows up one night at one of Daddy Holloway's gigs. He is introduced in this brief excerpt from the opening of the book:

We were playing a club in downtown L.A. the night Johnny Angel blew in. That is, the first time I noticed him. I never paid no mind to the savages when I was up there on the podium, but during intermission Daddy signaled me into the wings and pointed him out.

"Benny," he said, his eyes sort of narrow, "you dig that ofay punk in the George Raft shirt?"

I looked where he was pointing. A tall blond kid in a cream sports jacket and black shirt was holding up one of the pillars near the percussion end of the stand. He was about nineteen or twenty. Sharp and good looking. He knew it.

I said, "A punk, Daddy. What about him?"

"He taggin' us, Benny. He been at every date for the past month. What do you 'spose he want?"

"So what should I do, ask him?"

Daddy looked at his watch. "No use flappin' mouths with him Ben. Do we finish this next set, though, I wants you to watch him and Franky the Drum."

"You think he's a fag?"

It was no secret our drummer parted his hair on the wrong side. He was a little mulatto with eyes like a deer. The tall kid in the cream jacket didn't look the type.

And from farther along we read:

Either way you sliced it, I didn't like that punk in the cream colored jacket.

That punk is Johnny Angel, who will destroy everything and everyone he comes into contact with. It is only because Ben is such a talented musician, smart and bold, and a true survivor that he is not destroyed like so many others. However those others are not so lucky and Johnny Angel leaves a mighty pile of misery in his wake. Daddy Holloway is only the beginning. Daddy's a character who is as real as you or I am, a man with deep passions and emotions, one of them guys — you know the type — stand up guys who only seem to get bad breaks. His race is certainly the reason for a lot of his bad breaks, back then it was a brutal world for African-Americans to strive and even survive, but that is not the only reason for Daddy's problems. He's a good man, a trusting man, but when a monster like Johnny Angel enters your life — beware!

Ben opens his story by telling us a little bit about himself to allow us to get to know him and a real feel for his story. Now remember, he's telling us about things that happened in 1939 — in a book that was published way back in 1960 — 57 years ago! It is a black and white world in more ways than one, and no one crosses the color barrier. Cameron does not sugar coat the racism of the era, nor the racial aspects of situations that often effect his characters — both black and white. In the book Ben regularly calls blacks spades, even blacks who are his friends, but never uses the "N" word — and when other whites like Johnny Angel use the "N" word in his presence he angrily calls them out for saying it. Meanwhile, Daddy and other blacks regularly use the words ofay and cracker to describe whites. In this book, because of the times it depicts, words like "spade," "ofay," "cracker," are not always the derogatory words sometimes were used merely as descriptive words. Crude certainly, but descriptive and not hateful among the jazz folk, as they were often used during the times among too many regular people. It was that kind of world. You dig?

Another interesting factoid about this book, it contains what may be the earliest use I've found in popular fiction of the word "gay" for homosexuals. In one part of the book, the subject of the black drummer's homosexuality comes up. Ben and he are friends, but Ben uses the word queer to describe Franky's sexual preference. The drummer tells Ben that he doesn't like that word, that he prefers the word gay. This from a book in 1960. The word "gay" was a term not used in the general culture at that time, but was used for years in the subcultures of jazz, drugs, race, and of course, the beginning gay culture. Just one little interesting part of this book that adds to the ring of truth. Franky definitely had his problems being a drug-using, gay, black man, in a jim crow segregated world, but his worse problem of all turns out to be Johnny Angel.

In *Angel's Flight*, Ben Parker narrates his amazing journey through the world of jazz and his battles with Johnny Angel over the years. It's a wild ride and one rife with deep emotional damage and titanic struggle as Ben plays his gigs, makes his records, tries to break through the crooked payola system to get his music heard. Ben even stoops to playing on risqué stag party records to put food on the table.

Along the way Ben meets a gorgeous singer named Ginger Tracy. She's the gal that Mitchell Hooks has depicted so well in his painting used for the cover of the original vintage Gold Medal paperback.

Ben gives us a description of Ginger's appearance and her singing talent:

The song was supposed to be funny. It wasn't. It left every male in the joint with an empty ache in the pit of his gut. Ginger Tracy was cruelty to animals.

Ultimately, Ben Parker is a survivor. But so is Johnny Angel. Johnny Angel however is not only a survivor but also a user, a betrayer and a con man — not to leave out he's a prime louse and crook. Throughout this book the two men keep crossing paths until there is a final confrontation that will stun you with its utter viciousness and sheer…evil. Johnny Angel turns out to be anything but an angel.

With all that fine story behind it you might assume the title of the book references Johnny Angel himself. It does not. In fact, Angel's Flight is an actual place, a scenic lift in Los Angeles, a place where Ben and Ginger meet for a date that turns to disaster. Four decades later top crime author Michael Connelly would use the title for one of his famed Harry Bosch crime novels *Angel's Flight*, which also concerns events at that historic LA landmark.

The author, Lou Cameron (1924-2010), is well known as an American writer, but he was also an accomplished comic book artist. As a comic book artist, he illustrated Classics Illustrated and horror comics before becoming a writer. Then as a writer, Cameron became the author of dozens of excellent Gold Medal paperback original crime and spy novels written from 1960 to 1992. He also wrote 15 books in The Stringer western series, and dozens of paperback original westerns in The Longarm series under his pseudonym Tabor Evans — he wrote at least 52 books in this series which defined the then new "adult" western genre, in a series that ran to over 400 books. The Longarm series was later continued by James Reasoner. Cameron wrote many other books under many other pseudonyms including John Wesley Howard and Ramsay Thorne, and he wrote many film-to-book novelizations. In 1976, Lou Cameron won the WWA Spur Award for the best western novel of the year for his novel, *The Spirit Horses*.

Angel's Flight from 1960, was Lou Cameron's first book. Judging by this first effort, I am sure many of you will be on the lookout to read his other fine novels. In *Angel's Flight*, Lou Cameron created a be-bop jive jazz noir novel that sings loud and true with terrific characters, has real heart and is a joy to read. Without a doubt it is an under-rated and unacknowledged noir masterpiece. So stop wasting your time with whatever book you are reading now and turn this page so you can begin to take a dive into this vintage story of cool jazz and hot murder. I tell you true, you're in for a real treat!

—Brooklyn, New York
November, 2016

ANGEL'S FLIGHT
Lou Cameron

First time I ever saw Johnny Angel was 'way back in 1939 A. D. when I was still blowing bass with Daddy Halloway and his Hot Babies. Remember the group? Not many people do these days. Not even the longhaired jazz aficionados who argue the merits of Chicago versus New Orleans style.

I don't know what style we played with Daddy. We didn't know we were going to grow up to be Americana. We just blew hot. As hot as we knew how. And Daddy blew the hottest.

We had some good boys in that band. Daddy hired by ear. Didn't matter about your complexion or sex life to old Daddy as long as you blew good. I was one of the three white boys in the band. The others graduated in tone from Tommy the Axe, who could almost pass, all the way down the color scale to Daddy himself, who was black as his piano and damned near as heavy.

We were playing a club date in downtown L.A. the night Johnny Angel blew in. That is, the first time I noticed him. I never paid no mind to the savages when I was up there on the podium, but during intermission Daddy signaled me into the wings and pointed him out.

"Benny," he said, his eyes sort of narrow, "you dig that ofay punk in the George Raft shirt?"

I looked where he was pointing. A tall blond kid in a cream sports jacket and black shirt was holding up one of the pillars near the percussion end of the stand. He was about nineteen or twenty. Sharp and good looking. He knew it.

I said, "A punk, Daddy. What about him?"

"He taggin' us, Benny. He been at every date for the past month. What you 'spose he want?"

"So what should I do, ask him?"

Daddy looked at his watch. "No use flappin' mouths with him, Ben. Do we finish this next set, though, I wants you to watch him and Franky the Drum."

"You think he's a fag?"

It was no secret our drummer parted his hair on the wrong side. He was a little mulatto with eyes like a deer. The tall kid in the cream jacket didn't look the type.

Daddy said, "That ain't what eats me, Benny. Li'l Franky's getting a lag on the beat. I been watching him close. Franky don't blow that drum right, Benny. He on cloud nine!"

I raised a mental eyebrow. It figured, when you thought about it. Dope always starts in the rhythm section. First the drums, then the bass and guitar, on down through the brass to the piano. Don't ask me why. That's just the way it happens.

"You figure this punk's running snow to Franky?" I asked.

"I hope so, Benny. 'Cause if he ain't, he a narcotics man and we in the most of a jam."

"I'll see what I can find out," I said. Daddy nodded. The sweat stood out on his dark face in little beads. He looked at his watch again and said, "The natives is gettin' restless. Let's blow them some vibrations."

Back on the bandstand, I eased in back of the doghouse and waited for Daddy to sound his A. I looked out through the smoke haze at the crowded floor and this kid just leaned against the pillar like he was watching bugs on a pin.

Daddy brought his hand down and stroked the piano like a kitten. The drums picked it up with a soft roll of the brushes and I hit a deep one on the bass. Then, as Daddy walked up the eighty eights, the brass blared out the first eight bars of Angel's Flight. Only that ain't what we called it then.

Fact is, we never called it anything. It was just Daddy Halloway's opening. He'd been blowing it that way for so long most of us forgot how it sent you the first time you heard it. It was the best thing Johnny Angel ever stole.

Yeah, I know the ASCAP credits read Johnny Angel on that and a lot of other hits. I know he's supposed to have written more standards than anybody since Tchaikovsky. And I still say Johnny Angel never wrote nothing but a mess of bum checks.

So who wrote them? Stick around, man, and I'll cue you in on how you get ahead in the field....

If Angel was planning to steal Daddy Halloway's opening the first night I saw him, he didn't show it. Every cat in the joint was jumping by the time we were halfway through it. The chicks wore their skirts short that year, remember? The jitterbug bit was getting big and these babes were throwing legs all over the room. This kid in the Mafia suit just stood there with a coffin nail pasted to his lower lip and looked at us through sleepy bedroom eyes. It was creepy.

I stole a gander at the drums and little Franky was wearing his heart on his sleeve. It would have been funny if it hadn't been so pathetic. Franky kept looking through the smoke at the ofay kid and licking his lips. There was a glassy look to his eyes and his nose was running. He was coked to the eyebrows all right, and in love.

Either way you sliced it, I didn't like that punk in the cream colored jacket.

Before you get the wrong idea about yours truly, I'd better fill you in a little on Ben Parker. That's me.

At a very early age I discovered I was queer, for women. I've never had to fight the bottle too hard, and you couldn't get me to take a puff on a stick, or a shot of stuff, at the point of a gun. In some circles this makes me sort of a square. But I survive.

As far as spades go, I can take them or leave them. Some, like everybody knows, act like they ain't been down out of the trees as long as the rest of us. Others have turned out to be right guys. One of the nicest spades I ever knew was Daddy Halloway. The other one was

Franky the Drum.

Sure, he was a junkie and a queer. But one time in Salt Lake City, when the depression was blowing hard and cold and I hadn't played a date for many moons, Franky got me third chair in a spaghetti joint down by the tracks. They paid off in minestrone, but it kept us off the streets during the winter of '32, and that was one cold winter, Dad.

Another time, when I was stranded on the Borsht Circuit, I wired a lot of people for a ticket back to the Big Apple. Franky was the only cat who sent me one. Later on, they told me Franky sent me his last skin and had to hit the blood bank before payday. Not many cats, black or white, will give a pint of blood for a guy. Franky was as queer as a three dollar bill but, like, a friend.

The kid who'd latched on to Franky took a powder just before the last number. I eased off the bass and stood there for a few beats, while the savages got the message there was no doom doom in this part of the great American classic, Love Me Baby, With a Boogie Beat.

Halloway looked up and raised an eyebrow. I pointed with my chin at the empty pillar and raised an eyebrow back at him. He nodded and I slipped off the stand into the wings.

I circled the floor. Trying to spot the cream jacket amid the flying fannies and swirling skirts of the jitterbugs. It was no go. The kid had vanished from the scene. I checked the john and the bar and the parking lot and came up with zero. By the time I got back the band was swinging Good Night Sweetheart with a boogie beat and the savages were leaving.

Franky took off like a big bird for the john and never came back while we packed the show away. Daddy got me off to one side and said, "You know where that poor fruit live, Benny?"

"Sure, he's got a walkup over on Central Avenue. Want

me to check it, Daddy?"

"You think you up to it, Benny? It open season on white meat after midnight in that part of town. I'd go along, only Blanche gonna worry I in the bag agin."

"You go on home, Daddy. I'll tiptoe over and see what gives."

"You lemme know, huh, Benny? I be up all night does you find out anything."

I left Daddy sweating with all his three hundred pounds and went out to the parking lot. I piled into my maroon V-8 and gowed out. I was worried about Daddy a lot more than I was our rash drummer boy. The worst thing that could happen to Franky was getting rolled or picked up by the fuzz. If Daddy worried himself off the wagon the finance company was apt to see a lot more of my Detroit iron than I was.

I parked the heap a half block off Central Avenue and got out. A trio of sullen spade kids came up and asked for two bits to "watch the car." I gave it to them. They wouldn't watch it, but they wouldn't decorate the fenders with beer can openers either.

Franky lived in a six family frame house up the block. I ignored the stares of the spades on the porch and went in. Halfways up the back stairs I heard the beat.

For a moment I thought Franky was practicing with the brushes, though I'd never known a side man to blow alone. Then I dug the fact that Franky wasn't on the traps. It was someone else. Somebody who handled the brushes exactly like Franky. But, somehow, not the same.

It was a cold beat. Fast and tricky and cold. Those skins were getting hell stroked out of them with both brushes but it came out cold. Whoever was on those traps blew fast, but so does a rattlesnake. And you can't swing to a rattlesnake's beat. Not you, not me, not nobody.

I hit the door a couple of times to be polite and walked in. Franky was spread out on the bed with his eyes open, staring at the ceiling but not seeing it. His sleeves were rolled up and I could see the blue marks on his coffee and cream skin. He'd been taking it in the main line and there was no use ringing his number until he came back from pixieville.

The cat in the Mussolini shirt was sitting in on the traps. His jacket was thrown over a chair and his hair hung down over his eyes. He was chewing gum a mile a minute with no expression on his robot pan. Talk about poker faces! This cat made Coolidge look like Jimmy Durante.

"Johnny Angel," he said, not looking up from the drums.

"I'm Ben Parker," I said. "What's up there, anyway?"

"What's up where, Dad?"

"Up there on Angel's Flight. It's about a block from the club, kid. Couldn't you have swiped a name from farther away? What's wrong with Griffith Park or San Pedro?"

He stopped like I'd cut his ignition and sat there for a minute, looking at me with those cobra eyes of his. Finally he smiled boyishly with his mouth. A crooked, "cute" sort of grin. The kind Mickey Rooney used to use in those Andy Hardy pictures. The only thing wrong was that his eyes stayed just as cold as ever.

"You're pretty sharp, Mr. Parker," he said. "Not many guys would have noticed the connection. But it's still Johnny Angel. It's a lot more commercial than the one my mother hung on me a while back."

"When was that, kid?"

"You writing a book, Mr. Parker?"

"I'm a friend of Franky's."

For the first time I saw a glimmer of expression in his eyes. A sort of nasty cold humor.

"Really?" He grinned. "Are you the boy or the girl?"

"You're pretty fresh, punk. How'd you like to try for a fat lip?"

Angel pasted another smile across his pan and said, "Relax, Mr. Parker. Sometimes I sound off before I think.

Hell, I wouldn't blame you for thinking *I* was a fairy, rooming here with Franky and all."

"Matter of fact, kid, I think you're a junk pusher. That worries me one hell of a lot more than your sex life. How long you think Franky's going to last taking it in the vein?"

Angel shrugged. "He's a big boy, Mr. Parker. He can take care of himself. Besides, I ain't giving it to him. He buys it off an old goat in a wheel chair near the park."

"And you've been running it for him?"

"Hell no. You know a nigger pusher won't sell snow to us ofay."

"Look, Angel, if you know enough to call a white man ofay, you know better than to call a spade a nigger in this part of town."

The kid shrugged and brushed at the brass like he was swatting flies. I still couldn't figure it.

I said, "O.K. Angel. I'll buy you being square. I'll buy you ain't on the junk or pushing it. Now tell me, just what in hell is your angle? You ain't rooming with Franky to hear him snore!"

Johnny Angel said, "He's been giving me lessons on the traps."

"He's been *what?*"

"You deaf or sumpin? Frank's been teaching me how to blow drums. He latched on to me up in Bakersfield and told me about all the dough you guys make. All the broads you get. I decided that was for me. Old Frank asked me to come down to L.A. with him and I said I would if he got me a chair in the band. He said I had to blow something. So I'm learning to blow drums."

"Goddam," I laughed, "I've heard of opportunists, but you get the gold ring, Angel. What about Franky's unusual views on love?"

"Aw, he gets gay once in a while. But I slap the little coon down and tell him I'm going to walk out on him."

"Yeah," I sneered, "I can see you walking out on a free meal ticket, Angel."

The kid laughed. His teeth were regular and even but they sloped inwards like a rat's.

He chuckled. "Not until I don't need him no more. But the dumb nigger don't know that. O.K. *spade*, then, call the fag bastard anything you want. He's still got to pay for breathing the same air as me."

"How long you think he's going to breathe, Johnny, with him on the snow?"

"Who cares?"

"I do, punk. Franky's a good guy. Even if he is a little mixed up."

"A *little?* Hah!"

"O.K. He's mixed up for real. He's latched on to a creepy little punk who won't even put out for him and now he's so gaga he has to take dope to control himself. Let's just say I'm a cold blooded bastard who doesn't want to see the combo open some night without drums."

Angel looked over at the sleeping hophead and grinned.

"Relax, Dad," he said. "Anytime Franky can't sit in you got somebody just as good."

"Yeah? Who?"

"Me. Who else?"

"You little crud. You couldn't blow washboards on the Grand Old Operee!"

"Don't make book on it, Parker. I'm taking lessons."

□   □   □

I drove over to Daddy Halloway's to cue him in. His daughter Blanche met me at the door. I could see she'd been crying. I started to put my arm around her to comfort her. Then I thought better of it. Blanche had that effect on me.

Her mother had been almost white, and Daddy himself must have had more than his share of non-African ancestry a ways back. In any country but the land of the free she'd have been considered a white girl with a dash of Negro blood. Here she was a spade babe with a touch of ofay.

I've got nothing much against crossing the color line if a cat's willing to pay the price of crusading. But not with a girl like Blanche. She was one of the few members of her generation who'd managed to come through the depression thinking the world was run on the level, and I wasn't about to be the bastard who taught her different.

Daddy was in the parlor, halfway down a bottle of scotch. One thing you had to say for Daddy. When he got boiled he got boiled on good sauce. I sat down next to him and said, "It's O.K. Daddy. I checked on Franky and everything's jake."

"Who this cat Jake?" he mumbled. "Have a li'l drink, Benny boy." I poured myself a shot. The sooner the bottle was used up the better. I asked Blanche for a bottle of Coke as a chaser. I could match Daddy shot for shot without getting boiled by taking the scotch in my mouth from the glass and spitting it in the Coke bottle while I pretended to drink the chaser. It was a trick I'd learned one time from a friendly B girl on the Sunset Strip. I taught her to play chess in return.

Blanche brought me the Coke and said, "Daddy, you have to get up in the morning, remember?"

"Sure, baby. Jus' le's have another li'l drink wif my ofay brother here."

Blanche gave me a hurt look of apology. I shrugged. A spade couldn't insult me by calling me white. But it cut a little to have it come from Daddy Halloway. We'd known each other long enough for the invisible clubs to be put away, if they ever are.

Halloway shook his head and looked at me with red rimmed eyes. "I sorry, Benny," he said. "Ol' nigger wounds bleedin' bad tonight and I gotta carve somebody. You the only white man around. Have a drink, Benny."

"I got one, Daddy. I came over to tell you Franky's O.K. That kid's just a little queer hustler looking for free eats."

"Dirty li'l no-count nigger," said Daddy, not hearing me. "Li'l ol' high yellow piece of uppity crud! You know me a few years, Benny, that right?"

"That's right, Daddy."

"An' in all them years you ever see me mess with ofay stuff, man?" Daddy looked down into his glass like it was a deep well and said, "Lord knows I taken a lot of crap off white folks, Ben. I older than you. I born in Montgomery when they still hung a nigger ever Fourth of July. My granddaddy was a slave. Regular cotton pickin' slave wif whip marks on he back. You know that, Benny?

"I taken a lot of it, white boy. More than the good lord should have heaped on one poor nigger. If I didn't know how to blow hot on the Steinway I reckon I'd have picked my share of cotton too.

"Nowdays it's *très chic* to listen to jazz, Ben. They writin' books about it today. A lot of crap about the blendin' of the African's blue tonality wif the disciplined harmonies of western civilization. Man! Ain't that a mouthful of big words?

"You know what jazz means, Benny? I tell you what it means. It's a nigger word for what polite folks calls lovin'. Do my mammy hear me sayin' jazz when I was a li'l delta country boy, she'd have washed my mouth out with soft soap. It was still a dirty word when I started blowing piano in a New Orleans whorehouse, Ben. White men what would have killed me for looking at they wives used to get their kicks from coming down to the quarter and layin' yellow gals while me and the boys blew Jazz for them. Man, you should have seen some of the dances them yellow gals put on when we played Jelly Roll. An' you knows what jelly roll really is, Benny?"

"Sure, Daddy. I know all about Jelly Roll, Sea Food, and Boogie Woogie. I know they don't mean what our

LOU CAMERON

"Shut up and drink you booze while I blows my history lesson, Benny. It's like I said. We started out low down and we ain't really come much higher. White man's let us move from the whorehouse to the dance hall, long as we don't want to marry his daughter.

"But it still there, Benny. It still there. I got me a nice hot li'l combo. Got me three ofay side men sittin' in, and everybody jump when Daddy hollers Froggy. But it don't do me no good, Benny. It don't wipe the black off."

"Aw Daddy, for God's sake!"

"Don' God's sake me, man. You white! Only time you gotta think about the mess is when you see one of us cats. When you walk down a street the odds is ten to one the next guy you bump into is gonna be white. But we got it starin' at us out of ever magazine. Out of ever store window. This goddam country's been taken over by the ofay, Benny. You know that?"

"Sure, Daddy. It's a communist plot. What's that got to do with Franky the Drum?"

"Franky? That li'l bitty high yellow uppity crud? I tell you what it got to do with him. It shame him. That's what it got to do with him. It shame him so bad he take dope and turn fruit just to get next to white meat. He make me sick. Him and niggers like him. They hears all they lives what crud niggers is until they believes it theyselves!

"I take a lot, Ben. I take crap off bitty high school kids who want to hear the big fat nigger blow boogie woogie. I know what they thinks of me while I up there on the podium, and I don't like it. I don't like it one little bit. It make me mad, Ben. It make me want to kill me some ofay. But it don't shame me! I know I just as good as they is and maybe better. I don't have to lay some mixed up ofay whore to prove it! You thinks I ain't had the chance, Ben? You think I too black to get me some white meat? I got news for you, Ben. I too *proud!*

"I too proud to get in the feathers wif a woman who think she better than me. Any gal thinks because her ancestors stopped eatin' each other a few thousand years before mine did makes her special don't have to do me no favors! She kin take her Toleration and shove it!"

I gulped my scotch. I needed it. I'd seen Daddy in the bag before but this was the worse crying jag I could remember. I hoped he wouldn't remember all this in the morning.

Daddy poured himself another drink. I wondered about taking the bottle away from him. It wouldn't do any good. He'd just get another. When he was this far gone he'd drink Sterno. I decided he was better off on good booze.

"Do Jesus, I talks too much." Daddy laughed, downing the drink in one gulp and pouring another. "I swear I sound like one of Ma Roosevelt's crowd."

"Forget it, Daddy. It's a lousy mess."

"Mess ain't the word, Benny. It *bad*, I mean. Everybody pickin' on everbody else. Rich man pickin' on poor man, poor man pickin' on niggers, niggers pickin' on dogs and dogs pickin' on cats. And the cats pickin' on the poor li'l mices. I wonders who the mices pick on? How you feel about mices, Benny?"

"They're O.K.," I said, "but I wouldn't want one to marry my daughter." Daddy Halloway looked blank and then his face split open in a wide grin.

"You *drunk*, Benny!" he said. I wished I was.

"You say this ofay kid with Franky's jus' a hustler?" asked Daddy in suddenly restored good humor.

"He's a cheap little stooge. Wants to blow drums. He's nasty but harmless."

Which just goes to show you how drunk I really was. A lot of cats thought Hitler was a comical little man in baggy pants at about the same time.

I got Daddy onto the subject of our next club date in

Santa Monica and left him in a smiling stupor after helping him off with his shoes and propping his feet up on the couch.

When I tiptoed to the door he was humming Yellow Dog Blues and feeling no pain. I stood for a moment in the doorway and thought, "Poor Daddy, it even hurts a man like you. No matter how big you get, no matter how many white friends you have, a snide remark from an ofay soda jerk can send you back inside that terrible wall you guys throw up at the first whiff of insult."

Blanche let me out of the apartment and followed me out into the hall. She touched my sleeve and said, "I want to talk to you, Ben."

"Sure, kid," I said. "What's up?"

"Not here, Ben. It's private."

I took her across the street to an all night diner. It was a spade joint. The counterman gave us a funny look as I ordered coffee. I wondered how cats who marry across the line take it. Blanche was well dressed, every inch a lady, and beautiful. Yet I felt more embarrassed to be seen on the street with her than a Fifth and Hill streetwalker.

"I'm worried about Daddy, Ben," she said.

"Who isn't?"

"You don't understand. It's something the doctors told me. Daddy's liver has gone bad, Ben. One more drinking bout like the last one will kill him."

I whistled silently. "As bad as that, huh?"

"Ben, you've got to keep him off of it!"

"How, honey? I'm not his mother!"

"Then you'll have to sit in until he gets one, Ben. I'm not kidding. If he starts up again like he did in Bakersfield he's going to die. And Ben, I love my poor old Daddy."

"So do I, kitten," I said. She touched my hand and the hairs on the back of my neck rose. "I know, Ben," she said in a low husky voice. I mumbled something asinine and paid off the smirking spade behind the counter. Outside, she said, "I'll cross myself, Ben. Daddy may be up. Promise you'll watch out for him?"

"I promise." We stood there looking at each other for a minute while I wondered if she was expecting me to kiss her, and what she'd do if I did, and how she'd feel if I didn't. She turned and walked across the street and I started to breathe again.

Daddy's daughter had sure as hell become a big girl in the past few years. If a guy *was* going to be a crusader, Blanche Halloway wouldn't be such a heavy cross to bear.

"Trying to change your luck, buddy?" asked a voice in my ear. I turned and glared at the red faced cop who was watching Blanche approvingly from the curb. I said, "Just an old friend, mac." I wanted to punch his grinning mouth, but he was bigger than both of us and I didn't know what it would prove. As I walked towards my car he laughed. "I wish I could meet some friends like her, buddy. And you spell that meet, m-e-a-t."

I didn't answer. Blanche could be a very heavy cross, after all.

□   □   □

A few nights later, driving to the club, I stopped the heap near Angel's Flight. I hadn't taken a close look at the thing lately. I was thinking about the punk who called himself Johnny Angel as I stood and watched the overgrown sand toy. It was sort of fascinating to watch. Like a steam shovel, or a hanging.

Angel's Flight is a funicular railway up the steepest hill in the L.A. city limits. There were two ways to get to the top of Angel's Flight. One way was by the incredibly long staircase that wound up through the Mexican slum that clung like lichen to the slopes of the hill. The other way was a bit more adventurous.

A triple gauge track ran up the slope at an impossible angle. It looked steeper than a playground slide. Running on the tracks were two dinky yellow cars attached to opposite ends of the same steel cable. At the top of the hill stood a winch house where a big steel drum pulled one car up as the other one went down, like a yo-yo. The cars were built like lopsided Toonerville Trolleys that got stepped on. They were all out of shape so that the passengers could sit upright as they rode up the hill. The floors of the cars were built like flights of stairs and gothic windows were staggered like steps up the yellow sides of the cars. I guess you might say they were quaint.

There was a ding ding from one of the cars and it started up the slope of Angel's Flight. A girl screamed. One always did. Beside me, somebody said, "I wonder what's up there. Up there on top."

"Same thing as down here," I answered. "Couple of bars, a chili parlor, and a whorehouse." Then I saw it was Johnny Angel.

"Just the same," he said, "I'm going up there, Ben."

"Not on my nickel, junior. And don't be so goddam formal. Just call me Mr. Parker."

I turned and walked towards the club. Angel followed me. He'd traded in the cream jacket for a zooty number with lavender pin stripes and no lapels. Either he was fruit for black shirts or he only owned one. He'd also latched on to a gold satin necktie with black musical notes painted on it.

"You don't like me, do you?" Angel asked. He didn't sound like it bothered him.

I said, "Kid, that is the understatement of the year."

"Any particular reason?"

"How do you want them, alphabetical or numerical order, punk?"

"Oh, very very funny. I'd rather look at a plate of worms than your fat face anyways. But I figure we might as well be polite to each other. We're practically the only white men in the group."

I laughed. "What makes you a white man? And who said you were in the group?"

Angel shrugged and said, "Frank says I can fill in for him on the traps when he's feeling low."

"That's real nice of Franky," I said. "Only the band happens to belong to Daddy Halloway."

"Well, sure, I know I got to get his O.K."

"Wrong again, junior. You have to get *my* O.K. I'm second chair and bandmaster. When I ain't blowing doghouse I write the book and do any hiring or firing that's needed. And, Angel, you are one cat who's fired in advance!"

There's a law against clouting angels in the L.A. city limits. I couldn't stop him from tagging along to the club. I made a mental note to tell Franky he'd better keep his boy off the street at night and ankled in the side entrance. The house man didn't stop Angel so I knew Franky'd given him carte blanche. I was about to change this sad state of affairs when Chico the Sax came over and said, "Benny. Daddy ain't here yet!" I looked at my watch and forgot all about Angel. We were going on in fifteen minutes and the Hot Babies were missing three chairs.

Tommy the Axe was living with a white girl in Culver City and usually just made it before the doors opened. Daddy was always up at the Steinway half an hour before the date, but he wasn't there now, and Franky the Drum was nowheres to be seen. I turned to Angel and said, "O.K. Angel, where's your lover boy tonight?"

"Last time I seen him he was headed downtown."

"When was that?"

"'Bout ten in the A.M. I guess. He never came back."

"Goddam. He could be anywheres. Was he hopped up?"

Angel grinned as if the idea amused him. He shrugged and said, "Not so's you could notice it, Ben."

I said, "Chico, Franky call in tonight?" Chico the Sax shook his head and I started to sweat. It was too late to

get another drum. If you've ever heard a jazz combo trying
to blow boogie woogie without a beat you'll know why I
was sweating.

Daddy Halloway blew in a few minutes before they
opened the doors to the savages. He was listing to star-
board. Blanche was trying to keep him on his feet with
the aid of a cab driver. It wasn't easy.

Tommy came in with his axe. A guitar is maybe the one
instrument a jazz combo can make it without. But our piano was boiled and our traps were nonexistent. I turned
to Chico and said, "Get some hot coffee." Daddy heard
me.

"Wuffo' you wants hot coffee, white boy?" He laughed.
"I don' need no bath! Jus' lead me over to them eighty
eights and stan' back! I *hot* tonight, chillun. Tonight we
gonna purely *fly!*"

Blanche said, "He's been like that all day, Ben. What
are we going to do?"

"He'll be O.K., kid," I said. "Daddy plays better in the
cracks than most cats do on the keys. What I'm worried
about is our drum. You seen Franky?"

"No, Ben. I thought you said he was O.K."

"That was a couple of nights ago, honey. A long long
time in the life of a junkie. I'm going to have to call the
union and see if we can't stall the savages."

Daddy was spread out across most of the piano stool.
He'd taken off his jacket and the sweat plastered his white
linen shirt to his elephantine back. He looked at his watch
and said, "Open them doors, chillun. Daddy ready to
blow! Hey! Where that no-count yeller boy?"

Before I could open my mouth Angel had slipped past
me and said, "Old Frank can't make it, Daddy."

"Don' call me Daddy, white boy. I ain't about to take
the rap! Wuffo' you say Franky taint make it, boy? Where
he at?"

"Well, he's like *dead.*"

Daddy's eyes got big as ping pong balls. He grabbed a fistful of Angel's shirt and roared, "You *funnin'* me, boy? How come you say Franky daid?"

"Because he is, Daddy. He died at ten this morning. The interne on the meat wagon said he must have got some bum snow. Old Frank hit the main line at three in the A.M. and by ten he was stiff as a frozen flounder."

Daddy looked down at his keyboard and murmured, "Po' li'l uppity nigger. How we gonna blow hot now that we got no beat?"

"I blow drums good, Daddy," said Angel. Somehow, this didn't come as much of a surprise to yours truly. Angel grinned and said, "I blow real good. Ask Parker. He's heard me!"

Daddy said, "That right, Ben? This cat got a steady beat?"

I said, "So does a leaking faucet, Daddy. Listen, Angel. How come you didn't tell us earlier about Franky? How come you wait until opening time to tell us he's been stiff all day?"

Johnny Angel looked me right in the eye and grinned like a coyote in a chicken house. He said, "Why should I? That would have given you time to get another drummer."

"Man, he *bad!*" laughed Daddy. "How come you so bad, boy? You daddy whop you too much?"

"I never had a daddy. We was too poor."

"Oh. You funny too? Tell me sumpin, white boy. You really blow drums hot?"

"A lot hotter than Frank can, laying on that cold white table down at the morgue, Daddy."

Daddy looked at his watch. His, big shoulders sagged. Finally he said, "Ease in behind them traps, boy. You better blow them drums hot as you say you do."

"Thanks, Daddy. You won't be sorry."

"I better not be, boy. We gonna *fly* tonight an' we needs

us a beat. Do you mess up that beat, boy, you better give
your soul to Jesus, 'cause your tail belong to Daddy!"

□   □   □

That's the way Johnny Angel broke in with Daddy Halloway and the Hot Babies. It turned out better than I'd
expected. The kid had a weird style.

Lifeless and hot, if you can picture it.

He hit all the right beats at the right time, you understand. Drunk or sober, Daddy wouldn't have let him finish
a set if he was off the beat. And he'd developed a flashy
style with the sticks the savages went for. It didn't do a
thing for the music. But it was sort of commercial.

He was a good looking kid in a reptilian way, and when
he went into a drum solo he'd twirl the sticks like a drum
majorette. He'd chew his gum a mile a minute, jerk his
head so the blond hair fell down over his eyes, and throw
that Mickey Rooney grin at the gals.

I didn't like him even then, but I had to admit he was
less grief to the group than Franky the Drum had been.
That was a funny thing about Angel. He never got into
trouble. Dope, dames, or sauce never threw him. And he
had an uncanny knack of spotting trouble before it happened.

We played Venice and Chico got in a fight with a Mexican who said the only part of Mexico Chico'd ever seen
was Harlem. Before it was over I'd busted a knuckle on a
zoot suiter and Daddy had to throw a savage with a shiv
through the bass drum. When the law arrived and things
simmered down to a roar, I noticed that Angel hadn't
even got his hair messed. He'd been sitting in the bar during the whole mess.

Up the coast in Santa Barbara we had another Hey
Rube with the leather jacket set when the management
wouldn't let them ride their motorcycles through the front
entrance. Tommy the Axe got a cut on the head from a

flying bottle that needed sixteen stitches before he stopped bleeding all over his guitar. Angel, after the whole thing was over, wandered in from the parking lot where he'd been making time with a chick from U.C.L.A.

He bought himself another shirt and a cream colored sports car. One of those Derrin Packards that were going so big before the war. It had phony leopard skin upholstery and a genuine silver fox tail on the radiator cap. Once a chick slid her fanny into that rolling sex wagon she didn't have a chance. Johnny developed a pseudo Charleston accent and a duck's tail haircut. He looked exactly like the savage's picture of a jazz drummer. Maybe that's why I didn't like him.

Guys like Daddy, Bix, Fats, and even myself, never went into the field to make a buck. God knows not many of us ever did. Oh sure, a name musician pulls down a three figure salary, when he's working. But who in hell couldn't, if he worked fourteen hours a day at it and never thought about anything else? Hell, a dedicated plumber can make more than most of us ever did. We weren't in it for loot. We were in it for the sound. We were in it because we had a beat in our brains that had to come out. And let's face it, because most of us were too hipped to hold a job at anything else!

Angel was different from the beginning. He had an ice cold dedication, not to music, but to *being a musician*. There's a difference. To Angel, music was a way to make money. Nothing else. He never sat in on our impromptu jam sessions until Daddy ordered him to one night. On a date he'd sit there on the podium, the sticks making flashing arcs around his blond head and shattering the smoke with a voodoo beat, and all the time his mean little eyes would be coldly sizing up the savages for a willing broad.

I watched him all the way up Highway 101 and he never failed. He never goofed, either. He had the damndest instinct about broads who meant trouble.

By the time we got to Frisco, I'd stopped worrying about Johnny Angel. I was a lot more concerned with Daddy. He'd been in the bag since L.A. Blanche had followed the band up the coast. It was that bad.

Daddy'd had a sawbones in at Monterey. The doc gave him a shot of B-12 for his shakes and told him he'd better stop drinking. For this they sent the cat to medical school.

We were playing this North Beach date in Frisco. This was before the day of the Beatnik and North Beach was still an Italian suburb of Fisherman's Wharf. The California School of Fine Arts, up on Russian Hill, had attracted a few beards to the neighborhood, but mostly the crowd was a bunch of Italian kids planning to grow up and join the Mafia.

The joint we were booked into burned down during the war, and they never rebuilt it, which was just as well for the customers, but it left a mess of cockroaches homeless. Either it was supposed to be inside a cave, or the walls were plastered by a friend of the family. Like, rough. The tables were covered with red and white and tomato sauce checkered calico. The management saved on their electric bill by propping a candle in a chianti bottle on every other table. The bread sticks had been baked in the Frisco fire and tasted like plaster of Paris. The wine was a good substitute for red ink and the spaghetti tasted like strings of dried glue. We were supposed to blow so hot the customers wouldn't lynch the waiters.

We'd all checked into the same hotel down on the Embarcadero. It was a no questions asked joint. You didn't ask about the spade down the hall beating his woman and they didn't ask the boys about the broads they brought in with them. It was a hell of a place for Blanche to stay but I could just see myself checking her into the Mark Hopkins, even if we'd had the loot.

The second or third night we were there the manager called from the club and said he wanted to open early that night. He was paying for it so I told him I'd get the boys ready. That's how I found out about Blanche and Johnny Angel.

He had a room on my floor and I didn't bother ringing him on the house phone. I got Tommy and Chico out of the sack and told them to round up the others. Then I went down to bang on Johnny's door. Only I didn't. I heard voices. Loud.

One of them was Blanche. She was saying, "But, Johnny, what if it's the real thing?"

"Relax, chick. You're only a month overdue. Maybe you got a cold."

I stood there like a jerk while my guts tied up in knots. I tried to convince myself it wasn't Daddy Halloway's daughter in there with Angel, but it was no go.

"Johnny honey," she sobbed. "What'll we do if it's true?"

"Search me, kid. You should have been more careful."

"You didn't talk to me that way before, Johnny. You... you said you loved me! Well, didn't you?"

"So I said I loved you. That's the way the bit goes, chick. What in hell was I *supposed* to say, how's about a little stuff, Blanche?"

"Please, honey. This is serious! What if I'm really in trouble?"

"Well, kid, at least it'll have good breeding on my side."

I knocked on the door. There was an intake of breath and a scurry of mice through the door. Then Angel opened it and looked at me with a phony grin. He was wearing pajama bottoms. I had a good idea where I'd find the tops. He said, "I was in the feathers, Ben. What's up?"

"The date's been moved up an hour." I heard my voice say it like a victrola. My eyes flicked past him to the empty bed. There were two hollow places in the pillows. She must have been in the closet.

He said, "O.K. Ben, I'll be there with bells on."

"You do that, Angel. With funeral bells."

I went to find Daddy Halloway. He wasn't in his room. I tried a couple of bars near the Embarcadero and went back to the hotel. Daddy wasn't in his suite when I got there, but Blanche was, with her clothes on.

I told her about her old man's vanishing act and asked if she had any suggestions. Blanche shook her head. You kind of got the idea she had other things on her mind.

I said, "What's wrong, kid? You got troubles?" I knew damned well what her troubles were, but how do you tell a nice girl you know she's been in the hay with a wrong guy?

"It's nothing, Ben," she said. "Nothing at all. I guess I'm just feeling a bit poorly."

I couldn't look her in the eye. I said, "Like, Blanche, if there's anything you need, anything I can do. Oh hell, you know what I mean, kitten. You in a mess, just call on Uncle Ben."

The girl turned away. She put her hand up to the side of her face and I felt like a jerk.

I said, "Well, I got to blow, kid. I'll plant you now and dig you later."

"Later, Ben," she said. "God bless you."

"Wuffo, sugar? I didn't sneeze."

□   □   □

Daddy was still missing when I got to the club. We were a little early and, I'd never known Daddy to miss a date boiled or sober. But every time Daddy bent his elbow, death took another little bite out of him. It was enough to make a cat wish they'd bring back prohibition.

As long as I was steamed anyways, I figured this was as good a time as any to have it out with Angel. I led him out to the parking lot and put it right on the line. I said, "O.K. Angel, how long you been fooling with Daddy's kid?"

Johnny looked at me steadily for a moment and then said, "Since Pismo Beach, Dad. Why? You want some of it?"

That's when I hit him.

Did you ever have that dream? The one where you're fighting a guy in thick air? That's the way it was with Angel. Oh, I hit him. I belted him so hard I felt it down in my toes. He fell back against a parked car and bounced to the asphalt. Then he got up, brushed himself off and said, "Now what does that prove, Ben?"

I hit him again. I put all the steam I had into it and caught him on the mouth. His head jerked back and pomade flew off his blond hair in a greasy cloud of vapor. Angel just wiped the back of his hand across his bloody mouth and said, "Good thing I don't blow horns, Ben. I think that one busted my lip."

"Fight, you dirty crud!" I yelled.

Angel grinned. "Why should I?" he sneered. "Even if I win I'm sure to get hit more than a dozen times. One thing I've learned, man. I never do what the other guy wants me to. I make him play the way *I* want to. It cuts down the odds a lot."

"If you don't fight I'll beat your brains in!"

"No you won't, Ben. That's why you talk so much. You may hit me a couple more times, but then you'll have to stop. Guys like you always do."

"Don't count on it, crumb. And don't count on it when Daddy finds out. That three hundred pounds ain't all blubber. When he finds out you knocked up his daughter, boy. You better start running."

"How's he going to find out, Ben? You sending out cards?"

"I got news for you, junior. In about four months nobody's going to *have* to tell him."

"Hell, I'll be long gone by then."

"Yeah?" It was too good to be true. "You mean the

Hot Babies is losing their pet rattlesnake?"

"That's right, Ben. I been latching on to them new Gene Krupa sides. You ever dig that cat on the traps?"

"He blows drums good. What about him?"

"Oh, man, I blow just like Krupa now. I been following that lad with the brushes in my room. I got every lick down better than Mister Victor's wax. I too big for this ji-gaboo band, Dad. Before Blanche starts to show I aim to be swinging with Glenn Miller."

I said, "What about Blanche?"

"Well, what about her?"

"Look, you bastard. What about the baby?"

"Dumb broad should have taken care of herself. What in hell you want me to do about it, marry her?"

"Somebody ought to."

"Be my guest, Dad. It'll be a cold day in hell when I marry a nigger."

I was going to hit him once more for the road, when Chico stuck his head out and yelled, "Hey, Benny! We got trouble!"

It was Daddy. The doors would open in ten minutes and Halloway was spread out in the middle of the dance floor on his back. Out like a light.

"Get some coffee?" asked Chico. I shook my head. There was only one way that might get a trouper like Daddy Halloway on his feet. I said, "Come on, you cats. Let's get up on the stand and start swinging."

"But Ben, we ain't open yet."

"I know, thank God. Let's see if we can't bring Daddy around with the opening."

Somewhere in my misspent youth, along with snooker pool, I'd picked up a few piano chords. I slid behind the eighty eights and hit the big A. Then I started walking the bass with a boogie beat. It didn't sound like Daddy, but it set the tempo. Tommy started strumming his axe, filling in for my missing doghouse at the same time. Angel shrugged and picked up the beat with the brushes and then the brass cut loose with that sad opening wail. It was good. We were playing to an empty house and a dead drunk spade, but it swung.

A heavy hand came down on my shoulder and a breath you could have blown up the building with mumbled, "Move over, white boy. Daddy gonna show you how you blows a piano."

Good lord I wish we'd had tape recorders in those days. That last night up in Frisco should have been put down on wax. A lot would have had to be cut, to put it out on top of the counter. Daddy sort of let himself go on the lyrics of Mandingo Baby. You know how meaningless the words to that old blues number are? That's because they've been cleaned up for the trade.

We did Yellow Dog, and Sea Food, and Jelly Roll, and Daddy sang them the way they were written. The way he'd sung them in a New Orleans whorehouse back in the days when Jazz meant something else when you wrote it on a wall.

The cats ate it up. The worried looking manager headed for Daddy and I cut him off in the wings. His English was lousy, but the four letter words Daddy was using are the first ones anybody learns.

"He is singing *dirty!*" the manager sputtered.

"He's singing *jazz,* buddy. Pull up a chair and latch on to the real thing. You may never hear it again."

"We'll have troubles with the police."

"Relax, Mario. He's not taking his clothes off. Look how the cash paying customers are eating it up!"

I wasn't just woofing, either. The North Beach kids were shocked but they weren't leaving. The girls seemed to like it more than the boys. That's something you learn on a bandstand, Dad. Ladies are primitive little beasts once the drum starts their pelvis moving. Jazz seems to move the female pelvis more than it does the male. The Krafft-

Ebing set could learn a lot did they tour one season with a boogie woogie combo.

Daddy had the house mike on the piano. Right next to a bottle of gin. He was sweating like a mule and coon shouting into the mike.

> "Git you' hand off of it!
> It don' belong to *you!*
> Git you' hand off of it!
> It don' belong to *you!*
> I wouldn't give you none of it
> No matter *what* you do!"

His eyes were rolling like a horse down in the shafts and he was belting hell out of the gin. I was starting to wish I'd left him laying there. The crowd was shagging on down and jumping around the bandstand. Daddy wiped a trickle of gin off his chin with the back of his hand and shouted, "Tha's right, chillun. Step right up an' hear the big black nigger sing dirty!"

"Oh oh," I thought. "We're on the race bit again." I figured it was about time to cut the mike. If I knew Daddy, he was leading up to Ofay Gal and lyrics can only get so blue before somebody busts a bottle on the edge of a table. I was looking for the outlet plug when Daddy suddenly crashed both hands down hard on the keyboard and shouted, "Ben! Where you *at*, Ben?"

"Right here, Daddy. What's the matter?"

"Who turn out them lights, Ben? I caint see you!"

I looked at Chico and the two of us got on either side of Halloway. I threw an agonized look at Tommy and said, "Fake the ending and blow intermission. I'll be in the green room with Daddy."

"Where you at, Ben?"

"Right here, Daddy. Me and Chico's taking you to the green room."

"What happen, Ben? They blow a fuse? Where the lights?"

"Take it easy, Daddy. Chico's going for a doctor."

"Wuffo I needs a M.D. man? I feel *hot* tonight. We rockin' the joint! You hear them ofay goin' wild, Ben? Tonight I gonna *fly!*"

"Sure Daddy, only..."

"Only what, Ben?"

"Only the lights ain't out."

"Oh."

That's all he said. He just sat there like a big teakwood Buddha until the meat wagon from St. Francis Hospital rolled up to the side entrance off the green room. As they were taking him out he suddenly said, "Hey, white boy!"

"Yes, Daddy?"

"Not you, Ben. You ain't white or black. You just people. I means that white boy on the drums."

"Johnny Angel?"

"Yeah, tha's him. Get rid of him, Ben. He ain' no good. All you chillun hot tonight but him. Drum sounded like a uppity woodpecker. Only a woodpecker got mo' heart. That boy got no heart, Ben. That cat blow for cold cold cash. Come next date, I wants me some new drums. You dig me, Ben?"

"Sure, Daddy. I'll get rid of him."

"'Nother thing, Ben."

"What's that, Daddy?"

"You tell Blanche I gotta check in with the pink elephants, hear? You look out for her till I gets dried out again. Will you, Ben?"

"Sure, Daddy."

As they carried him out to the meat wagon I could hear him saying, "Well, all you li'l lavender spiders and big yaller cockroaches, make room fo' Daddy! Daddy back in the wet sheets agin! The gin ain' what gits you, chillun. It's them cotton pickin' DTs!"

Daddy didn't have the DTs that night. Or any other
night. When I phoned the hospital after we got back to
the hotel, he was dead. I went over to the window and
looked out. You couldn't see the stars that night. A ruddy
glow from the lights of Oakland made the bay a dark
pool of red wine. I looked up into the fog and thought,
"Good luck, Daddy. You said you was going to fly tonight,
and you did. I hope they dig your sound out there in the
big dark."

□   □   □

The funeral was something to see. Daddy couldn't be
buried with the white folks but there were as many white
faces in the crowd around his grave as there were black.
People sent flowers from all over the 48. Musicians,
mostly. Daddy hadn't much of a following outside the
trade. But side men know a talent when they hear one,
and Daddy was a right guy.

Blanche didn't show for the funeral. It figured. Who
wants to cry for a mess of strangers? Johnny Angel was
the only member of the band missing. It was just as well.
We didn't figure him as part of the group anyways. And
the graveyard was no place to fire the cat.

Blanche had told me to write the book until the North
Beach date was finished. It was her band now. Still a valu-
able hunk of property. But she didn't seem interested.
Told me to take care of things until the date was finished.
I didn't have to ask her plans for the group after the date
was over. Without Daddy, the Hot Babies sounded like
they'd lost their mammas.

The first night we opened after the funeral, Johnny
Angel blew in about a quarter to nine. We were all sitting
in the green room moaning low and wondering if it was
worth going on. It was a rainy night and Daddy was
dead. We were blue.

"Well chilluns," said Angel, standing in the doorway in

a white trench coat. "I got good news for you-all. We're booked into the Oakland Casino across the bay for the next two weeks. Johnny Angel and his Devils. How does that sound for a new name, Ben?"

"You have a very lousy sense of humor, Angel. Also, you are fired as of now. It was Daddy's last wish."

"Hah hah. Very funny. No bull, men. I been scouting up a buck while you cats sat around on your cans. I sold the combo across the bay this afternoon. We check in right after this date."

"What's with this Johnny Angel bit?" I asked. "This is Daddy Halloway's band, punk."

"Not any more, Ben. Daddy's dead. Gone and forgotten."

"Not by *me* he ain't!"

"Look, Ben. Don't fight the facts of life. You know where they put Daddy's obit? On page fourteen, right under an ad for concrete sewer pipe. You got to admit Johnny Angel and his Devils sounds more commercial than the Late Daddy Halloway and his Orphans."

"Sure, Angel. Only you're forgetting one thing."

"What's that, Ben?"

"This is still the Halloway band. Blanche owns it, now that Daddy's dead. And I'm still the manager of it until Blanche says different."

"You don't want me writing the book, Ben?"

"You are so right, punk. Daddy told me to look out for Blanche and that's what I'm doing. I've got a check made out for your time and just as soon as Blanche signs it there's not a goddam thing around here for you but a fat lip. You are, at the risk of repeating myself, fired."

Angel didn't smirk. He didn't have enough warmth in his face to call it a smirk. But I don't know what else you could call the expression on his pan as he reached inside the white trench coat.

"I'm sorry you and me can't work together, Ben." He

grinned. "You got a certain amount of brains and I could have used you. But I see we just ain't cut out for each other. I don't think you like me, Ben."

"That's for sure. What's that in your hand? Your draft papers, I hope?"

"Not exactly, Ben. It's a marriage certificate."

"Congratulations. Who's the unfortunate girl?"

"Blanche Halloway, Ben. We were married two days ago in Reno."

So what could I say that he couldn't top? He stood there like a guy whose horse has just come in and gloated. I shook my head and muttered, "O.K. Angel. So you're not fired."

"But you are, Ben. As of right now."

I looked around the green room and nobody looked back. I shrugged and stood up. "Have it your own way, creep," I said. "But I'm going to hang one more on you for the road."

I took a step towards him and balled up my fist. He pulled out a nasty little whore pistol from the pocket of his trench coat and said,

"Wrong again, Ben. I don't like to stand in for your punching bag."

I said, "Is that thing real?"

"Start swinging, Ben. You'll find out."

"I presume you have a permit?"

"You presume rightly, Dad. I told the cops there was a jerk who got his kicks out of bruising my lip and that I carry large sums of gold around. You start something with me in front of my band, daddio, and I'll fill you so full of lead they won't have to bury you. You'll, like, sink through the floor, man."

"Well," I sighed. "That just leaves me with one thing to say."

"What's that, Ben?"

"Goodbye."

□   □   □

Johnny Angel and his Devils opened in Oakland on the third of September. A day the astrologers said was good for supermen. I was headed east to fill a vacant chair with Claude Thornhill.

I was on my way to the Big Apple on a coach car left over from the Civil War. In the middle of the Nevada desert the candy butcher came through the coach with oranges and newspapers. I ate an orange on a train once, so I bought a paper. The headlines read:

NAZIS INVADE POLAND

By the time I rolled into Penn Station the British and the French had gotten into the act. But old F.D.R. wasn't about to let the balloon go up before the campaign. So I had a lot less to worry about than them cats in Warsaw.

I washed four nights road grime off my hide and changed into a clean shirt in the coin operated washroom in Penn Station. I'd sold the V-8 for a few clams on the coast, so I had the nickel for the subway. But man, who rides the earthworm his first night in the Big Apple?

In case I've missed you with that one, Dad. The Apple is a side man's home town. But there's just one *Big* Apple, and that's New York.

I ankled up Seventh Avenue towards 42nd Street and the big town hit me in the face with its big smell.

I walked through a cloud of roast peanuts, orange peels, scorched tires, asphalt, mildewed newsprint, burned out electric wires, expensive perfume, and cheap dames, to that glittering tawdry waste of good electricity known as Times Square.

The crawling headlines of light around the Times Building read:

FRENCH RUSH TROOPS TO MAGINOT LINE.
... B.E.F. LANDS IN FRANCE....

I exhaled the last few breaths of clean Midwestern air,
took a deep breath of Manhattan and said, "Well, you
old whore of a city, Ben Parker's back. So why don't you
lay down like a good girl and give in?"

New York didn't even answer with a sneer. She's a cold
hearted broad. You can lay your head on the BMT tracks
and she won't even notice. She just don't give a good goddam for anybody. Maybe that's why so many guys bust a
gut trying to make her.

I checked into a cheap but clean hotel, refueled, and
picked up a stripper billed as Ching Lee. The next day,
still tasting fried rice and broke, I got my first lump of the
season. Thornhill turned out to be one of those Paul
Whiteman type cats who blew from a map! Like, hell,
man, none of the old bunch from the South Side ever
learned to *read* music. Even Bix had trouble blowing off
a map and he was the goodest. We just latched on and
blew the stuff.

I checked with the local. It was the same all over. The
Dorseys, Herman, Miller, even Ben Bernie. They all wanted
cats who could read.

It was the era of the big band. The country had crawled
out of the depression with a yen for bigger and better
sound. By the end of the dirty thirties the savages were
asking for Swing, and jazz was dead as a dodo. Everything
but Swing was old hat. And you couldn't blow a Glenn
Miller arrangement off the top of your head. The big
bands of the forties swung like a team of West Point
cadets on parade. Every goddam note meant something
and it had to land in the right groove.

After I'd latched on to some of the sides the lads were
cutting I would have been sour graping it to say it wasn't
solid. But it still left me feeling like a kid with his nose

pressed to the candy store window. I began to understand how the poor dinosaurs must have felt.

I landed a chair with a marimba combo over on 49th Street in a Latin joint too poor to afford a juke box. I was just able to pay for the cheapest room in the Somerset Hotel, a pigeon loft under the water tower. At least, I thought, I was *next door* to the Palace.

It must have been Halloween I saw my first ghost. Considering I'd never seen a ghost before I think I played it pretty cool. Coming down the street towards me in a fall rain was Franky the Drum!

I said, "God Almighty! I thought you were dead!"

Franky the Drum looked blank at me for a minute and then he said, "Benny, how perfectly *charming* of you to notice me! Now step aside, white man. I got places to go."

"No apcray, Franky, what happened? We heard you were stiff."

"I'll just bet," he said in that bitchy voice only a fag can put on. "Johnny told me what you and Daddy said about me after the fuzz picked me up."

The penny dropped.

I said, "Hold it, Morgan le Fay, a picture is emerging from the mists. Before you go on your nightly cruise, doll, you and me are going to compare notes."

I dragged Franky into Whelan's Drug on the corner and planted him on a stool while we consumed a couple of cups of joe.

I filled Franky in on the way Angel had eased into his chair and now owned the band. Franky listened and his hurt looking eyes got big as golf balls. When I finished up with the creep canning me he said, "Oh man, that cat is *bad*."

"Cue me in, Franky. What happened at your end?"

"The brass on that cat!"

"Granted. Angel is the kind of guy who'd murder his

mother and father and ask the mercy of the court because
he was an orphan. Now take it from the top, Franky.
What happened?"

"Well, 'long about ten in the A.M. a couple of narcotics
fuzz bust me in my room and drag me down town. Didn't
even give me a phone call. I spot Johnny in the hall and I
yells for him to tell Daddy and you I got pinched. They
take me down to the Federal Building and they got the
pusher and his runner. Somebody blow the whistle to the
law."

"Five will get you ten you know who that somebody
was, Franky."

"No bet, Dad, now that my brain's hitting on all four.
But I still thought Johnny was my buddy. Old Johnny
come down to the Federal Building that afternoon and
they let him in to see me. He say he try to get bail from
you and Daddy but you brush him off 'cause I a gay cat
and Daddy say he don't want no junkies or snow birds in
the group. He say all he get from you-all is a big fat
brush!"

"Why didn't you call the club, Franky?"

"Oh man, they only gives you one call every seventy
two hours, Ben. Didn't you know that? I bet Johnny did.
He got me to call a cat in Santa Monica he said could fix
the rap for me. The cat gave me a mess of double talk and
Johnny cut out. I never see that boy no more. What happened then, Ben?"

"He came to the date and said you were dead. With the
narcotics fuzz in the picture, none of us bothered to check.
Chico had a few joints stashed in his socks and marihuana
gets you sent up just as far as H, even if it don't kill you as
fast. How'd you beat the rap, Franky? Isn't it a little soon
for your graduation?"

"Oh man, I messed them fuzz up good. The pusher and
his runner took one look at me and said they never see
my handsome puss before. Only one they caught with

snow on him was the runner and all they could hang *him* with was possession, so the rest of us cats keep our traps shut. They slam me in a cell by my lonesome to sweat. They real smart fuzz. They know a bitty gay coon like me gonna be crawlin' the wall in a few hours without I get a fix.

"Only I fool them, Ben. I figures the odds on going seventy two hours without a fix and plain cold turkey nothing if I crack. So I grits my teeth and hangs on. Man, that was a long seventy two. The longest, I mean! I got sick and puked up every thing I ever ate since I was three years old. Red ants was crawling under my skin and I kept throwin' up in the toilet bowl until a fuzz came to the door and said, 'Hey junkie. You ready to turn state's evidence?'

"I look him over, Ben. You know something? Did he be a spade or even a nice ofay I might have done it. I was sick and scared and ready to die, Ben. I knew they wouldn't give me a fix, but just the one in a million chance that they might would have made me tell him anything he wanted to know. But this fuzz had a mean face. He looked just like the big fat Georgia cracker my old man used to work for.

"'Bout the first thing I ever remember is my old man loading cord wood on a Model T pickup while this white man yells, 'Hurry up, you lazy black bastard!' Far as I know he never hit my old man or even treated him mean, but I always hated that red faced sonofabitch more than I did my father. And man, I *really* hated *him*. He used to take crap off his white boss all week and then get drunk on gin Saturday night and beat hell out of my ma and us kids.

"So I just looked this fuzz in the eye and all the malice I'd ever felt came up and stiffened my back bone. I wiped the puke off my lips and told him what he could do. Old fuzz didn't get mad. He just grinned. He thought he had me all figured. He thought old Franky gonna be climbing the walls come nightfall. He just shake his head and walk away."

"So you made it for the full seventy two, Franky?"

"Yeah, man. It wasn't easy, but I made it. You should have seen the faces on them ofay when morning of the third day roll round and I holler, 'All right, man. Either book me or let me go. That's the law, man. You held me all the time the law allows without you press charges.' So they talk it over for a while and there ain't a cotton pickin' thing they can do but let me and the pusher go. I helped him down the stairs in his wheel chair and we went out and got a lawyer for the runner. He copped a plea and got a year. Man, it was worth it to see the look on that red faced fuzz."

I shook my head and ordered another round of coffee. Little Franky had some sand in his craw if you looked under all the perfume and skin bleach. I said, "I get the picture now, Franky. By the time you got out you were too steamed to check with us, right?"

"Yeah, man! I headed east where the fuzz didn't know me. Got a chair with a frantic set on Lenox Avenue and I'm feeling no pain. But man oh man, did that Johnny bastard take us all!"

"While we're on the subject, Franky. I want to ask a personal question about you and Angel. Was he queer?"

"*Please*, Benny. Don't *say* that. Say we're *gay*. We don't like to be called queer."

"Sorry, I haven't been reading my Havelock Ellis. So what was with the creep? Were you getting your money's worth?"

Franky grinned and licked his lips. "You think I pay a cat's way from Bakersfield to L.A. just to hold his hand?"

"I'm seeing a clearer picture of our boy, Franky." I grinned. "He's one of those AC-DC types. Plugs in either way for his sex life. Must make a cat pretty independent."

Franky's eyes clouded over. He said, "You don't understand that cat yet, Benny. He bad. I mean, he bad all the way! I been around an' I seen me some action, but Johnny Angel the baddest action there is! You want to know what make that boy so bad, Ben?"

"Shoot, what's so bad about him? Aside from being a liar, a ghoul, and a fairy, I think he's kind of cute."

"You don't like gay boys, do you, Ben?"

"You know that, Franky. You're a good egg, but your personal life turns my stomach."

"I know, Ben. Either a cat's gay or he ain't. It something you born with, I guess. You my friend, Ben. But I knows the first time I put a hand on your knee I gonna draw back a stump. Now Johnny Angel, he's not like you and me. He not square and he not gay. He just plain don't *give* a damn! That boy'd climb in the feathers with a three day old corpse, if you made it worth his while. Male or female! He's bad, Ben! Bad and cold. Only thing that boy queer for is money!"

I shuddered. Blanche was living with the creep. She was having a child by him. I wondered how it was going to turn out. Black, white, or cobra.

□   □   □

Like I said, it was the era of the big band. A few cats like Fats Waller and Jack Teagarden were still holding the fort. But gut bucket went to sleep for a while. The big bands blew swing and the little bands blew "Fwee ittee fiddies inna iddy biddy pool." The kids were yelling for new sounds and the side men were giving them all the new sounds there was. Then, on New Years Eve, a new sound burst on the scene like a big blue rocket. The swing record that outgrossed them all, Angel's Flight, by Johnny Angel and his Devils!

Needless to say, it was Daddy Halloway's opening, with

a big band beat and a really solid arrangement by Con Conners.

I heard it on my radio under the water tower and nearly jumped off the roof. Talk about steamed? I was parboiled, fried, and served!

Stealing Daddy's theme was like taking the pennies off a dead man's eyes. But a lot more profitable.

While he was getting rich, I was running like hell in the opposite direction. I heard about an opening in Hoboken where a skinny kid named Sinatra was knocking them dead. But, like everyplace else, they wanted a lad who blew from a map.

Unless I learned to read music I was liable to end my days as a busboy at the automat. I dropped in at the agency the next day and told my tale of woe to Buddy Epworth.

"You South Side guys kill me," he said. "You double on a dozen instruments, you look down your noses at any cat who never sat in with Bix, and not a damned one of you can read music!"

"So I'll learn. I learned to read English, didn't I? And I was only six years old. Where can I find a cat to teach me?"

"Free?"

It was a good question. I owed two weeks rent and only the fact that I knew a Hungarian waitress from Queens better than her husband did kept me from starving to death.

I was just wondering if it was too soon to put the bite on Ep when all hell broke loose on the street below. We went to the window and looked down. A fire engine red Rolls Royce convertible was parked in front of the hydrant and a character in a vanilla sports jacket and Hollywood sunglasses was beaming up at us.

Ep waved and said, "It's Con Conners. He said something about buying a car to drive out to the coast."

"He bought one."

"That's for sure. Let's go down and see if we can't make him stop blowing his horn. He won't until he shows off his new toy."

We took the elevator down, along with half the girls in the office. Conners stopped blowing his horn when we arrived at his court. He stood up in the car and waved an imaginary sword at Ep. He said, "I dub thee knight, Sir Epworth."

Epworth said, "Ben, this is Con Conners. He's a pixie, but harmless."

Conners looked gravely at me with his big brown eyes and said, "I am a Jew."

I said, "I'm not. The name's Parker. Glad to know you, I think."

Conners said, "I like to get it straight, right off. People hear the name Conners and think I'm a Harp. Next thing you know they make a crack about the Jews and I have to belt them."

"So why'd you change the name to Conners?"

"I didn't. My old man did. It used to be Cohen. I've been thinking of changing it back since this Hitler business. But I'd have to have the name changed on all my ASCAP files and it would cost me. Just wanted to let you know where you stand. Since the Reichstag fire I've developed a very thin skin."

Ep said, "Con's the cat who wrote Angel's Flight, Ben."

"I didn't write it," said Conners. "Johnny Angel wrote it."

I said, "Bull."

Conners opened the door of his car and said, "Was that an antisemitic bull, or just a general bull, Parker?"

Epworth got between us and said, "Ben's trying to learn how to read music, Con."

"That's interesting. Do you want to fight, Parker?"

"It depends, Conners. Did you ever hear of a cat named

Daddy Halloway?"

"Sure, I caught his act one time in Chi. He blew good. What about him?"

"That's who wrote Angel's Flight, Dad. Johnny Angel stole his band, his daughter, and the opening, when Halloway kicked off."

"Really?" asked Conners. He was either a good actor or he didn't know Johnny Angel too well. He said, "No spades in the band now, Parker. I ran into Angel last fall at Avalon. He was swinging with an all white band. Asked me to do some arrangements for them."

It figured. I said, "You meet his wife, Blanche?"

"He got a wife? He was making out with his vocalist, a little redhead from Pomona who's busting a gut trying to sound like Helen Forrest. She don't make it. The whole outfit sounded like a bad imitation of Glenn Miller. Most of the bad bands do. He had a frantic type with a crew cut blowing the opening on the eighty eights. Not very well. I took the theme and rehashed it. After a while it swung and Johnny cut a side of it. You know the rest."

A cop wandered over as if he was about to join the conversation. When a Broadway cop looks at you that way it's time to move on.

"Climb in, Parker," said Conners. "You interest me strangely. I'm headed west to do a musical with Johnny Angel and you know things about him that I don't."

I slid in beside him on the leather upholstery and he said, "By the way, can you drive?"

"Sure," I said. "But I'm getting off this side of the Holland Tunnel."

"Why?"

"Why? Hell man, because it costs a nickel to get back from Jersey and I've got uses for my nickels. I'll fill you in on the cat between here and the tunnel. After that, you're on your own."

"I got an idea," said Conners. "You drive and I'll teach

you to read music. Maybe between us we can figure some way to get this guy out of the picture."

"Wait a minute," I said. "You mean, you want me to drop everything just like that and drive out to the coast with you?"

"Why not? You got something else to do?"

When you put it that way, I didn't. I wasn't about to get my suitcase down from the fourteenth floor without paying my bill, and Hollywood is a better place to be broke than New York. Not that Hollywood gives a damn, either. But starving to death under a palm tree seems easier, somehow.

With Conners footing the bill, we headed west. I don't know if the country's recovered from that trip yet. I know I haven't.

In Harrisburg we stopped to refuel the car and pick up a couple of broads. The gasoline and the dames lasted as far as Pittsburgh. There we ditched them. Con said he had the greatest respect for the Mann act. Besides, he knew a waitress in Columbus who had a friend.

In Indianapolis, we found out why we were getting so many miles to the gallon and burning so much oil. An unbelieving mechanic, who'd always wanted to see a Rolls engine, lifted the hood and informed us we had a Model A mill in the "bargain" car Con had bought.

"Oh well," shrugged Conners, "it's got twin pipes, and the babes never look under the hood, anyways."

We were grinding up the 800 mile hill to Denver when the car threw a rod in Wichita. It must have been malice aforethought. Wichita was dry that year and we nearly died of thirst before they said the car would live. The mechanic in Wichita knew what he was doing. The car lasted all the way to the coast. Con didn't.

A few miles outside of Denver, in a roadhouse shaped like an Indian pueblo, Con suddenly coughed and grabbed for his handkerchief. He covered his mouth and staggered outside. Throwing a ten dollar bill on the counter beside the fine spray of ruby red drops.

The counterman shook his head as he counted the change. He said, "He's got it bad, huh? I see them all the time. Coming to Denver to grab a few more months at the sanitarium."

I nodded and went out to the car. Con was doubled over with his head between his knees. The floor of the car was slick with blood.

"T.B.?" I asked.

Con shook his head and gasped, "I'll be O.K. Ben. Just get me to the Brown Palace in Denver. I know a chick who works at the bus depot across the street who..."

"You're going to a hospital, you jerk!" I said. I floored the gas pedal and burned rubber gowing out.

Near Aurora a state trooper on a suicide wheel flagged us over to the side and looked like he was going to eat me alive, until he saw Con.

"What's with him?" asked the trooper.

"T.B. Hemorrhage," I said.

The cop said, "Follow me." And got back on his wheel. We blew into Denver as fast as four cylinders would take us. The cop's siren was really rattling the windows as we pulled up at the emergency entrance of the Catholic Hospital. An interne took one look at the bottom of the car and they whipped Con out of his seat like his life depended on it. I guess it did.

I stood there in the driveway, looking at the trickle of blood dripping off the running board onto the asphalt. The cop said, "Well, I got to get back on my beat." At least he had someplace to go.

I spent most of the night in a Laramie Street movie. Trying to sleep through Hopalong Cassidy and not making it. By the time they threw me out the night was half shot and I killed the rest of it trying to pick up a Mexican waitress in a chili parlor near the Union Depot. God knows what I'd have done if she'd taken me up on it.

I wasted the price of breakfast on calls to the hospital. Finally, at six in the morning, they said he was out of danger. Visiting hours were nine to eleven. That gave me just time to walk it. Con was sitting up in bed looking like a million dollars, if you didn't pay any attention to the rubber tube stuck in his arm. He was flirting with a pretty nun when I arrived.

"Benny, you old basser," he said. "You saved my life."

"So what else is new?" I said.

"Really, the old doc was just in here telling me. He says if you and that cop had been ten minutes longer I'd have been making like mackerels down in the cellar. On a slab, I mean."

"Forget it," I shrugged. I was wondering how to put the bite on him and he was making it tough.

"Forget it hell, man. Half the cats I know would have rolled me and swiped the car. I ain't forgetting this, Ben."

"Okay, let's segue into eight bars of Hearts and Flowers. How long the MD say you're in for?"

"Coupla weeks anyways." The nun looked startled and he grinned. "They want to check me into the gasping academy and collapse my lung." He shrugged. For a minute he looked at the crucifix on the wall near the foot of the bed. Finally he said, "You know what's wrong with this Jesus bit, Ben? You know why we can't buy it? Because he was a poor nebbisch."

The nun sniffed and went out of the room. Con stared morosely at the crucifix and sighed. "See no evil, hear no evil, huh? Poor kid. Such a goddam waste of good curves."

"You didn't have to make the crack, Con. This is a Catholic hospital," I said. Wondering why I've never learned to keep my trap shut.

"O.K. I'm a bastard. But you know why this Jesus business bugs me? For two thousand years you Christian cats been using the poor guy as an excuse to throw rotten eggs at us Hebes. And who was Jesus anyways? I'll tell you who he was, Ben. He was a nebbisch.

"Like, this Jesus cat blew into Jerusalem moaning high and low about his Daddy. He say his Daddy was the lad with the power. He say his Daddy make all the wheels go round and he was going to lay it on the line for the rest of us cats. From the top.

"First thing he does is put the muscle on the racket guys hanging around the temple. He goes tossing all their schlock out in the street and messing up the good thing the shamus had going for himself. Oh man, he talked big.

"So when they gang up on him, what's he do? Does he get his Daddio to open a big zipper in the sky and holler, 'Take your cotton pickin' hands off my boy!'? Why, hell no! He just stands there like a hophead copping a plea and lets them hang it on him! You call that common sense? The poor guy even carried his own cross!"

"What would you have done, Con? Called a cab?"

"I'll tell you what I'd have done, Ben. I would have fought 'em. I'd have given them cats a run for their money. I'd have got the best shyster in town and fought them all the way. Hell, Jesus was right in the middle of Jerusalem and didn't have enough moxie to get a good Jew lawyer.

"And if they *had* hung the charge on me, Ben, you know what I'd have done? They'd have had to carry me, kicking and biting and scratching, every goddam foot of the way! They might have nailed me to that cross, Ben. But they wouldn't have gotten me to carry it!"

"So what's that got to do with this deal?" I asked. "Why give the medical profession a hard time?"

"Hell, Ben. Don't you see it? It's the same thing! You think I'm so goddam anxious to crawl around on this second class planet a few months longer that I'm willing to do it in a wheel chair?"

"Better a wheel chair than a silver handled box, Con."

"Horse turds. We only pass this way one time, Ben. We

get all the laughs we can out of this rat race before they pat our noses flat with a shovel. We gonna be dead a long time, Ben. While we're alive, man, I want to live!"

"You sound like a Crosby record, Con. How long you figure to whoop it up, with one lung, on a bottle and three dames a day?"

"Stick around, Ben. You'll find out."

It was a good opening. I said, "I have to stick around. All I got in my pockets is belly button fuzz and a ticket stub from the Roxy."

Con nodded. "That's what I wanted to talk to you about, Ben. I got to stay here for a couple of weeks at least. I want you to drive the car to the coast for me. I'll fly out and join you. In the meantime, here's the key to my house. Get my dog Susie Q, out of hock at the vet's and see that she gets plenty of chopped chicken livers. It's all she'll eat. Oh yeah, you'll have to sit in for me while the contracts are being drawn up for the picture. I've written up a power of attorney for you and—"

"*Hold it!*" I said. "I don't know what you're talking about!"

"Nobody does," he said. "Just tell them you're my manager or something. Stall until I get there. If the studio finds out I'm sick they might get Arlen or one of those guys to take my place."

He reached into the bedside stand and pulled out a sheaf of papers with a Denver notary's seal on them. I looked at him and said, "Hell, Con. You don't know me."

"I know you well enough. You didn't steal Angel's Flight, did you? And you could have rolled me a dozen times by now. Besides, I *have* to trust you. You know who's going to be at that meeting?"

"Johnny Angel, I presume?"

"You are so right, Dr. Livingston. From what you've told me of that cat, he'll bear watching. And you know him gooder than me, Dad. How much do you need to operate on from here to the coast?"

"Credit card'll feed the car. I need five bucks a day to eat like a white man on the highway."

"You think too small, Ben. What you going to do for company? Motel room cost you seven dollars minimum with no questions. I'll tell you what. Take my check book along and write it as you go. Those papers ought to cover the bank."

"You're nuts, Conners," I said.

"You won't do it?"

"I didn't say that. I just said you're nuts."

The pretty nun came in and shooed me out. As I left Con said, "See you under the La Brea tar pits, Ben."

"O.K. Dad. Bring your own dame."

□ □ □

You don't drive into Los Angeles. The City of the Angels creeps up on you like a big chicken wire and plaster ameba. After you've crossed a few hundred miles of desert, wondering if the gray gravel and joshua trees extend all the way to Hawaii, you start hitting suburbs. The first one is called Las Vegas.

Los Angeles consists of hundreds of lost suburbs in search of a main drag. A big blob of pastel stucco spread over what used to be five hundred miles of worthless desert. Some folks still wonder if Los Angeles is any improvement.

One of the lost suburbs, a couple of miles of nouveau riche architecture, snuggles against the base of the scrubby brown Hollywood Hills. The hills are covered with mesquite, yucca, beer cans, chaparral, used contraceptives, California poppies, and poison oak. You won't find a sprig of holly south of Oregon.

People think Hollywood is where they make all those pictures. A few animated cartoons are turned out in back of the Hollywood roller drome. Or were at the time. Most of the studios are in the San Fernando Valley, Culver City, or Long Island. I hope I haven't disillusioned you. Hollywood is O.K. to live in but you wouldn't want to visit it.

When I drove to the house where Con said he lived, I noticed a light in the window. Either I was at the wrong place or Con had left the lights on all the time he was in New York. Not as unlikely as it sounds, knowing Con.

I opened the door with the keys he'd given me and went in. The girl was lounging on a red velvet sofa under a large painting of the Charge of the Light Brigade. Her hair was bleached. This was not idle guess work on my part. She was stark naked.

"Don't you feel a draft?" I said by way of an introduction, when I got my breath back.

She looked up at me, took another bite from the navel orange she was eating, and said, "Hello. I'm Dorothy."

"I'm the Wizard of Oz," I answered. She didn't get it.

She took another bite of the orange and asked, "Are you a friend of Con's?"

"You might say that." I grinned. "And then on the other hand you might not, if you don't get some clothes on."

She looked blankly at me for a moment and then grinned. "Oh. I'll bet you're wondering why I'm in the raw?"

"Sort of."

"Well, it's a hot night and my light print dress is in the cleaners. My linen dress makes me sweat and that ruins my skin tone for the class."

"That's tough," I said. "What class?"

"The art class, silly. I'm an artist's model. That's why I don't mind having men stare at me when I have no clothes on. It used to bother me but not any more."

"It bothers me, honey," I said. "I'm not an artist. I am a hard drinking side man. Jazz musician to you, doll. When I see naked dames it brings out the beast in my libido."

"Really?" asked Dorothy, as if the idea somehow failed

to terrify her. "You men are all alike, thank God. But let's not get grabby so early, huh lover? It's early yet and I very seldom go to bed before midnight."

I shook myself, turned around, and went to the nearest liquor store. Then I sent Con a wire.

> HOUSE HAUNTED BY A DOROTHY. DOD OH DOD. WHAT DO ME DO NOW.
> > CONFUSED

I took the fifth of scotch and my clear conscience back to the house. Dorothy hadn't put any clothes on, but she was frying eggs. It was very disconcerting. The least she could have done was put on an apron.

I'd finished my second plate of eggs and a good part of the bottle when Con's reply came. He'd wired:

> IS SHE STILL THERE. SHE CAN GO FOR THE DOG. SUZIE Q LIKES HER AND AS FAR AS I KNOW SHE HAS NEITHER BRAINS AMBITIONS OF MATRIMONY NOR SOCIAL DISEASES. HAVING WONDERFUL TIME. WISH YOU WERE HERE AND I WAS THERE.
> > BUFFALO BILL

"Is that from Consi?" Dorothy asked, "What does he say?"

"He says for you to go and get Suzie Q at the vet's."

"Tonight?"

"In the morning, honey," I said, flipping off the light. "The morning will do just fine."

An hour later I got around to telling her my name.

□   □   □

Dorothy came in very handy. She couldn't cook anything but eggs and she drank pink gin. But I forgave her these minor lapses from civilized behavior. She had other talents.

The most useful of which was feeding the damned dog. Suzie Q was a black chow the size of a timber wolf. She took one look at me and went for my throat. Dotty managed to talk her out of killing me by feeding her a plate of pâté de fois gras. That was all the mutt would eat. With truffles, yet.

As long as I was stuck with the mutt, I figured I might as well keep the Dorothy. She made up in bed for her lack of household skills and never voiced matrimonial sobs at the breakfast table.

I might have done better in front of the Chinese Theatre, but I might have done worse. I had other things on my mind. Most of them were Johnny Angel.

As Con had filled me in, the studio was cashing in on the record's success by producing a low budget picture of the same name. The plot was the usual pablum about a poor but honest trumpet player who is hot for a debutante with overdeveloped mammaries. Sulking in the wings is a poor but honest carhop (female) who has panting fits every time she looks at the poor but honest trumpet player.

Somewhere between the time the boy meets the girl in a doorway during an April shower and the time he gets her girdle off, we were supposed to blow enough jazz to fill in the holes in the plot.

Angel wasn't acting in the thing. There'd be a couple of shots of him waving an idiot stick at the band of overaged adolescents who were Mel Davis's idea of side men.

Con had been hired to do the arrangements so Angel's band, while they were dubbing in for the actors, wouldn't sound as bad as they were. My job was to stall until he got out of the hospital. We both knew how long Angel would take to cut him out of the scene if he thought he could get away with it. From what Con had said, Angel was already steamed that they'd given Con a credit line on the record.

He'd teamed up with a wig named Marvin Knopff. A frantic type who'd been blowing eighty eights with him. Knopff wore a crew cut, horn rimmed glasses, and a knowing look. Need I say more?

I met them in the producer's office. Angel's hair was chopped flat across the top, like a Prussian drillmaster's. He was wearing a mauve camel's hair jacket, a flaming magenta sports shirt, and square rimmed sun glasses with purple frames. He looked like he was about ready to say, "Take me to your leader."

Instead, he grinned nervously with his rat teeth and said, "Hey, Benny boy! Slip me some skin, man!"

I said, "Burn a few inches off and I'll consider it."

Mel Davis, the producer, wandered in before Angel could think up a devastating reply. Davis was a worried looking type who looked like he'd really be a lot happier in the going out of business business. A harassed little cat in a handmade suit that had set him back more than all the threads the rest of us were wearing. But he still thought we were maybe one up on him.

Davis had produced a long gray line of Hollywood fluff. He'd never won the Academy Award, but he'd never produced a picture that lost money at the box office. He was a genius of the mediocre. This isn't as easy as it sounds. Any cat can produce a bad picture. Mel Davis produced bad pictures that appealed to the great unwashed. He'd shoot anything from a western to a bedroom farce off the top of his head and a script scribbled the night before on the back of a Brown Derby menu. He wouldn't have used more than three sets and Griffith Park to shoot War and Peace, and the sets would be left over from another picture.

His actors were either has beens or the never wases who hang out along Gower Gulch. His best pictures seldom came to the standards of a high school play, and his bad pictures were frightening. But, to the ever smiling delight of the auditing department, he never made one bad enough to keep the matinee hausfrauen from paying to see it.

People who should know better may laugh at guys like Mel, but he and producers like him built all those swimming pools in Beverly Hills for the studio execs. They were, and still are, the backbone of the industry.

I filled Mel in on Con's absence. Said he was in bed with a sick friend named Mabel. It was the best thing I could think of that couldn't be checked. Davis wanted to know where Mabel lived, and right off the top of my head I gave him the only address in Salt Lake City I knew. It was the Mormon Tabernacle, but I didn't think he'd know that.

Mel Davis couldn't have looked more unhappy if I'd stabbed him. He pointed a finger at me and said, "Mister Parker, do you mean to say Con Conners is not ready to start work on the picture?"

A stooge in pin stripes and advanced acne said, "We've heard about this Conners, Parker. A good man. A very good composer. But not very reliable."

Another said, "I heard he lost out on that last Fred Astaire, Ginger Rogers picture because he was too drunk to make it to the studio."

I kept waiting for Angel to grab his cue. The lad had smoothed off some of his rough edges since I'd seen him last. Instead of putting the shaft to Con in front of God and everybody, he let his stooge do the hatchet job.

Knopff shook his head and pulled out a slide rule. I never have figured how the damned things work, but I know you don't write music with one. Nobody else in that room knew, though. It was a neat bit of one-upmanship.

"This is very bad," said Knopff, fiddling with his slip stick. "Very bad indeed. According to my calculations we're a week behind schedule now."

Davis looked like he was going to have apoplexy. He clutched at his side and said, "My God! Did you hear that? Already we're a week behind schedule and this goniff hasn't even crossed the desert!"

I was feeling a little like the Dutch boy with his finger in the dike. I said, "Relax. Con's already written the score for the picture. I bet the rest of you haven't even figured out how the girl loses the boy after she meets him the first time."

"As a matter of fact, we have a cute situation worked out," said Davis. "This girl has a room mate, see? A real spiffy brunette. We're dickering for Anne Miller in the part if we can get her to cut her price. Anyway, this other babe's hot for the hero, see? And... Look, are you on the level? Have you got the arrangements with you?"

"No, but I can get them any time you need them."

"We need them."

Angel cut in. His voice was soft as honey. You'd think I was his old flame instead of the cat who'd once busted his lip. He said, "All we've got to work with, Ben, is the opening crawl and the theme. We're using Angel's Flight for both. But we'll be up the creek without a paddle if you let us down."

Davis looked like he was going to throw up. He popped a little pink pill in his mouth and said, "Maybe we better shop around. I hear Sid Mitchel's in town. If we can figure a price, he writes pretty good schmaltz. That's what this picture needs. Lots of schmaltzy music."

I expected Angel to jump at the chance. Instead, he grinned at me and purred, "Hell, it's not as bad as that, Mel. Ben isn't a lad to let us down. I know Ben. He used to blow bass for me. He'll have the roughs in for us by Monday, won't you, Ben?"

I could have shot him. I said, "Sure, I guess so." Angel had nailed my feet to Monday morning and now he was ready to push me over backward.

To change the subject, I said, "You're using the tune for the crawl, huh?"

Knopff said, "Yeah, I've written a real ragtime boogie arrangement for the crawl. It really swings."

"I'll bet," I said. "Only you don't rag boogie woogie."

"Oh come now, Parker. Let's not get technical. You know what I mean when I say ragtime."

"Sure I do," I grinned. I could play one-upmanship if I had to. I said, "The only trouble is, I don't think you do. Boogie woogie is eight beats to the bar, blues are twelve, and ragtime is a march with an accented weak beat in four parts, each sixteen bars long. It started with white bands in the Midwest and has no more relationship to Gulf Coast boogie woogie than it has to a waltz by Strauss."

Knopff looked like he'd been hit in the head by a dead fish. He was being beaten at his own game and he didn't like it. He smiled weakly and said, "All right, professor, while you're giving me a free course in music appreciation, suppose you define jazz."

I sidestepped the trap with Satchmo's classic quotation. I said,

"Hell, man. If you don't know what jazz is by now, *don't mess around with it!*"

Knopff went into a purple sulk, mumbling to himself about what he called Progressive Jazz. He was a little avant garde with the term. Only a few wigs from Central Avenue had even heard the term in those days.

Davis, who knew a good punch line when he heard it, actually smiled at me. The water cooler brigade went back to the commissary. Mel showed us out and patted me on the back as he said, "I'll expect you Monday with something on paper, Ben. Right?"

"Right," I muttered. Angel bugged me. He was grinning at me like a weasel in a chicken coop. He looked like he knew I was stalling. He didn't just look it. He did.

The lad was smooth. Not any nicer, but smooth. He waited until we were out of Mel's earshot before he dropped his bomb.

"Too bad about Con," he said. "I hear the sanitarium in Denver is about the best."

"How'd you find out?"

"Buzzy West just blew in from the Midwest. It's on the front page of the Denver Post. I imagine the wire services will have picked it up by Monday."

I couldn't see his angle. I said, "Why the sudden silence? Why didn't you knife me in Mel Davis's office?"

Angel shrugged and exchanged glances with his stooge. Knopff looked at me sincerely, and said, "We didn't want to louse you up, Ben. Us musicians got to stick together."

I said, "Bull. What's the weenee?"

Johnny Angel laughed. "What he really means, Ben," he said, "is that Davis would get another boy if he knew Conners was down with T.B. We sort of figured to keep it in the family."

"Meaning?"

"Meaning Marvin has written a few catchy little tunes. He's very talented. But I think they could use a little polishing by a hep talent like you."

Knopff said, "Aw, Johnny."

"Shuddup! Like I said, Ben. If the three of us got together on this picture we might make a bit of change."

"What's in it for Con and me?"

"Just you, Ben. For you there's money. Con's got a name, but so have I, now. The name sells, and you and Mary got everything else I need."

"You mean, you're dealing Con out?"

"Hell, Ben. He *is* out! Is it my fault he breathed them bugs? Besides, who needs him?"

"You do, creep!" I said. "Con Conners has more music under his fingernails than you have in your whole crummy combo!"

"You won't throw in with me?" he asked. He looked like he really couldn't see why a guy wouldn't double-cross a friend while he was in the hospital. To Johnny Angel it would be a golden opportunity.

I said, "Give the man a cigar. He just made halfwit."

Angel shrugged. "You're a funny guy, Ben," he said. "That's why you never get noplace. First you latch on to a dying nigger and now you're passing up a big break for a sick Jew."

I flashed a look at Knopff. Either I was wrong about the name or he had very thick skin. I said, "How's your wife, Angel?"

Johnny grinned sheepishly. "You mean Blanche?" he said. "Long time no see, Dad. Got me a Mexican divorce many moons ago. You want her telephone number?"

"What about the kid?" I asked.

"It was a girl, I hear. Never saw the brat. I got the divorce before it was born."

"Right after you took her band away from her?" I growled, I felt a familiar twitch in my bicep. Johnny Angel's face was just meant for my right cross.

"The hell with Blanche, Ben." He laughed. "That's all water under the bridge. What I want to know is, where are you going to come up with a score for the picture by Monday morning if you don't join me and Marv?"

He had me. I really didn't know. I said, "I just need something on paper to keep his nibs from slashing his wrists until Con gets in."

"Sure, Ben, but let's not kid each other. You don't have it. I read you like a book, Dad. You're sweating bullets. Now Marv has some good sheet music laying around doing nothing. All it needs is a good jazz beat to make it swing. You run it through the piano for Marv and he can write it down."

Knopff said, "Listen, Johnny. It's got a great sound already. I don't want no squares making it sound like Dixie."

Angel stopped in midstride and said, "Beat it, Knopff. You're bending my ear."

"Aw, Johnny."

"You heard me. Wait in the car. I got things to talk over with Ben."

Knopff slunk off with his tail between his legs. He must have needed the job.

I said, "Where'd you get the idea that everybody in the world was your stooge, Johnny?" I really wanted to know.

Johnny grinned, and before I could stop him, snatched off my panama hat. He said, "Watch this, Ben. You'll learn something."

"Hey, that hat cost me eight bucks!" I yelled. It was too late. The jerk threw the hat like a pie plate out into the studio street. The wind picked it up and started rolling it in the general direction of Glendale. As I took a step after it he stopped me and said, "Take it easy, Ben. Just watch."

A heavy set man in a blue serge suit ran out from the opposite curb and chased the hat. He caught it two or three cars down the street and brought it, puffing like a winded water buffalo, back to me.

I mumbled thanks as he smiled and handed me my hat. When he'd turned away, Johnny Angel said, "You know who that was, Ben? Joe Meyers. He's the production head on this lot. A very big wheel. When Joe Meyers yells froggy, all the studio cats jump. So why should he bring you your goddam hat like a puppy dog retrieving a rubber ball? He don't know you from Adam, Ben."

"He's a nice guy, I guess," I said. I didn't get the point. I'd chased hats myself. Hasn't everyone?

"Nice guy my foot!" laughed Angel. "You should see that lad at a director's meeting. Yet he knocks ten minutes off his life chasing your hat. It's a built in reflex, Ben. He sees a dopey looking straw hat go flying by and goes after it like a hound dog chases cars. It makes him feel good to chase hats. He'd have done it for any grip on the goddam lot."

"So he's democratic," I said.

"You *still* don't dig me? Christ, you're thick!"

"What's to dig?"

"The way a smart operator can make the conditioned reflexes of the slobs pay off! I've studied them, Ben. Pavlov studied dogs. I study people. There's not a hell of a lot of difference. You show a dog a chunk of liver and ring a bell, Ben. After a while the dog's mouth drools every time he hears the bell. You don't need the liver any more. The damned fool dog isn't thinking. He's reacting. It's the same way with people. They don't think. They react. You show them a picture of a blind girl hugging a puppy and they get lumps in their throats. Wave a flag and they stand up. Show them a picture of Hitler and they hiss. Insult their mother, even if she was a drunken whore and they know it, and they take a swing at you. It's like you're pushing buttons, Ben. You watch for the built in patterns and taboos. After a while you get where you can call the shots."

"Yeah?" I sneered. "So what am I going to do Monday?"

"You bug me, Ben. You're one of the only guys I can't figure. Give me enough time to size up the average cat and I'll march him off a cliff for you!"

"Please. Don't do me no favors."

"You should thank me, Ben. I'm trying to show you something it took me a long time to learn. Are you getting the picture? Are you starting to dig what I'm blowing you, Dad?"

"All I dig, you bastard, is that you used *my hat!* Next time gives a fat lip!"

"I guess I'll never understand you, Ben," sighed Angel. I left him at the entrance of the parking lot, shaking his head. It was mutual. I didn't understand him either. I didn't want to. I was having enough trouble with my digestion.

It didn't get any better as I drove back to Con's. A newsboy in front of the Chinese Theatre was waving a banner headline. It read:

GERMANS ENTER PARIS. CITY UNDEFENDED.

It didn't make me feel any better to know other people had troubles that night. It was Friday evening, and unless I had something looking like a musical score to show Mel Davis by Monday morning, Johnny Angel was going to see a Parker with egg on its face.

I stopped off to wire Con in Denver.

ANGEL KNOWS ALL. HAVE STALLED UNTIL MONDAY. ANY SUGGESTIONS.

His answer came as Dorothy was burning eggs for dinner. Con wired:

DON'T JUST STAND THERE. FAINT. IF YOU CAN STALL AT LEAST TWO WEEKS I MIGHT TUNNEL OUT OF HERE.
           THE COUNT OF MONTE CRISTO
P.S. CHECK MUSIC IN PIANO STOOL. MAYBE YOU CAN USE SOME OF IT.

I tossed the wire aside and tore open the piano stool in front of Con's baby grand. It was full of penciled sheet music. It was about as much use to me as a Sanscrit Veda, but it was music.

I asked Dorothy if she knew a cat who could read from a map. She thought prettily for a moment and said, "There's my husband, Tom. He used to play the cello."

"Don't you know anybody but your husband? He's liable to take a dim view of life as he finds it on the Sunset

Strip."

"Oh, Tom won't mind, Benji. He's very progressive."

"He'd have to be," I snarled. "Is there anybody you haven't slept with who reads music? For that matter, is there anybody you haven't slept with?"

"There's Alex. He's sort of squirrelly and he drinks too much but he plays a piano in a night club. I think he reads music."

"Bless you, my child. What's his number?"

And that's how Alex Bodanoff came into my life. A weird experience. Alex was a tall distinguished type who worked, when he was sober, at a White Russian samovar joint in Beverly Hills. He came over about an hour after Dorothy had called him and shook my hand in a matter of fact way. Then he threw himself at Dorothy's feet.

"Dorothy, my little Dorothy. Alex Alexandrovitch loves you!" he sobbed.

Dorothy, who was wearing an open kimono in deference to my feelings of delicacy, stamped her foot prettily and said, "Alex, don't be so silly."

Bodanoff threw me a tortured look and sighed. "You see how cruel she is to me? The only woman Alex Alexandrovitch has ever loved and she is spitting on me!" He was playing Mischa Auer that night. Half the White Russians I ever met did, when they weren't being Gregory Ratoff. I've never figured it out whether they were kidding or not.

I handed him a sheet of Con's music as he knelt at Dorothy's sandaled feet and said, "Can you read this well enough to play it for me on the Steinway?"

Alex eyed the penciled notations coldly and said, "For why should Alex Alexandrovitch play this crass American crud?"

"For a dollar an hour, Dad. More if I see I can use you."

He blinked a few times as his pickled brains translated a buck an hour into the vodka it would buy. In those days

it bought more. He got to his feet and patted me bearishly
on the shoulder. "Mister Parker," he said. "I like you!"

"I like you too, Alex. Do we have a deal?"

"First I need a drink to steady my nerves."

Dorothy said, "Sit down at the piano, Alex. I'll get you
boys a drink from the kitchen."

As she left the room Alex sighed at her swaying figure
and said, "My God, what a magnificent animal! If I didn't
need the money I think I'd kill you both!"

I didn't answer. After he saw I wasn't going to pick up
my straight lines he relaxed a little. It's tiring to be a
clown. Most drunks are either clowns or they want to
fight. If they'd just shut up and drink their booze nobody
would mind them. But I guess if they had that part figured
out they wouldn't be drunks.

Dorothy came back with two eight ounce tumblers filled
with lemon soda and pink gin. Alex shuddered and drank
his. I said, "For God's sake, Dorothy, do you expect a
white man to drink this?"

Alex said, "Speak for yourself, John." And drank mine
too. I told Dorothy to put on some clothes and go get
some scotch and cokes while I eased Alex into working
for a living. It wasn't easy.

Once I got him started he blew pretty good. A lot of
jazz men won't admit it, but a classical background never
hurt a guy's style none. A lot has been made of the African
rhythm and blue tonality elements of jazz. But without
European atonated melody, Dad, all you've got is a lot of
cats beating on hollow logs.

Bodanoff had very little syncopation, and he blew pianos
like he was mad as hell at them. But Con's sound came
through. Conners was a mean man with a melody. Even
without a bass and guitar, they swung.

The stuff in the piano stool was mostly unfinished chord
patterns with no bass. But bass was my middle name. I
made Alex pick out the tunes while I slapped the doghouse

in my mind. I made him play it all from the top. By the time he was finished he was sweating and his tongue was hanging out for anther drink. Drinks we had. Dorothy kept spooning it to him just fast enough to keep him from seeing snakes and slow enough to keep him from passing out. She couldn't cook, but she was a very talented girl.

I picked out eight or nine good melodies and started fooling with them. I told Dorothy to water the Alex and took his place at the Steinway. I let my left hand blow improvisations on the bass while my right stayed in the groove so the melody wouldn't get lost.

Maybe I couldn't read music, but I knew how to blow it. By three in the morning I was ready to have Alex start writing some of it down. He was busy.

I opened the bedroom door and said, "Dorothy. All I said to give him was a drink."

From the shadows, Dorothy sighed, "I know, Benji. But I just can't stand to see a man cry."

Alex emerged, wearing my pajamas and a guilty grin, at eight in the morning. I'd worked the music out by then to where I could blow it in my sleep. I nearly was. Only the grim gray thought of Monday morning with no score kept me awake.

"Are you angry with me, Ben?" Alex mumbled.

"Oh Christ, Alex," I said. "It's too early in the morning for Noel Coward dialogue. Are you ready to put some of this down on paper?"

I started blowing the sweet and hot theme I'd picked for the love scenes. It even swung to me. I'd used Fletcher Henderson's solid gimmick of harmonizing the solo line, adopting a call and response pattern, and thrown in a lot of riffs for the cats to swing on. It sounded big band.

Alex nodded gravely all through the set and then said, "I like it."

"That's big of you," I said. "Now look, Dad. You've drank all the booze and made all the dames in the house.

Are you ready to go to work, or do I have to beat your pointed head flat with an ice mallet?"

Alex grinned. "Cossack!" he said. "Out of my way. I, Alex Alexandrovitch, am ready to play. I am in the groove and the spirit is moving me. We are going to *jam*, dad-dio!"

He wasn't just a woofing, either. I'd hit eight to twenty-four bars and he'd blow it back and transcribe it to the paper. The only hitch was when I had to let him stop for a break, or another drink.

Then he'd insist on at least fifteen minutes conversation about the origins of the incest taboo, Zoroastrianism, or the dental condition of Melanesian cannibals after being forced on a low protein diet. His favorite topic, the one I had the most trouble getting him off of, was his theory of Luciferism.

According to Alex, we weren't living on the planet Earth at all. He insisted we were all in Hell. The world was run by Lucifer instead of God and we were all here to pay for sins in another world. The reason nobody knew it was that if we knew we were in Hell it wouldn't be so bad. This way, thinking it was run on the level, we knocked our hearts against a stone wall of frustration while the devil laughed. He pointed out that the good die young as proof. The good were the spirits of people who'd been just a little bad in the other world. The longer you lived, in other words, the bigger a bastard you must have been wherever we really came from.

Life was one big horrible climb up a greased pole to nowheres, according to Alex. A greased pole that rose out of emptiness below us and disappeared into a black dream above us. Only the drunks had enough sense to see the top was just as horrible as the bottom and slide. The rest of us cats sneered at them as they slid down past us, he agreed, but where in Hell did we think we were climbing to?

Life was just one big frustration anyways. Alex pointed out some choice examples. The millionaire who owned half the oil wells in Texas and had an idiot son and cancer. Or the movie star who was the idol of American women. A man who could have any woman he wanted except that he was a hopeless homosexual. Then there was his pet example. The French engineering officer who devoted his life to building the impregnable Maginot Line, and had the fun of watching the Germans march around the end of it through Belgium.

It was crazy, but it bugged me. I was dead tired and half crocked anyways. As we worked on the music over that long crazy week end it made a certain grim sense. I thought of poor Daddy Halloway, Franky the Drum, and Blanche. All mixed up inside by something that happened before anybody alive today was born. No matter how many white friends they made, a beady eyed skipper of a Yankee slave ship was still cracking his whip at them from his weed grown grave.

And Con Conners, who wouldn't carry a cross, except the one he made for himself out of expensive booze and cheap floozies.

There was Alex, drinking away the Russian Revolution and hiding his talent behind a burlesque of Ivan the Terrible. And Dorothy, so afraid of being considered square that she made a roving punch board out of her body.

And there was Johnny Angel. What was Angel's cross? What was the carrot hanging before his nose that made him pull his cart over everyone else's toes?

Somehow, in spite of all the chatter, we got it down on paper by four in the A.M. on Monday morning. Alex played it back at me off the map and it swung.

The only reason they gave the Academy Award to Rebecca that year was because Angel's Flight was a lousy picture. It had good music though. That piano stool of Conners' was a gold mine.

I got to Mel Davis's office at nine thirty. The great man wasn't there yet. Johnny Angel and his stooge were. Angel was looking smug as a buzzard over a battlefield. Marvin Knopff was making like an intense young man of the progressive school. He had an ostrich skin brief case in his lap. I hoped he'd worked as hard as I had over the week end.

"Heard from Conners yet?" asked Johnny smoothly. I promptly pasted a worried look across my pan and said, "I can't seem to reach him. But I guess Davis will give us an extension."

The pair of them exchanged knowing glances. I tried not to laugh.

Davis must have been worried. He blew in before ten, like one of the hoi-poloi. The first words out of his mouth were, "All right, Parker, what about the damn score?"

I shrugged my shoulders and said, "I haven't heard from Con yet, Mel. But I've got a few notes we can kick around until he gets here."

Marvin Knopff pounced like a hungry cat. Waving his expensive brief case, he said, "Don't worry, Mel. I've got the opening and the love theme all worked out. I can have the rest of the score by the end of the week."

I didn't say anything. Davis frowned and said, "What about it, Parker? We can't wait much longer."

Knopff cut in, "The hell with Conners, Mel! The jerk is laid up with T.B. in Denver. I've got the music. Right here and now!"

"What about that, Parker?" asked Davis.

"Eager, isn't he?" I smiled. I knew Davis didn't like to be told how to run his picture by a snotty kid like Knopff. Little Marvin was pushing his luck. I helped.

"What can we lose?" I shrugged. "Let's hear what the boy has to blow. If it comes out of a piano like it comes out of his mouth, we have another Gershwin."

Davis smiled crookedly. Knopff said, "Every moment

counts, Mel." Johnny Angel didn't say anything. He just lay low, like Brer Fox watching the Tar Baby. You could almost hear the little gears in his head going tic tic tic while he waited to see which way the wind was going to blow.

Davis said, "O.K. Let's hear it." And led the way down the hall to a soundproof room. He'd punched a button somewhere along the way, and the water cooler brigade filled in after us to help the great man think.

There were a dozen chairs and an upright piano in the room. Davis sat down in one of the chairs, folded his arms across his chest and looked like he was waiting for something to happen.

So there we were, with Davis waiting to see what his staff thought of Knopff's music, and his staff waiting with carefully cultivated dead pans to see what Davis thought before expressing an opinion.

Knopff grinned nervously and spread his sheet music on top of the keyboard. He forced a stage chuckle and said, "They laughed when I sat down to play.... I didn't know the bathroom door was open."

I guess it was supposed to be a joke. Nobody laughed. I started feeling a little embarrassed for the creep. Don't ask me why. I guess I'm a soft hearted slob.

Knopff started pounding the piano. I'd expected him to be bad, but this was ridiculous. It was so bad it scared me.

The boy in the horn rimmed glasses wasn't blowing jazz. I didn't even know if you could call it music.

He'd swiped a lot of Stan Kenton, who was already blowing pretty wild sounds, and twisted it until it howled in agony. The melody would go in one direction for a few bars and come to a dead stop. Then he'd either play a snatch of something else, or start making with something that sounded like a trio of morons with big feet marching towards A flat. From time to time, Knopff would raise both fists and bring them down on the keys like he was mad at them. It was *strange*, man. The strangest. I didn't know it, at the time, but these hideous sounds were the birth pangs of Bop.

Mel Davis couldn't have carried a tune on a comb wrapped in toilet paper, but he'd heard a few bars in the years he'd been producing low budget musicals.

As Knopff kept throwing the upright out of tune, Davis started looking worried. The yes men started to look worried, too. Not enough so they couldn't change their minds if Davis decided he liked it, but worried.

Brer Angel didn't say nothing. He jest lay low.

"This is the opening?" asked Davis when Knopff had finished.

"The love theme," said Knopff proudly. Davis shook his head in bewilderment. "So who in hell is making love, *zombies?*" he asked.

Knopff looked hurt. He said, "It's the new sound, man. In a year or so every band is going to bop this way."

"They're going to what?"

"Bop, you know, Rebop?"

"Never heard of it," said Davis. Neither had I. I thought he was making it up out of his own goof balls at the time.

Knopff said, "This is the new progressive sound, Mel. The public is tired of Glenn Miller and them square swinging cats like Harry James. Man, any high school band can make like Benny Goodman. This is what you need for the picture, Mel. Progressive jazz!"

"What I need for a musical," said Mel Davis, "is music. Jesus H. Christ! I got my choice between a composer who ain't here and zombie music!" He threw me a hurt look.

I said, "Well, it's not as bad as all that, Mel. Con will be here by next week and he's already written eight numbers...."

"Eight numbers!" shouted Davis, "We only need six! Goddammit, why didn't you say you had music with you?"

He looked like a prisoner in death row who'd just been handed a reprieve. I shrugged and pulled out the sheet music from my brief case. I didn't look at Knopff and Johnny Angel as I walked over to the piano. I would have busted out laughing.

Coming after Knopff's god awful noises, Con's numbers sounded even better. I batted out solid big band swing for half an hour before I turned around.

When I did, Mel Davis was beaming at me like a long lost son. The water cooler set looked ready to hoist me to their shoulders and march me once around the lot to the tune of a Nelson Eddy picture.

Only Angel and Knopff weren't joining in the fun and games. Knopff looked bewildered. Looking back on it, I guess he was.

Angel shot me a crooked smile across the room, like I'd just knocked off his queen in a surprise chess maneuver and he hadn't figured his next move.

I gave the sheet music to one of the studio musicians. He took it from me reverently and carried it away like the Holy Grail. Mel Davis stood up and said, "I knew I could count on you, Ben."

Angel came over. His mouth gave me the Mickey Rooney smile while the little snakes in his eyes hissed at me.

"I told you Conners was the man for this picture, Mel," he said. "I was a little worried when I heard he was sick, but with Benny here on his team, we haven't a thing to worry about."

Knopff had gotten the idea he was persona non grata around Mel Davis right now and had slunk off to wait for Angel.

Davis lowered his voice an octave and said, "Confidentially, Johnny, where did you dig up that Knopff character?"

Angel shrugged and grinned sheepishly.

"I guess it's my own fault, Mel," he said. "I wanted to give the kid a break. How was I to know he was squirrely?"

"I thought you said he blew good," I said, twisting the knife.

Again I got that cold smile. The smile of a boyish rattlesnake.

"You know me better than that, Ben." He laughed. "You used to blow with my band. Did we ever blow that... that zombie music?" He chuckled and sighed. "I had a couple of my own arrangements for him to play, Mel. Not as good as Con's, but good enough to fill in if he should, God forbid, not make it.

"Knopff has been bugging me to play this crazy bop stuff the Central Avenue cats have been experimenting with. Remember how I told him it wasn't ready yet, Ben? Anyway, I guess the kid thought this was a good chance to slip some of his own stuff across. I never heard it before today."

"The little bastard!" snapped Davis. "You'd better watch him! I know the kind. Some guys will cut their mother's throat to get ahead. If I were you, Johnny, I'd get rid of him."

"I already have," said Angel. Somehow, this didn't come as such a complete surprise to me as it should have. I'd tried to drop the boom on Angel's head and he'd managed to shove poor Marvin Knopff under it.

Knopff was a jerk. A no-talent schlemihl who was trying to ride a reptile's coat tails to the top. Guys like Marvin Knopff should be stepped on, like beetles, before they multiply.

And yet, as I walked out into the bright June sunlight, I felt kind of sorry for Marvin Knopff.

Like a guy might feel sorry for a wolverine who'd been bitten by a snake....

□   □   □

Johnny Angel stayed out of my way for the next few months and that was the way I dug the most.

Con had blown in by DC-3 halfway through the third week on the picture and I let him carry the ball from there. He and Alex decided they liked each other almost as much as they both liked Dorothy and invited me to join them in a novel social experiment.

I guess I'm just a Midwestern boy at heart. What Alex called polyandry was known as gang shagging on the South Side. It didn't appeal to me then any more than it had when I was twelve years old and Froggy Wilson talked Maria Tallerico into taking off her panties in the garage we used as a club house.

I was working on a social experiment of my own named Lenora. A bit player on the lot who thought I could open doors for her. When she found out I couldn't, she left me for a klieg light man who said his brother in law was a friend of Errol Flynn.

So there I was, all alone in the cold gray dawn of Santa Monica. And, Dad, they don't get any colder or grayer than that. I'd rented a furnished pad with a view of Catalina, on a clear day, from the bathroom window. There aren't nearly as many clear days in Santa Monica as the California chamber of commerce would have one believe.

I didn't mind. Nobody but tourists go to Santa Monica Beach to swim. Californians know better. In the summer the beach shivers under a moist blanket of seaweed scented fog. The winters aren't so foggy. Plenty of rain but not much fog.

What the beach lacked in sunshine it made up for in quail. The girls came down to pick up the overdeveloped types wandering up and down Muscle Beach under a thick coating of sun tan oil and liniment. After the chicks got the message that the muscle men were only interested in each other's biceps, some of them were ready to settle for a slob like me.

They could have done worse. Con had put me on salary and I'd hocked my soul for a cream colored '36 V-8 with white sidewalls, twin pipes, and reclining seats. Mister Ford never made a nicer looking heap than the '36, unless you count the old Continental, and the babes thought I was what they'd come to California to find.

At least, that's how it looked till I met Ginger Tracy, the only girl in the world with lavender eyes.

It was the night we previewed the picture. Mel Davis had scheduled a sneak in a Burbank theater. I went with Con and Dorothy. I brought along a lovely little moron from Laguna with a blonde streak in her pompadored hair and a loose gear in her differential. I think her name was Hazel.

We had to sit through a Walter Pidgeon detective picture and a western before the crawl of Angel's Flight flashed on the screen. I was amazed to see how many people stayed to see it.

The picture was as bad as I'd expected it to be. The only bright spot in the whole dreary episode was when my name flashed among the credits. Right under Con's. It was nice of Con to give a stooge a credit line. "Music by Johnny Angel, Con Conners, Ben Parker." If Marvin Knopff's name was there, I never saw it.

Once I'd thanked Mel Davis and Con for the plug there wasn't much I could do but sit through the lousy picture. Hazel chewed gum as I absently massaged her left breast and tried to stay awake. She cried when the nice girl in the picture broke off with the poor but honest trumpet player to marry the handsome playboy who could offer her everything but love. Diamond tiaras, a fleet of yachts, and a penthouse, yes. But not, alas, true love. It figured. That was what you picked up on Muscle Beach.

After the picture, Con insisted we go out on the town. I'd had all I could stand of Hazel with her clothes on, and after twelve or thirteen years on a bandstand, a night club was not my idea of Shangri-La. But Con was paying for it, and he was the cat I worked for.

Dragging my feet, I let them haul me to a small club just off the Strip. Halfway through my third drink, Ginger Tracy came on to sing. And that, Dad, is what kept little Hazel pure for her true love, the Pacific Fleet.

I took one look at Ginger Tracy and died a little. Dames that good looking ought to be against the law. Her hair was the color of a starling's wing against the cameo skin of her bare shoulders. Her torso belonged on a Greek goddess, and how she got it inside that tight purple dress without busting it wide open is a mystery I never solved.

As soon as she opened her lush mouth to sing, I was had. The sound that came out of that thrush was the most.

Picture Wee Bonnie Baker and Lena Horne at the same time. I know it's tough, Dad, but that was the sound Ginger had. A little girl and jungle cat all rolled up in one velvet voice. The song was supposed to be funny. It wasn't. It left every male in the joint with an empty ache m the pit of his gut. Ginger Tracy was cruelty to animals.

Con shot a sardonic look across the table. "Not a bad looking pig, is she, Ben?" He grinned.

"Please," I said. "You're speaking of the woman I love."

"Relax, Ben," said Con. "Better men than you have tried. That lovely thing is a lez."

"You're kidding!"

"Wish I was, Ben. But everybody knows it. She'd be the biggest thing since Sophie Tucker if she wasn't such a crazy dike."

I looked at the lovely girl with lavender eyes and raised my glass.

"To Lucifer." I shrugged, and downed the drink.

Dorothy perked up at the name. "You've been talking to Alex," she said brightly. "Him and his goddam Lucifer."

Hazel asked, "Who's Lucifer?" Somehow, I'd expected it. Before Dorothy could inform her we were all in Hell I tried to change the subject.

"What do you think of us giving those destroyers to England, Con?" I asked. I'd just read where F.D.R. had slipped fifty over-aged tin cans to Churchill. Just in case Hitler didn't know which side we were on.

"We should have hung on to them," said Con. "We're going to need them."

"Think we're going to get in it?"

"Hell yes, within a year," he snapped. "And all I can do is play piano and hang around with cheap broads."

Dorothy pouted, "Consi, that's not very nice of you."

Conners shook his head as if he were trying to clear it. He'd had too much to drink and his face was a pale mask with two bright red cheeks. He grinned and said, "I'm sorry, Dottie. I'm drunk."

"It's still a helluva thing to say to a nice girl."

"You're right. I said I was sorry. Just let's not talk about the war. It sorta bugs me."

"But Consi dear, you don't have to worry. Even if we get into the war, they won't take *you!*"

Con looked bleakly at me across the table and for a minute I saw the death's head we all carry less than an inch under our smiling faces. His lips twitched and he said, very gently, "That's right, baby. They won't take me."

Hazel said, "Why?"

It figured. I kicked her under the table and said, "Ixnay on the estionsquay." Con grinned and sipped his drink.

"It's all right, Ben. The little lady is entitled to know all." His voice sunk to a low conspiratorial tone as he said, "You see, Hazel, the army won't take me because my seeing eye dog has flat feet." It was a pretty stale gag, but I guess it was the best he could do while he was crying.

Ginger Tracy'd finished her set and I'd managed to file her away among my fond memories. I put her right between Clara Bow and Jean Harlow. I never made them either, but it didn't kill me.

So it came as a surprise when she joined us at our table a few minutes later. Up close she was even rougher on the glands than she was on the stage. She smiled brightly at Conners and said, "Con! How nice to see you again."

Con shot me a wry look and mumbled an introduction. He didn't offer her a seat. I could have killed him. Hoping my voice wouldn't crack like a kid's, I said, "Won't you join us, Miss Tracy?"

So you could have thought of a better line with your collar choking you to death?

Sliding into a seat across the table in a cloud of perfume, she said, "I've got a problem."

Con looked sardonically at me and cracked, "What's her name?" Ginger either didn't get the innuendo or she didn't give a damn. She dimpled prettily and went on talking as if we were all her life long friends. I was.

"I'm having trouble with the manager," said Ginger. "First he asked me to mix with the savages between sets. You know what that sort of thing can lead to."

"Sure," grinned Con. "Big tips."

Ginger shot him a look that should have melted him and went on. "So now he's getting grabby. Wants to take me home to see his collection of early American contraceptives. I was wondering if you folks would help me out...."

"How?" asked Con. "I never use the things, myself."

From the way he was ranking her, I got the idea she'd stepped on his toes one time. Hard. Con was a sweet guy. Why was he acting like a heavy in a Tom Mix picture?

I could see the flicker of scared tears in those lavender eyes and it made me feel like the marshal of Dodge City. I said, "Hey Con, you're reaching for them tonight. What do you want me to do, Ginger, tell the cat I'm your tough cousin from Detroit?"

Ginger smiled. She'd been playing up to Con and it was the first time I got the full force of her disintegrator beams. I wanted to roll over and butter myself for her.

"You don't have to bulge a muscle at the poor man." She laughed. "But I thought maybe I could leave with you folks after the next set."

A sharp toe dug into my ankle under the table. Dorothy was too far away, so it must have been Hazel. I ignored the warning and said, "You can ride with Hazel and me. We'll be glad to drop you off."

"Off the Pacific Palisades," muttered Hazel.

Ginger smiled fondly at her and stood up. "I don't know how to thank you, Ben," she trilled. "I'll join you right after this next set."

When she'd gone and I could breathe again, Con said, "You notice how she remembered the name, Ben? That's a sure sign."

"A sign of what?"

"Of a lez, you jerk! No normal female remembers a guy's name the first time she hears it, unless she's flipped for him. But when a she-dike wants something out of a man she spreads it on thick. She digs the male ego better than most broads. That's 'cause she's got one herself!"

I growled, "You're worse than Franky the Drum. He's got nine thousand ways to spot a gay type. Most of them wrong. I remember one time in Sioux City he made a grab at a local pea picker who had the corner of his handkerchief sticking out of his hip pocket. It seems that in certain circles a hankie in the hip pocket is an open invitation to buggery. Only it ain't in Sioux City. Franky wound up with his head in a urinal and his wallet among the missing. The pea picker hadn't heard the bit. He didn't know he was gay and it annoyed hell out of him to hear it from Franky."

Con laughed. "Why didn't I think of that? I should have rolled the little bitch!"

"Consi?" asked Dorothy. "Did you get fresh with that girl?" Both babes leaned forward expectantly, with that dirty look only a female face can get, while they waited for Con to cue them in on Ginger Tracy's sex life.

Con sipped his drink. The red spots on his cheeks were brighter and his mouth was twisted in a bitter grin. "I never," he said with drunken dignity, "discuss my affairs publicly. That is, unless I score."

Hazel said, "Tell us about it. Where did you meet her?" The three man combo was blowing tinkle music and I grabbed Hazel's arm.

"Let's dance, chick," I said. The two of them were getting Con wound up and I didn't want to hear. He was my pal and I didn't want to belt him while he was drunk. He might hit back.

A million years went by. Ginger came back out and did a few more novelty numbers with very blue lyrics and then segued into a torch song that made every man in the joint feel younger, and every woman but Ginger look older than God.

As soon as the set was finished she threw a lynx jacket on over the purple gown and rejoined our party. As we headed for the parking lot a pudgy type in a night club tan and tux gave me the evil eye.

"Eat your heart out, you poor jerk!" I thought. As I opened the door for Ginger, my rolling bedroom seemed as classy as Harold Teen's Jalopy. She had that effect on everything. Compared to Ginger, everything in sight was sort of third rate. Me included. It was inferiorating.

Ginger offered to take a cab. An expensive business in L.A. I told her to save her money for heroin and offered to drive her home. This went over with my date like a lead balloon. Hazel lived in Laguna Beach. Ginger was staying at the Beverly Wilshire. Only a few dozen blocks away in Beverly Hills. Guess who I took home first?

Hazel steamed silently between us all the way to Laguna while Ginger and I twinkled. I must say the girl from Laguna was a good sport about it. She didn't shoot me.

I offered to walk her to the door. "Don't bother!" she snapped. "I had a lovely evening. Thanks for nothing!" And then she walked out of my life and into the arms of the U.S. Navy.

"I hope I haven't loused you up with your date," purred Ginger when we were alone. I started the car up and laughed. "There's more than one Hazel on the beach. Where do we go from here?"

"Home, James," she trilled. "I've enjoyed the ride, even if you did haul me halfway to San Diego in the process, but I've got to get to bed and take care of my youth."

"Really? Why didn't you bring him with you?"

Gravely, Ginger said, "You stole that from Noel Coward."

"I always steal my material from the best," I said just as gravely.

We were wheeling and dealing up Highway 101. The moon was hanging over the hills to the east and the Pacific was sending phosphorescent breakers ashore. It was the kind of night that makes you want to drive fast and far. Right off the end of the world.

I said, "I really ought to have a full orchestra and a voice like Nelson Eddy for a night like this. Then maybe I could talk you into sticking around."

"Really, Ben, I've got to get home."

"Look, Ginger, I'm not on the make." She didn't answer. I said, "Well sure, I guess I am. I'd be nuts if I wasn't. But what I mean is.... Well, hell. Can't we do *something*? I've just met you and it's too early to say goodnight. I'll behave

myself. I'll buy you a hamburger at Simon's, or take you
for a ride in the electric boats at Westlake Park, or even
take you grunion hunting."

Ginger laughed. A skylark laugh. "What in the world is
a grunion?" she asked.

"Little sardines," I said. "They swarm ashore along the
coast every full moon in the summer. The kids go down
to the beach with buckets and catch them with their
hands."

Ginger looked at me and raised an eyebrow. "What in
the world do you do with the grunions after you've caught
them?"

"Beats me. I've never caught one. Eat them, I guess."

"Sounds kind of icky. What do the silly little fish swarm
up on the beach for if all these cannibalistic adolescents
are waiting for them?"

"Well, it's where they mate. The full moon and all that."

"I might have known that was what was on your mind!"
She grinned. "I think I'll settle for a hamburger at Simon's.
It's only a few blocks from the hotel."

"Westlake Park?"

"It's closed at this hour."

"The La Brea tar pits?"

"In an evening gown and lynx jacket? To Simon's, James.
And home!"

□   □   □

She wasn't kidding, either. When she ordered hamburger
with Bermuda onion at the drive-in, I knew all was lost.
The lobby of the Beverly Wilshire is kind of public to
hold a wrestling match, so I let her go at the elevator with
a handshake.

I was halfway home before I figured out how I was
going to see her again. I made a U turn in the middle of
Sawtelle and drove back to Con's place on the Strip. Con
was up, alone, when I got there. He was sitting at the

piano in his undershirt blowing sad and blue. There was a half empty bottle of gin on the music rack and Con was feeling no pain.

"Con," I said. "I'm cutting out on you."

He blinked and stopped playing. "Et tu, Brute?" he sighed. "Was I really that nasty tonight? First Dorothy and now you."

"Dorothy's gone?"

"Like the snows of yesteryear," he said. "I said something she didn't like on the way home and she walked out in a huff. She claims I insulted her. Though God knows how anybody could. She took Susie Q and three bottles of gin and left me Alex. I guess it's my fault, but I'll miss the little bitch."

"Don't worry, Con. You'll get her back."

"I hope so. Susie Q was a pretty expensive dog."

Con took a swig from the neck of the bottle and put it back on the music rack. "I'd offer you some of this," he said, "but it might kill you. And, Dad, I don't mean the booze. The damned little bugs are getting so thick I can taste them. Was I really that bad tonight, Ben?"

"Hell no," I said. "I'm not cutting out because I'm mad at you, Con. It's just that I finally got some place to go."

"Thanks."

"Come off it, Con. You know I've just been stooging off you at a higher price than I'm worth. You took me out of the gutter and I'm grateful as hell. But I'm about ready to stand on my own two feet again. I don't want to do it on your time."

"You got a job?"

"No. I'm going to start my own combo. I'm thinking about cutting a record or two now that I have a few connections."

"With Ginger Tracy on the vocal," laughed Con. It was a statement, not a question. I grinned sheepishly.

"Can you think of a better way to get next to her?"

"Not without getting twenty years," said Con. "You ever hear of Don Quixote?"

"What's he got to do with me, Con?"

"I'll tell you what it's got to do with you, you poor schnook. Ginger Tracy is poison. You think you're the first guy who heard her sing? Sure she's got talent. And she makes Lana Turner look like a Harvey girl. But she's meshuga. She's a bitch on wheels and as queer as a three dollar bill."

"Why, Con? What's eating her?"

"How should I know? All singers are nuts anyways. They're worse narcissists than actors, and that's saying a lot. A dame can't be that beautiful and still be sane anyways. Folks spoil her rotten all her life. Other girls hate her and guys start making grabs at her before she's old enough to know what they're grabbing for. A beautiful dame don't need to think. Nobody's interested in her brain. So it turns into perfumed mush. Some of them turn into Dorothy types and others go the other way and get so goosie they won't let a man open a door for them. That's the kind of a broad Ginger is."

"She don't act goosie."

"Wait until you make a grab, Ben! I did. It was only a little grab. It wouldn't have insulted my mother. Ginger climbed the nearest wall and started screaming rape. The worst part is, when a dame yells rape, somebody always believes her. She got me thrown out of my hotel."

What Con said shook me up a little. I'd never be the ladies' man he was in a million years. But I'd started my plot for the ruination of the girl with the lavender eyes and I decided I might as well bulldoze my way through.

"Look, Con," I said. "Even if she won't play footsie with me I think the dame is a great talent. On top of that, I guess I'm on the level with her. I'll worry about that when the time comes. What I want to know is, can I cut a disc of your East of Sunrise? I can line up a few of the old bunch from the Hot Babies and with Ginger on the vocal we'll have Jack the Bellboy spinning that turntable until he's sick of your name."

Con swayed to his feet and rummaged around in the piano stool. He handed me one of the numbers we hadn't used in the picture. A blue torch Mel Davis hadn't thought was commercial. I wanted to prove he was wrong.

"Help yourself, Ben," said Con. "And I wish you a lot of luck. But you're going to get hurt."

He swallowed a stiff belt from the gin bottle and went into a coughing fit. He put a handful of damp kleenex to his mouth, but not before I spotted the red froth on his lips.

"You need a doctor, Con," I said.

"What in hell for?" he snapped. "To tell me what I already know? I should pay some gonnif half a C to tell me I'm dead?"

"It's as bad as that?"

Con nodded. "I'm living on half a lung and gin," he said. "In Denver they said I had maybe a couple of years if I cut out booze and dames and late hours. I asked the sawbones how long I'd last if I didn't. He said not long."

"So can't you cut down on the eat drink and be merry?"

"What the hell for? To live two or three years as a goddam vegetable?" Con shrugged and looked down at the floor. He spoke in a quiet tone, like he was thinking out loud instead of talking to Benny Parker.

"My grandfather was a rabbi," he said. "A nice old Polish Hebe with a beard down to his belly button. My father hated his guts. I can still remember when the old man died. My dad changed his name a couple of weeks later, and I grew up fighting kids who thought an Irish kid with a Jewish face was funny as hell.

"I never had any religion. I never met a dame I could level with. I never found anything that meant a goddam thing to me except the keyboard and having a ball. And lately, with the streetcar getting near the end of the line, the dames and the booze have gone kind of flat. Did that crazy Russian fill you in on the Lucifer bit?"

"Who, Alex? Yeah, he thinks we're all in Hell."

"Maybe he's got something, Ben. Look at me. I got a top ASCAP rating. The dough rolls in as regular as the sewage at Redondo Beach and I've never had any trouble keeping my bedroom occupied. And the only thing I want to do I can't."

"What's that, Con?"

He grinned sheepishly. "You'll laugh. It's sillier than you wanting to climb in the hay with Ginger Tracy."

"I won't laugh, Con. Promise."

Con took a deep breath. "I've never told a goddam soul, Ben. I know it's silly as hell. But, knowing I ain't going to be around much longer makes it worse."

"What is it, Con? What do you want to do?"

"Well, if I wasn't sick, I'd go up to Canada and join the R.C.A.F."

I'd promised not to laugh, so I didn't. He nodded and went on.

"That's right, Ben. I'd join up. I used to fly, you know. And God knows they could use me over in London right now. But they'd just laugh at me. The jerks. Sure, I got half a lung and I couldn't fight my way out of a wet paper bag. But so what? Isn't it better to use guys like me instead of young kids with their whole lives ahead of them? If I could take maybe one or two Nazi bombers with me I'd feel I'd done something to pay the bastards back and I'd rather go out in a blaze of glory than wait around for the bugs to kill me."

He grinned and said, "Hell, I sound like G-8 and his Battle Aces! I don't even know why I have an axe to grind with Hitler. God knows I've never been a good Jew. Until this concentration camp bit started, I used to say I was a goy. Guys like my grandfather creep me. They smell of kosher salami and they cry too much about God. But they're my people, the poor nebbisches. And when I think of some poor old Polish Hebe like grandpa Cohen digging his own grave because the Hitlerjungen who wants to kill him is too lazy, it bugs me. Do you suppose I'm nuts?"

I laughed and rolled the sheet music up to put in my pocket. I said, "Hell no, Don Quixote. Care to join me in a go at the windmills?"

"Yours is built better than mine," he said. "Where are you going, Ben?"

"Thought I'd go home and hit the sack," I said. "It's almost morning."

Con licked his lips and took another drink from the bottle. He looked out the window and said, "It'll be daylight soon, Ben. Do me a favor?"

"Sure, Con. What is it?"

"Stick around until the sun comes up? I'm afraid of the dark."

□   □   □

Finding the remains of the Hot Babies was tougher than I'd expected. I hadn't seen Blanche Halloway since that last night at the hotel in Frisco. I'd meant to look her up when I hit L.A., but what the hell was I supposed to say?

But now that I had an excuse that didn't have nothing to do with Johnny Angel, I tried to find her. She'd moved from the valley address Chico the Sax gave me. I finally located her new address. She was living in a frame house on Diamond Street. Not the worst neighborhood in the Mexican district, but a long ways from the best.

I played a hunch and called from a bar on the corner. It was a good hunch. A thick Spanish accent answered the phone. I didn't ask who he was. But he wanted to know who in the hell I was and what I wanted with Blanche. I told him I was looking for the phone numbers of some people we knew. He said, "What the hell you think this is, information?" and hung up. I decided to quit while Blanche was ahead.

I'd already found Chico and we dug Tommy the Axe out of a tuna cannery in Monterey. He was so glad to stop stuffing fish in tin he agreed to work on spec. Not that I had anything else to offer.

Tommy knew a cat from Pismo who owned his own vibes and knew how to blow them. I got Stretch Voss to make with the horn while I went back behind the doghouse. Now all we needed was a set of traps and a canary. Franky the Drum was on the east coast and I'd already made up my mind not to have any junkies or queers in the group. I finally latched on to a kid from Venice who could make a set of brushes talk pretty and called up Ginger Tracy.

O.K. So I wasn't Paul Whiteman. What in hell did she expect? Most unknown singers would have thrown their mother's guts into a revolving fan to cut a record. Even with us. I had to twist her arm.

When she finally agreed to at least look at the studio she brought along a frosty looking dame in a mannish tailored suit and a short haircut. "My lawyer," she said.

I shrugged it off. What Con had said about her being on the gay side was getting harder to laugh off. But no man really believes a woman can give him competition with a chick.

Ginger thawed out a little when she saw I really had a contract for her to sign and a distributor lined up. You couldn't really blame her. Telling a babe you're going to put her in a picture or on a disc is a favorite line. By the time we were ready to cut the platter she even left her lawyer behind.

You might have heard that side. It was mostly Ginger. We just tooled along in the background while she wrapped her husky voice around Con's lyrics and purred. Stretch did a little improvising along with the vibes and sax in the break, but it was Ginger's record. She should have sky rocketed with that one platter. She didn't. And I lost every dime I sunk into the deal.

I'd heard about the trouble ASCAP was having with the networks. ASCAP, the song writers' and publishers' union, was holding out for more dough. I don't know who was right and who was wrong. I'm an ASCAP man myself, but in those days who wasn't?

BMI had never been heard of and ASCAP was the only union there was. So when the networks turned down the union, ASCAP pulled every pop song since Jeannie With the Light Brown Hair off the air. This naturally included everything Con Conners ever wrote. So while the radio blared Stephen Foster and Red River Valley for the next few months, East of Sunrise gathered dust in the warehouse. I hear they finally unloaded most of them at nineteen cents each on Sixth Avenue after the war.

The day they called me about the record ban was about the lowest I'd ever felt. The lowest came a few days later. The day Con Conners shot himself.

Alex Bodanoff called me at four in the morning. He was scared sober and I could hardly understand him. He kept lapsing back into Russian as he begged me to come over. I piled in the heap and drove to Con's place. There were more people there than Coney Island on a hot day. I elbowed my way in past a brace of cops.

"You a reporter?" asked the cop.

"No. I'm a friend of Mr. Conners'. I came over to see if there's anything I can do."

"You can help us get hold of his relatives. Has he got a wife?"

"Not that I know of. When did he kill himself?"

"He didn't."

"Con's still alive?" I asked, relieved.

"Six of one and a half a dozen of the other," shrugged the cop. "He shoved the barrel of a Luger in his mouth and pulled the trigger. First time I ever heard of a guy doing that and living."

"Didn't it go off?" I asked.

He pointed at a stain on the rug and what looked like hamburger smeared on the wall near the kitchen door. He said, "It went off. Tore his left mastoid and half his jaw out by the roots and scattered them around. He missed his brain pan and spinal cord by a spider's eyelash. Silly bastard didn't even black out. It took Bodanoff and two prowl car boys to hold him on the mat till the meat wagon got here."

"Where is he now? Which hospital?" I asked. The cop shrugged.

"The one down on Pico, I think. You won't find him there, though. Soon as they patch him up they'll ship him to the county bughouse."

"Conners?" I gasped. "Hell, there's nothing wrong with him. He's been waiting around for a dose of T.B. to kill him and I guess he wanted to go with the lights on. But he's not crazy."

The cop shook his head. "You wouldn't want to bet on that, would you? Like I said, it took three guys to hold him down. All the time he was spitting blood and cursing them in Yiddish. Zuckerman, one of the prowl car boys, says he thought they were taking him to a concentration camp."

Alex came out from the bedroom. He was dressed in Con's bathrobe. I didn't have to ask why he'd changed his clothes. I felt a green ball of scream gathering in my throat and swallowed hard. Alex was as sober as I'd ever seen him. His Russian accent was missing. He came over to me and gravely shook my hand with both of his.

I said, "It must have been pretty rugged."

He nodded. "I saw worse things in the revolution, Ben. But it's been a long time. It wasn't the blood. It was his eyes, Ben! It was like looking into Hell! I was in the kitchen, fixing sandwiches for us, when it happened. I heard the gun go off. When I came out Con was standing there with the gun in his hand and blood all over the front of him. He stood there staring at me, as if he was surprised to be alive. I guess he was.

"He didn't say anything until I took the gun out of his hand. Then he started to laugh. My *God!* The way he laughed, with gouts of blood running out of his mouth and gurgling in his throat like a toilet flushing. I called the police while Con stood there and giggled. He was all right until he saw the uniforms. Then he really started climbing the wall!"

I slipped Alex a ten spot. I knew he didn't have a dime and couldn't stay in the apartment now. Then I went outside and threw up all over the trunk of a palm tree.

A voice near my elbow said, "What's the matter, Ben? You sick?" It was Johnny Angel. I felt like an idiot.

I wiped my mouth and said, "What are you doing here, creep?"

"I just heard about Con," said Angel. "I thought maybe I could help out."

"You could pick up the gun and rid the world of a louse," I snarled. Johnny looked hurt.

"What are we fighting about, Ben? We had a few run-ins in the past, but that's all water under the bridge. Maybe I stepped on a few toes on the way up. Maybe I stepped on yours. But I was hungry, Ben. I'm not hungry any more. Even with this record ban I'm pulling in much loot with my band. Besides, there's nothing in it for me to hurt you, so you don't have to be afraid of me any more."

"Who was ever afraid of you, creep?"

Angel smiled. That knowing, sneering smile. I wanted to cave his teeth in for him. But there were a dozen cops within earshot and I knew Johnny Angel would holler for them if I spit on the sidewalk.

I went back inside and dictated a statement to the cat

from the D.A.'s office. Then I lit out before they showed the blood to Johnny. I didn't throw up again until I got home.

One thing you have to say for Angel. Johnny didn't do anything halfway. When he decided at an early age to become a bastard, he didn't settle for pedestrian bastardry. He was a bastard with talent. It was the only real talent he had. But it was almost genius. For instance: even after I'd heard a couple of Con's unpublished numbers over the air, right in the middle of the record ban, I didn't get the connection. I didn't have that much imagination.

Con had been taken out of the county laughing academy by ASCAP and put in a private sanitarium. Even with the record ban on he had enough back dough coming to keep him in style.

I went up there one day with Alex to see him. It wasn't the biggest ball I ever had. They had Con in a padded cell with what looked like leather handcuffs on his wrists. The head shrinker said they'd had to do that after Con had pulled two gold caps off his teeth with his bare fingers and hidden them in his rectum so the Nazis wouldn't get them.

They'd patched up his ruined jaw pretty well, although he still had some plastic surgery to go, and arrested the T.B. But there wasn't much they could do with Con's mind.

His latest kick was that this whole bit was a movie. The day I was there he was being Warner Baxter in the old movie about Juaquin Murrieta called Robin Hood of El Dorado. This was where they had Juaquin in jail and he was planning to have Leo Carillo bail him out. As the doctor opened the door for us he glared at him and sneered, "You'll never hang me, Sheriff. Just wait until Three Finger Jack gets here with my gang!"

Knowing Con, I was sure he was kidding. He looked at Alex and me and said, "Who are you?"

I said, "Buck Jones. I'm on your side."

A look of low cunning crossed Con's face. He spit at my feet and sneered, "You dirty bastard. Who do you think you're kidding? Buck Jones isn't in this picture!"

The head shrinker touched my arm. "You'd better go, Mr. Parker," he said in a low voice. "When he's like this visitors excite him." He didn't have to twist my arm.

Driving back to L.A. with Alex, I flipped on the car radio in time to hear the last fourteen bars of one of the mysterious records I'd been worrying about. I said, "Alex, don't that sound like one of Con's numbers? One of those half-written things he had in the piano stool?"

Alex listened for a moment and said, "I think you're right, Ben. And that novelty number about the two birds in the nest sounds a lot like that one Mel Davis turned down along with East of Sunrise."

I was getting a sick feeling in the pit of my gut. I slowed down and shot Alex a look. "Damn!" I said, "The piano stool! In all the excitement I forgot about it! What's happened to Con's furniture?"

Alex said, "They put it in storage for him. Bekin's Warehouse in Beverly Hills, I think."

I said, "Yeah, but what about the sheet music, Alex? Did you see it after that night?"

Alex struck the heel of his palm against his forehead. "Benny!" he shouted. "I just remembered!"

"Yeah," I grunted. "Johnny Angel was there that night."

Back in town, I called Con's publisher and was told he hadn't sent the sheets to them. I called a D.J. I knew and asked who in hell had written them.

The songs had been published in the east by a certain Marvin Knopff. I called Angel at his hotel. When I got him on the phone I said, "You sonofabitch. I'm going to beat your brains in."

"Any particular reason, Ben?" Angel yawned. "Or are you just feeling beastly?"

"You goddam ghoul!" I yelled. "You swiped the sheet music out of Con's piano stool in front of the L.A. police force."

Angel chuckled. "That would have been kind of crude, Ben." He laughed. "Lt. Hegar *gave* me the sheet music I'd ordered from Con."

"He *what?*"

"You heard me, Ben. I told Hegar I'd come over to pick up the score for our new picture. He said it was a little irregular but he sort of looked the other way when I told him we had a deadline to meet."

In spite of myself I was curious. Johnny's only weak spot was his sadistic delight in telling you what a clever little boy he was. I said, "So how come you let Marvin Knopff take the bows for those sides, Angel? With practically nothing to play, the networks are wearing those discs out. Knopff must be making a mint."

"You know better than that, Ben," laughed Angel. "I can't put them out under my handle. It would put me in bad with ASCAP. And they might win."

"So Knopff is sticking his neck out for you while you collect the loot on those records?"

"You and me should work together, Ben. We think along the same lines. Only you haven't got the intestinal fortitude."

"Is that what you call stealing now?"

"That's what I call guts, Ben. Something you ain't got. Muscles yes. But no guts. So if you're through crying I'll hang up. I've got a redhead from Sioux City here who thinks she can sing better than Maxine Sullivan. I want to see what her other talents are before I sign her up."

"You bastard. I'm going to ASCAP with the whole story."

"Be my guest, Ben. Do you think anybody will listen to you?"

I said, "I can sure as hell try."

Angel chuckled. It was not a friendly chuckle. He said, "You little jerk. If you get under my feet I'll step on you like a bed bug." And hung up. It shook me.

Sure, I could whip him any day in a fair fight. But who fights fair any more? Nowadays men don't fight with swords or even fists. They fight with money and the brutal power money can give. A little jerk you could break over your knee in a minute can send you to jail or run you out of town if he has the right connections. And Johnny had connections.

I realized he'd been playing cat and mouse with me for a few amused minutes until the game bored him. Then he'd bared his claws and told me to get lost. The worst part was, I had a nasty feeling that was about all I could do.

Angel had a foot on both bases. If ASCAP won the strike he was in like Flynn. And if this new BMI outfit got off the ground he was in with them too, through his dummy, Marvin Knopff. And all I had was a mess of un-paid bills.

So I went on the road with my hungry little combo. I tried to get Ginger to go with us but she acted like I was asking her to take up prostitution. I got a thrush named Mabel. Never mind her last name. She lived on jelly beans, sang off key, and shacked up with Stretch Voss the third night out.

Looking back on it since, it was a lot of laughs. We lost Mabel in Baltimore to a local yokel who offered her more than Stretch to park her slippers next to his. We picked up another thrush who crossed the color line for Tommy the Axe. Which was all the same with me, but we had to cancel a couple of bookings south of the Ohio to keep Tommy from decorating the end of a clothesline.

We'd swung down Route 66 from Chi, planning to play the coast by Christmas, when it happened. Chico came tearing into the club waving a screaming headline. It read:

JAPANESE PLANES BOMB PEARL HARBOR!

I didn't know if Pearl Harbor was a place or the name of a Hawaiian stripper, but I knew what it meant. It meant the balloon was going up. Con's war had arrived. Stretch and Tommy the Axe joined up the next morning. Chico got the vocalist.

I thought they were nuts, but I didn't say so. People were pretty hysterical those first few days.

The west coast was blacked out and a bunch of characters went running around waving blue-tinted flashlights, screaming, "Douse them goddam lights!"

In L.A. somebody saw something up in the sky and the army fired a million dollars worth of ammunition into the smog. The falling shell fragments busted roof tiles and windows all over town, but it made people feel better.

It got kind of rough to be an oriental on the coast. A whole page of the Constitution got lost while a few thousand American citizens who were unlucky enough to have Japanese grandparents were rounded up and hauled off to concentration camps. We knew the Germans were lousy to do it to the Jews, but this was different. "These bastards are Japs." It got so Chinese waiters were going around town with American flags and pictures of Chang Kaishek in their hatbands. Some of them got beat up anyways.

I had other things on my mind. The war didn't interest me half as much as a certain girl with lavender eyes. The closer I'd gotten to L.A. the more Ginger had been on my mind. I'd had a lot of time in the past year to torch it over her. I'd tried every way out I could think of and it was no go. It was pretty silly for a big brave boy like Benny Parker, but I was ready to admit defeat.

Ginger was playing a small club right across from the one where Johnny Angel had slithered into my life. It's a small world. I dropped in one night to catch her act. I was hoping she might have gotten fat or grown a beard. I was out of luck. Damned if she didn't look better than ever.

I had a hell of a time getting her over to my table until she saw who it was. Then she beamed at me clear across the room and joined me between sets.

"Ben Parker, it's good to see you again," she said, smiling.

I said, "What's with this last name bit, Ginger? I'm your tough cousin from Detroit, remember?"

"Oh, sure, cousin. I remember you now. We used to hunt grunion together." Either she didn't have many dates or I'd made a hell of an impression. It had been over a year ago.

I said, "It seems to me we cut a record one time, too."

"Please, Ben," she groaned. "Don't remind me! It looked so good until the bubble busted."

"I know," I said. "That's one of the things I wanted to talk to you about. The record ban is over now. How'd you like to cut another side with me?"

"On the level?"

"Honey," I said, "you don't know how level I am with you. The record is just one of the things I've got planned. How about letting me take you home?"

"By way of Seattle this time?" she laughed. "I'm staying at a hotel just a few blocks away, Ben. And I'm on a diet."

"You don't give a guy a fighting chance, do you?" I grunted. "Can't I even *walk* you home?"

Ginger smiled and I could feel my ears redden like a school kid on his first date. "I'll see you after my next set," she purred.

The trip up Angel's Flight was an inspiration. I'd forgotten the damned thing was there until we passed it on the way to Ginger's hotel. One of the cable cars was about to leave for the top. I grabbed her arm and said, "Come on. I've always wanted to see what the hell was up there."

Ginger looked dubiously at the little yellow car. "I've got to get home, Ben."

"Live dangerously," I said.

She dimpled and gave in with a shake of her head. "This is silly," she said. We took a seat near the rear platform. At this hour the car was nearly empty. The conductor ding-dinged a signal to the winch house up on the hill and we started with a lurch. Ginger stiffened and I put my arm on the back of the seat. She edged away and I eased off. Con had said she was goosie, but this was ridiculous.

The trip up was a lot of fun. Like a roller coaster ride without the drop off at the top. The streets we'd left fell away below us until the people on the sidewalk watching us looked like toys. It was a short ride. We got off and walked out of the station on top of the hill. The street that ran along the crest was dark at this hour. There was what looked like a closed grocery store down the block and a beer sign flashed on and off in the distance. Ginger looked around at the cluster of small buildings on top of Angel's Flight and said, "Is this all there is up here?"

"Yeah." I laughed. "It's hardly worth the ride up, is it? I know a guy who ought to see this."

"So," asked Ginger, "now that we're up here, what is there to do?"

"Go back down, I guess. But first I want to talk to you about something." I walked her over to the crest of the hill. We could look down at the spider web of lights below. A mist was blowing in from the sea and it looked like as good a background as I was ever going to get. I said, "Look, kitten. I got something to unload. I know I should have the sound track playing something on the schmaltzy side from behind that board fence. The fence ought to be covered with roses instead of worn out whitewash and I ought to have a better script, but—"

"Please, Ben. Let's not get biological."

"Shut up and listen. I'm not propositioning you, you dumb broad. I'm asking you to marry me!"

Ginger laughed suddenly. "That's the most romantic thing I've ever heard, Ben. Who writes your proposals, Raymond Chandler?"

I threw her a sheepish smile and said, "I'm not in practice, kitten. I don't usually go for broke with a dame. Look, Ginger. I know it's too soon to expect an answer. What the hell, you hardly know me. I just want to get it straight with you what my intentions are. I mean, I want you. I want you so bad I can taste it. But I'm on the level with you. I want to cut the record with no couch casting deal attached and maybe take you out a few times. And then, if you think you can stand the idea, I want to spend the rest of my life on your team. I'm having a hell of a time getting the words out, Ginger. I love you sounds so goddam corny. There ought to be another word for the way I feel about you. Something that hasn't been used in so many parked cars. I'll tell you what. I'll make up a word for the way I feel about you. Something bigger and better and nicer than love. How does beejum sound?"

"I don't care for beejum. Starkle sounds more romantic, Ben."

"All right," I said. "I starkle you." Then I kissed her. It would have been safer kissing a grizzly bear.

She bit. Hard. She sank her teeth into my lower lip until they met. I've still got the scar. I pulled back and just had time to say, "What the hell?" when she raked me across the face with her nails. "You dirty animal!" she hissed. Her eyes were wild and glazed with terror. Tears ran down her cheeks and her mouth was a square of hate around her bared teeth. "You stinking, hairy, lecherous ape! You men are all alike! All of you!" Her voice rose to a wail and she turned and started running down the street.

I yelled and started running after her. And then it hit me how I'd look to anybody who saw us. Ginger tracking down the street in tears and me with my face ripped open and blood all over the front of my shirt. Any cop who didn't shoot first and ask questions later would be nuts.

I stopped and dabbed at my ruined mouth with my handkerchief. I could hear her high heels clicking off into the misty night.

"Crazy bitch!" I muttered. I looked around me at the nothing much on top of Angel's Flight. There wasn't anything left to do up here now but go back down.

□　□　□

I don't know if it's fair to blame my joining up on the girl with the lavender eyes. I guess I'd have gotten into the war sooner or later anyways. Just about everybody did.

If you were around at the time, you know about the war. If you weren't, you might look through about two hundred back issues of Life, or read Tolstoy. He said everything there is to say about war and this is a story about the music field.

So smoke a cigarette or something while you picture the time lapse and join me along about the spring of '46 in the rest room that used to be under Duffy Square.

The world was once more safe for democracy, the American way of life, the girl next door, and Mom's blueberry pie. I'd changed my ODs for a new set of blue threads and the only way you could tell Benny Parker had been away was that I'd traded my left knee cap for a brand new silver plate, and three or four gray hairs were sprouting over each ear.

I'd gone down into the john for the usual reason and who should I run into but Alex Bodanoff. For a minute I was tempted to give him a miss. My mustering out pay was gone and every time I'd ever seen Alex it had cost me a couple of skins.

But his eyes caught mine and there wasn't anything to do but say hello.

"Ben Parker!" he grinned. "What are you doing in New York?"

I said, "Hi, Alex. I was just about to ask the same thing."

He said, "I've gone legit, Ben. I'm playing piano for a man over in Jersey who makes dirty records."

"It's better than working," I observed. I was still groping for a way to cut out before he made a touch. Alex slammed his paw on my shoulder and said, "Go on and drain your carburetor, Ben. I want to introduce you to my wife. She's upstairs feeding the pigeons."

"Dorothy?" I asked.

Alex looked smug. He shook his head and said, "Last I heard of Dottie she was in San Francisco, married to an insurance salesman from the east and getting fat. You don't know this one, Ben. My God, what a delicious little beast!"

We went upstairs and Alex led me over to a rather vapid girl in doe eyed glasses and flat heeled shoes. She looked pretty young for Alex. Not more than twenty-three or four. Her name was Martha. She wasn't pretty until she smiled.

"Alex has told me so much about you, Mr. Parker," she said, "that I feel I know you." It was unimaginative, but the right thing to say. You got the feeling Martha was an organization type chick. A little country, but nice, and on her husband's side. It was a switch.

They insisted on dragging me uptown with them. I didn't have a thing to lose. I'd been planning to eat at the automat anyway.

The day had been full of surprises ever since I'd noticed they'd taken down the Chesterfield sign. Not only was Alex inviting *me* to dinner for a change, but the address he gave the cab driver floored me. He was living in a very chi-chi brownstone on the east side, up near the Queensboro bridge. The pad must have set him back a couple of bills a month.

Alex parked me on a mile long sofa in front of a for real fire place and I lied to him about the war while Martha pottered around in the kitchen making dinner.

She must have been afraid I was going to curl up and die of starvation before she finished the lasagna. She kept fluttering in like a little brown bird with trays of hors d'oeuvres. It was the first time I'd ever tried smoked oyster served in a dab of sour cream on a cheese cracker. It sent me.

As the evening progressed, I could see what Alex dug in his small bundle of mouse. Martha wasn't the best looking thing that ever came down the pike, but all her features were on straight and you wouldn't kick her out of bed for eating crackers. Her house was neat as a pin and her cooking alone was enough to get most guys to move in with her. She served a light Spanish wine with a smoky aftertaste that set well with the lasagna. Afterward, she curled up adoringly at Alex's feet.

I noticed she hadn't set any wine in front of Alex. He caught the look I tossed at the empty spot by his plate and grinned.

"I'm off the stuff, Ben. Or hadn't you noticed?"

I said, "Congratulations, Alex. But I feel kind of silly drinking alone. Can't Martha even have a glass with me?"

Alex shook his head. "Nope. She's an addictive personality too."

"Come again?"

"An addictive. Like me. Martha and I met about a year ago at an A.A. meeting. To tell you the truth, I'd just gone for the free sandwiches and coffee. Then I met Martha and kept going back to see if she looked as good to me sober as she did when I was drunk. You know what, Ben? She does."

Martha put her head on his knee and he reached down and patted her fondly on the fanny. It was kind of earthy, but on them it looked sweet. I felt like an intruder in some honeymooning couple's bedroom.

I said, "Well, I'd better be shoving along, Alex."

He said, "Nonsense, Benny. I haven't seen you in nearly five years. What are you doing, now that you're back from Lucifer's temper tantrum?"

"You still on that kick?" I laughed. "I'm trying to make connections with the old crowd, Alex. Things are sort of mixed up. I know what happened to Tommy the Axe. Him and Stretch Voss are swinging with Glenn Miller in the big dark. But I haven't found the rest of the boys."

"Do you need a job?" asked Alex. Like I said, it was a night for switches.

"Who do I got to kill?" I asked.

Alex said, "It's not as bad as all that, Ben. Have you ever heard of Hotsi-Totsi Records, over in Jersey?"

"You're kidding. Nobody would name a record company Hotsi-Totsi."

Alex laughed, "Nobody but George Flannery. He's the man I am working for. He makes recordings for stag parties."

I suddenly felt I liked Alex better as a drunk. I said, "You mean, you're working for one of those pornographic outfits?"

Alex winced. "It's not as bad as all that, Ben," he said. "And neither is Hotsi-Totsi Records. You've seen the ads in cheap men's magazines? The ones with a blurb reading, 'Something for really *adult* listeners?'"

"Yeah, they usually have a chick in panties and bra winking at the camera and bulging her lungs."

"Those are Flannery's, Ben. They aren't in very good taste, but the lads who send for them aren't art lovers. Or music lovers, either. They're only interested in the blue lyrics."

"You're going to wind up in jail," I said.

Alex laughed. "I don't think so, Ben. Flannery has a grubby little lawyer who knows just how far you can go without getting into trouble. He's been putting the silly things out for years now without a whisper from the cossacks."

I shrugged and said, "I don't know, Alex. It still sounds pretty icky."

Alex waved a hand at the four expensive walls and said, "It pays, Ben. Flannery doesn't pay a hell of a lot, but he keeps me busy. I couldn't afford this place playing in a restaurant."

One thing the army'd taught me, aside from what I picked up at V.D. lectures, was to keep my mouth shut and my ears open until I had something to offer to the conversation. I toyed with my glass while Alex kept twisting my arm.

"A few sides would put your wallet in pretty good shape, Ben," he said. "And we need at least *one* musician when we cut a record."

"You're selling me," I said. "Does this creep pay union scale?"

Alex sighed. "Of course not. With the talent he signs, he doesn't have to. On the other hand, Flannery pays off in cold green cash. You don't have to report it on your income tax. It comes out just about the same."

"You damned Russians are all anarchists at heart."

"Then I can count you in on the next date?"

"I'll think about it, Alex."

And that, kiddies, is how I wound up in the dirty record business. Only it didn't work out the way it was intended to. Not for George Flannery it didn't. If he'd known what Alex was doing that night, he'd have shot the two of us.

□   □   □

The same night I first cut a side for Hotsi-Totsi Records

I watched Joe Louis clobber Billy Conn on the ten inch screen in a Sixth Avenue bar. I don't know if there's a moral to this or not, but I sort of like to think I grew up with television.

George Flannery was a cherubic looking cat with a halo of snow white hair and a loose upper plate. He'd spent the better part of sixty-five years twisting his ratty little face into a picture of sincerity and upright honesty.

A lot of people, meeting Flannery for the first time, would have been surprised to hear he was in the dirty record business. After you got to know Flannery a little better, you couldn't picture him in any other racket.

He had the soul of a pimp and the ethics of an Arabian rug merchant. Flannery was one of those twisted little weasels who lie when the truth is in their own favor. He worked so hard at being a smart crook he was a lousy businessman. Half the time his left hand didn't know what his right one was doing and he was so busy picking other cat's pockets he didn't watch his own. Whenever anyone got the better of him, even if their name was O'Brien, he called them Jew Bastards. The Jews didn't mind too much. Flannery's dislike was almost a sure sign of a man's honesty.

Flannery's organization was spread out over three or four states. If he kept any books I never saw them. And whether you got paid or not depended on how tough you looked.

The first disc we cut was in a rented studio on 47th Street. Alex beat the Steinway, I slapped the bass, and a Puerto Rican kid named Tico Sanchez strummed the axe. The vocalist was Bunny. Never mind her last name. She's a top torch these days and I don't think working for Hotsi-Totsi Records is something she still brags about.

Like Alex had said, the lyrics were kind of slimy but not a hell of a lot bluer than you'll hear in some supper clubs. It was all double meanings. Nothing Anglo Saxon enough to have the post office down around our ears, but sexy enough to give grins to the young punks with skin trouble and the impotent old foofs who go in for that sort of entertainment.

Flannery paid off in cold green cash on the spot and we all filed out without talking to one another, like customers in a cat house. It made me want to go home and take a very hot shower, with lots of soap. I told Alex not to count me in on the next disc.

But he did. Two weeks later the dough was gone and I still hadn't latched on to anything good. Blowing bass for Bunny's low down and dirty voice wasn't my idea of a musical career, but neither was standing in line at the employment office waiting for a snotty type in a forty dollar suit to lecture me on being a bum before he handed me a lousy twenty bucks.

So I kept slapping the doghouse for George Flannery and taking the dough for it. After a while, it didn't bother me so much. I guess I worked two years or so for Flannery. God knows how many sides we cut in that time. And every week I'd tell myself it was time to get myself in gear.

I'd rented a comfortable pad in the Village for half a bill a month. It had a private entrance and the landlord furnished the hot water. How you heated the joint in the winter was your problem. I got Bunny to help me with the interior decorations. That girl had strange taste in colors. She put on a pair of old blue jeans and my flannel shirt and helped me paint the joint. Orange and burnt cocoa. Like, it glared a little.

But after the blue jeans came off I didn't really mind the walls glowing at me in the dark. Bunny lasted six weeks and the first thing I did when she cut out with a drummer from uptown was to buy five cans of French Blue latex paint and rest my eyes.

This is to sort of cue you in on why I just drifted along with Hotsi-Totsi Records. As you can see I had it made.

Not big but cozy. The pad was clean and I could afford to dress better than most of the cats in the Village. As a matter of fact, as the only guy in the building who was working as an artistic type slob instead of at White Tower or the garment district while I waited for the big break, I was somewhat of a celebrity.

Down the block there was this hole in the wall night club owned by a cat in a black turtleneck sweater who painted very bad imitations of Picasso because he didn't know how to draw people.

One day, as I was standing on the southeast corner of Washington Square gazing in horror at a couple of chicks in the New Look, Black Sweater strolled up beside me.

He had a monkey on his back. I don't mean he was on dope. This was a real live monkey. It had grayish green fur and had to wear little diapers because it wasn't housebroke.

Black Sweater, his name was Sam, said, "Pretty gruesome, isn't it?"

I sighed as I looked at the skinny ankles sticking out from under the long hemlines on the circle skirts the chicks had paid good American gelt for. "That frog, Christian Dior, has a lot to answer for," I said.

"You're a musician, aren't you?" Sam asked.

"When I ain't pushing dope," I grunted. I didn't know if he was after my loose change or my virtue. In the Village, it's usually one or the other when it ain't both.

"How do you feel about this crazy Bop music?" he went on. He'd already told me he thought it was crazy, and this was before crazy meant good.

I shrugged and said, "It's O.K. If you don't know how to blow music. Dizzy Gillespie makes it sound almost reasonable, but the weirdos who ape him are mostly no-talents who want to carve the rest of us cats by making a new sound, even if it's off key."

Sam tickled the monkey under the chin and drew back

his hand before it could bite him. "I got a combo playing now in my club," he said. "I thought they were going to play jazz. The hipster who leads the group says that's what they're playing. Bop jazz. It sounds to me like they're all nuts. Worse. It's driving the customers away."

"I thought this Bop stuff was going big with the Village set," I said. The two girls in the New Look were almost out of sight. You couldn't tell from here whether you were sorry to see them go or not.

Sam the black sweater said, "The hipsters love the stuff, but who wants hipsters? I'm a painter, not a music lover. I only run the joint to pay for my canvas and oils. When I want to get frantic, Dad, I do it with a brush."

"So what's that got to do with hipsters?"

"Man, don't be square. Them creeps ain't got enough gold between them to pay for their own beer. It's the cubes from uptown who pay the rent, and the place only sits fifty couples after I grease the fire inspector. Them hipsters scare the paying customers away!"

I had to laugh. I don't know if you remember the hipster. He wasn't around very long. Those of them who haven't grown up to be beatniks call themselves Hippies today. They're not the same breed of cat. The hipster was the wartime zoot suiter without the zoot suit. A sort of bastard cross between a hoodlum and a musician without the guts of one nor the talent of the other. His trademark was the D.A. haircut and the long key chain. He wore a porkpie hat and a dead pan. He was coooool, Dad. He was so cool he was almost dead.

Not being able to blow a kazoo himself, the hipster insisted on the musical integrity of everyone else. Jazzmen, over the years, had sort of built up a code and jargon of their own. The hipster latched on to this code and jargon and enlarged on it until he was using a musical term to pick his nose. After a while he was talking more music than the cats who blew it. He talked it until he convinced himself that anybody who didn't dig his jive was square. It wound up with Satchmo and the Duke being considered square and Cab Calloway was Uncle Tom because people who didn't smoke reefers liked his music. The world was a better place when he finally swapped his porkpie and key chain for rope soled sandals and a beard. Beatniks are just as obnoxious but they don't play as rough.

I took a chick from the Island, who'd always wanted to see the dark and mysterious byways of the Village, to Sam's a few evenings later. It wasn't hard to see what was driving his paying guests away.

There were two of them arguing with the doorman when we got there. A white punk in a purple suit and a Harlem chick in a green mohair sweater that didn't do a thing for her platinum blonde hair. She looked like the Bride of Frankenstein in blackface.

Sam had a small cover charge, which he wisely collected in advance at the door. The two hipsters didn't think it was fair.

"Like, let us in for free, man, and don't be square," drawled the male member of the duo, in a desperately casual voice. The chick sneered, "Don't you want us to latch on to real art? You want us to think you trying to stamp out progressive jazz? You ain' down south now, daddio."

The doorman let them in with a sigh. He wasn't paid enough to fight. Not that the boy would have had the nerve but the chick looked like she packed a shiv, and she was walking about two inches off the sidewalk with a faint aroma of marihuana mixed in with her perfume. We went in after them and sat down at the card table Sam had reserved for us.

My date had wanted to see a dive, and this dive was the most. The air was too thick for Earth people a foot above the floor. A fog of tobacco and Mexican tea took over from there to the ceiling. The drinks were watered worse than on Lexington Avenue during a Shrine convention and somebody at the next table needed a bath. It was pretty bad, but then it got worse. The band came in.

Either I'd been away too long or these wigs were just out of the wet sheets at Bellevue. The leader was a strange looking cat with skin the color of peanut butter and orange hair. He wore a bebop beard and a dirty T shirt. My date said, "Ben, is he colored?"

"Martian," I answered. I wasn't sure I was kidding. As the lad with the strange hair ignored us in pointed sullenness, the rest of the group filed up on the little stage at the end of the bar. Then, before the drummer had seated himself behind his traps and the tenor sax was wandering across the podium with a glass of beer in his hand, they started to blow. A trombone blasted in his ear and he almost dropped the glass and swung, before he remembered he was cool.

That was the deal these days. Coool, man. Playing it hot was Uncle Tom. These cats were the coolest. Not worth a damn as musicians, but you couldn't call them hot. I didn't.

The first thing I noticed was that they'd dropped the common courtesies of the side man. Each of them was submerged in his own sulk and only came out of it long enough to carve his buddies with incredibly long solos.

Usually, when a side man nears the end of his chorus he'll nod his head to the next soloist and give him time to get set for the break. Even in some of those frantic uptown sets where half the cats are swinging on dope, they used to at least *take turns*.

Not these boys. A wig would jump up and blow anywheres from two to twenty minutes of ear splitting bop and then stop short in the middle of a bar and walk off the stand to get a drink, leaving the rest of the band to pick up the pieces. If anybody'd ever done that to me on a date I'd have waited for him in the bus, and not to hold his hand neither!

Two of the group insisted on blowing with their backs to the audience. I didn't mind. It cut down on the volume. But I noticed a few cats leaving with a disgusted look. They were uptown types, too. The kind that order more than a beer.

After the set, Sam came over to our table and sat down. "What did you think of it?" he asked.

I shrugged and said, "The bass was off key."

"My God, how could you tell? I've got to get rid of these creeps before they ruin me."

I said, "They got a contract?"

"Hell no," he answered. "But I can't open without a band and all the cheap outfits are playing this junk now."

"Thanks for the compliment." I laughed. I didn't think it was very funny. Sam grinned and said,

"Let's not kid each other. Neither one of us is a big wheel or we wouldn't be down here in the goddam Village. I've heard you used to play with Daddy Halloway, though, and that's the kind of stuff I'm looking for. Nice quiet dinner music for the squares who come down here to see how the queers live."

I had to laugh. Daddy Halloway's boogie woogie being considered square. But it figured. Yesterday's avant garde is today's fuddy duddy. Jelly Roll Morton's old records sound tinny to today's ears, but when he made those Dixieland sides decent folks wouldn't let their kids listen to them. It made me feel old.

I talked it over with Tico and he said he knew a really cool cat who beat a set of traps better than Chano Pozo. He was full of crap but the kid was good enough for union scale and Sam wouldn't pay a dime more.

Alex was a nice guy, but from endville on the eighty eights. I passed him up for a Brooklyn kid named Freddy Zuber who hadn't been infected by the bop bug yet. A horn I used to know on the coast blew into the Big Apple broke and so I had the skeleton of a combo. And, as Sam observed, his monkey could blow as good as the wigs he'd just canned, and double as vocalist.

We opened at Sam's joint late in '49 and a funny thing happened. The word got around. A few minks dropped in to mingle with the black stocking set and Sam had to hire more waiters.

I could take the bows for it, but it was sort of an accident. I had these two Latin cats in the group and they couldn't blow Battle Hymn of the Republic without making it sound like a rumba.

Freddy and the horn and me blew Chicago, so it was kind of hectic at first. But nobody was out to carve the others and we all tried to meet in the middle. After a few sessions we had a new sound.

It wasn't just new. It was good. The Afro-Cuban kick was coming in to shove bop aside and for once in my life I was in on the ground floor of a trend. Carmen Miranda had brought the Latin beat out of the tango palaces, where it had been hiding since Rudolph Valentino died, with her big records in '46 and '47. Miguelito Valdes belted out Bobalu with a jungle beat that made Xaviar Cugat sound like Guy Lombardo, and dance floors all over town got scratched up by Cuban heels.

The stuff we were blowing at Sam's hit a happy medium for the cats who wanted to cha cha without throwing their sacroiliacs out. He was so pleased he offered us more dough. But not as much as a hotel uptown. I held out long enough to get a contract out of the hotel and told Sam to give the maracas to the monkey.

He'd made enough on us for a new car, and at union scale too. So don't feel too sorry for Sam. I didn't.

Meanwhile, back at the ranch, Alex had been pestering me to make another record for Flannery. I didn't want to. Not only because I didn't need his lousy dough, but I hadn't even been paid for the last three sides. I told Flannery what he could do with his dirty records. Not that I think they'd have fit.

Then something happened to make me change my mind. The second month we were at the hotel, I spotted Ginger Tracy in the audience. It wasn't an accident that Ginger had found me there. My face was plastered all over the three-sheet out front in the glass case. She kept those violet eyes trained on me all through the set and it took an effort of will to ignore her through the break.

I didn't want to start up with her again. Not ever. I was still bleeding from the last time and that had been a half dozen years ago. Tempus fugits, but it had been good to Ginger. A lot of water had passed under the bridge and a lot of girls had helped me paint my apartment since that night on Angel's Flight, but I was still bleeding.

When she was still sitting there after the next set there wasn't anything I could do but go over to her table. It was getting kind of silly pretending I didn't see her. She was the most gorgeous head in the room and knew it.

I noticed she was wearing a cloth coat and her dress wasn't as new as it used to was. If you looked closer you could see a few little crow's feet around the corners of her eyes. I don't know why God makes a beautiful woman if he's going to mess her up in such a little while.

I said, "Don't you know they got a law against un-escorted women in this town, Ginger?"

She smiled wanly and said, "I told them I was your tough cousin from Detroit, Ben." Her eyes were pleading. Not for me. But you could see she was on the make for something.

"How've you been doing?" I asked. I knew it hadn't been good. Girls like Ginger either hit big or not at all and I hadn't heard a thing about her since she'd ripped my face open.

"The usual, Ben," she said. "Club dates, the Borsht Circuit, a couple of sides that never went. You know the bit.

I imagine it's been the same with you."

"Not all of it," I said. "There was a short time out for a war."

"I noticed the limp, Ben. What happened?"

"I zigged when I should have zagged, I guess," I said. "Got hit with a chunk of eighty eight. Not the kind Mr. Steinway makes. One of the eighty eights from Essen made by Krupp."

"Was it bad, Ben?"

"It got me out of a lot of K.P.," I said. "And they gave me a purple ribbon that entitles me to ride the BMT any time I have a dime to drop in the slot."

I looked at my watch and said, "The war was a bore, Ginger. And I got to get back on the stand poco tiempo. So what's on your mind? You didn't come down here tonight to dig my tales of blood and slaughter."

She stammered, rapidly, "I wanted to talk to you, Ben. Will you take a walk around the Plaza with me after you close?"

"Want a rematch?" I asked, making my voice as hard as I could. "As far as I'm concerned, Ginger, you won the last time."

She reddened and sighed. "That's one of the things I wanted to talk to you about, Ben. I wanted to tell you how sorry I was about that night."

"I'll bet. Too bad you missed my eyes. I could have sat out the war behind a seeing eye dog."

"You're not making it very easy, cousin."

"I'm not trying to. I'm a dirty male animal, remember? So state your name, rank and serial number, doll. I got to go."

You could see her pride fighting with her hunger. The hunger won.

"Ben," she said. "I need a job."

I'd expected a bite, but this jolted me. I said, "You must need one pretty bad, kid." That turned on the faucet. Her lavender eyes welled up with tears and she started spoiling her mascara.

People were looking our way and I've never liked watched pretty girls crawl anyways. I said, "Look, Ginger. Wait for me in the green room, huh? I'll listen to your woes after the next set."

The novelty act that filled in between sets was almost over. I showed Ginger to the green room and went back to making a buck. We had a good crowd that night and the joint was jumping. Our horn couldn't blow as good as Prado, but he blew just as hard. I'd swiped Desi Arnaz's bit with the bongo drum and as a finale we formed a conga line and marched down off the stand into the savages. I'd yell something that sounded like Spanish and Tico would answer I was a dirty S.O.B. in the same. We got all the cats in the room to latch on to our snake dance and congad through the kitchen, out the service entrance onto 59th Street, and back through the lobby into the ball room again. Then we blew Good Night, Sweetheart, with a cha cha beat, and told the savages to get lost. As soon as the house lights dimmed I was off the stand and into the green room.

Ginger had repaired her makeup. She'd tossed her cheap coat over a chair and was trying to look like she'd been eating regular. I offered her a cigarette and waited for her pitch.

She looked uncomfortable and said, "Do you really hate me that much, Ben?"

I shrugged. "Not any more, I guess. You look like you've been drug through a key hole backwards, kitten. Care to tell me about it?"

"Oh, Ben, it's been awful! I've tried to get out of show business. I know I have no business in it with my squirrelly brain. But it's no use. I take a job in the dime store and I get fired within a month. Show business is the only business I know."

"You've got the prime advantage, cousin," I said. "Nobody who can do anything else ever stays in it long enough to get anywhere. You have to make up your mind at the age of three you'll either be an entertainer or starve to death. By the time you're thirty or forty you might make it. It's them lean years in between that get you."

"I know, Ben," she sighed. "I'll be dead before I see thirty again. And all I've managed is to louse myself up at every cheap roadhouse and summer resort in the Catskills."

I didn't argue the point. She knew what the score was better than me by now. When I didn't answer she went on, "Is it my fault I'm pretty, Ben? Is it my fault men think I'm sexy?"

"The girls in the five 'n' dime are bleeding for you," I muttered sarcastically.

She smiled sheepishly and reddened around the ears. "You think it hasn't been rough? My God, Ben. Men started making passes at me when I was nine years old! I don't mean just truck drivers and boys on the corner, either. I mean *every* man. My own brother made a grab for me when I was twelve. I fought off my stepfather with a bread knife when I was fourteen and my mother threw me out. She said it was my fault. It's been that way ever since, Ben. Men make grabs and their wives blame me! I can't go to the corner drug store without some man trying to pick me up."

"So call a cop," I grunted.

"You think cops don't make passes? Vice cops are the worst kind. Vice cops and hotel detectives. They see me alone in a hotel and right away they put two and two together and come up with six. I've lost count of how many small town vice dicks have tried to shake me down. And not for money, either. Hotel clerks, bellhops, taxi drivers, and every damned manager I ever worked for that wasn't gay have made a grab at me, Ben. And you can't trust the gay ones all the time, either. There's something about me that makes even a fairy want to get in bed with me. And every man seems to think he *can*."

She stopped and wiped at her eyes with a hanky. I had to admit she had a point. It was enough to make anyone goosie. But not as goosie as Ginger was.

She said, "It seems like every man I've ever met tried to make me, Ben. You're about the only one who was nice enough to ask me to marry him first."

I rubbed thoughtfully at the scar tissue on my lower lip.

She put her hand on my wrist. "I don't know what got into me that night, Ben," she said. "I don't usually fly off the handle like that. I've fielded a lot of passes without drawing blood. But something snapped inside me when you held me in your arms. I felt so... helpless. You're very strong, you know."

"Sure," I said. "Ben Parker, the Chicago Strong Boy, jumping through hoops for a pair of lavender eyes."

"No woman on earth could make you jump through a hoop, Ben."

"Nobody but you, cousin."

"What do you mean?"

"I mean you've got the job. We need a good vocalist anyways, and you're the goodest. Even if you do think I'm a sucker."

"Ben, that's not true."

"Nuts, Ginger," I said. "You're padding your part. You've got the job and you don't have to spread the oil about what a sterling type cat Ben Parker is. Just sing pretty for the supper crowd and for God's sake let me know if any of the boys get fresh. I got a good group and I don't want them scarred up."

□   □   □

Funny how you can go along on your lonesome while your wallet's flat. I'm not saying people were ducking into doorways during the time I was drifting in limbo, but it struck me odd how many old acquaintances wanted to get in touch with me after our combo moved uptown.

Franky the Drum wrote to me from a V.A. hospital where he was learning to blow traps with an artificial hand. He'd blown off the one his mamma gave him trying to toss a Jap grenade back to its owner. Seems little Franky'd saved a whole dugout full of G.I.s in the process. The army'd shipped him home with the silver star and told him he could bleach his hair again.

Sure, the letter was a bite. But I'd bit him a couple of times, and had both hands when I done it. So I wired him half a bill and told him not to believe I was as big as the three-sheet said I was.

Blanche Halloway didn't put the bite on me. The guy she was living with did. Said Blanche needed an operation and he was a poor but honest runner for an L.A. bookie who owed him dough and could I send him a few bills until his horse came in? I didn't answer it. I don't mind being a sucker but I knew Blanche would never see the dough and he'd probably get drunk enough on it to beat her.

A couple of army buddies nicked me for a pass to the club when they hit town. I had to pay the tab and tip the maître de for them so they'd think I was the big wheel they told their wives I was.

My old platoon leader had a kid brother who wanted to blow a horn. I didn't owe the bastard anything but a bullet in the brain. He'd been hound dog yellow on the line and chicken in the rear area. But I let the kid sit in with us a couple of times and squared it with the union. The kid couldn't blow, and on top of that he wanted number two chair because his big brother was my old army buddy.

Tico took him out in the service entrance one night and taught him not to call a Puerto Rican a spic where he can hear you. Last I heard of the kid he was hanging out in a coffee joint in the Village, telling folks what a louse I was now that I'd gotten a break.

So I wasn't too surprised when I looked out over the crowd one night and spotted a familiar face peering at me from behind a bopster beard. It was Marvin Knopff. He was with a Miami-tanned blonde who wasn't born that way and sent me a card in case I didn't know him under the shrubbery.

I was about to toss the card away when I looked at it. It read:

MARVIN (BIRD DOG) KNOPFF
DISC JOCKEY, DRUG ADDICT, AND BIRD
WATCHER
(OVER)

I turned the card over, and in small print it read:

(Confidentially, all other D.J.s are bastards.)

The penny dropped. I'd heard the program a couple of times without getting the connection. He was billed as Bird Dog Before Dawn, and had an all night spinning session operating out of a transmitter across the river.

If Knopff wanted to impress his girl with me I wasn't about to louse up his act. I never knew when I'd need a plug and I was willing to forget our feud if he was. After all, I'd won.

I went over to his table between sets. Knopff looked a little relieved and said, "Craaaazy, man. You blow the most!"

To dig half of Knopff's dialogue you needed a bop dictionary. Us poor cats who *worked* as musicians didn't have the time to keep up with the hippies. These cats spend their waking hours hunched over a cup of black coffee in Bickford's blowing jive talk at each other until *they* don't know what they're talking about. As soon as half the cats in town say Hep the avant garde decides the word is Hip. God knows what it is by now. I've been too busy paying my bills to keep up with it.

I let Marvin Knopff ramble on long enough to impress his broad with his jive and finally said, "Like, man, you're sending them over my head. Square it down so us Earth men can follow you!"

"Roger Wilco, Dad," said Knopff. "I was like saying I dig this stuff you're blowing the most. It's a little country, but very commercial."

"Thanks," I said. I was still trying to figure his angle. I sat tight while he ordered a round of drinks.

Then he said, "Like, Daddio, you planning to cut any platters? That chick you got on the vocal could blast off if she was handled right."

A little warning light went on in my brain. I said, "By any chance, did a blond creep named Johnny Angel send you, Knopff?"

I'd heard Angel had four bands touring under his name. How he'd missed the war was more than I could figure, and stealing Ginger out from under me just as we were set for a new contract would be the kind of thing Angel specialized in.

Knopff looked blank for a minute and then said, "Johnny Angel? That rat bastard? I ain't seen him since the war. Remind me to send him a bomb sometime when I've got the postage. I owe him one."

"Et tu, Brute?" I laughed. Somehow, it didn't come as a complete surprise that Johnny Angel had done something to annoy brother Knopff.

Knopff was so mad he forgot his bop talk. "Do you know what that rotten bastard did?" he snarled. Knopff didn't allow himself many snarls and he wasn't pretty when he did. A clown with his fangs bared is kind of spooky.

"What happened?" I asked. "Last I heard, you and him were dividing up the music he stole from Con Conners after Con blew his cork."

"Is *that* where he swiped that music, Ben? I was wondering."

"I'll bet."

"No, honest! I didn't know anything about it. I knew he'd swiped it from somewhere. Angel couldn't write eight bars of morse code. But I didn't know who he'd swiped it off. Not that I gave a good goddam. I paid for my education. I figure other cats can pay for theirs." Somehow, I believed him. Knopff would sell you his sister for money but he didn't cut throats just for practice. He shook his head sadly and said, "I should have made a pile on that deal, Ben. Old Johnny flew in from the coast a week after I got my draft papers. How in hell they got to my name so fast is a mystery. I guess somebody had to go first. But the damn war didn't start till I was almost out. Anyways, Johnny perked up as soon as he heard I'd been drafted. You know, he sort of brushed me after the deal with Mel Davis fell through. I should have known what he had in mind, the dirty bastard. You know what he did, Ben? He had this sheet of music he wanted to publish, see? Only the record war was on then and he didn't want to get in bad with ASCAP. So he talked me into putting my John Henry on the sheets and told me he'd split with me."

"Needless to say he didn't," I said. "Didn't you have a contract?"

Knopff shook his head. "Sure I had a contract, Ben. You think I got rocks in my head? Johnny sent me the first check a week after I hit Fort Dix. It was the only check he ever sent me, and it bounced."

"Couldn't you sue him?"

"While I was agitating gravel with a forty pound pack on my shoulders? The check was on a paper corporation that went bankrupt and left Johnny covered. He'd ducked in behind such a smoke screen of dummy publishers and fake agents that the best shyster lawyer in Brooklyn couldn't even get him to small claims court. And I ought to know. The best shyster in Brooklyn is my uncle Max."

"And you were all tangled up with Uncle Sam at the time and couldn't get time off to fight him?" I asked.

"I couldn't get time off to go to the can, Ben. F.D.R. must have known we were going to get into it, and they worked our fannies off trying to get our depression army into shape for the big date. By the time Pearl was bombed I was too tired to fight Angel. And after that I was too busy staying alive. I'd been in on the ground floor and Uncle decided to give me a break. They made me a second John and stuck me out in front of a rifle platoon in the South Pacific. Did you ever look at the casualty lists on second johns, Ben? The army killed off more shavetails than paratroopers."

"Yeah," I said. "But look at all the fun you had making the enlisted scum salute you, Knopff. All I made was tech sergeant. Our platoon leader was too yellow to get killed and give me a battlefield commission. Like, it was *rough* in the E.T.O., man!"

Knopff laughed. "Don't talk to me about the E.T.O., Dad. At least them frauleins was white and none of them had leprosy. Johnny Angel should have been in the Pacific. All by himself."

"By the way," I asked, "how'd our fair haired gonnif manage to miss the blitz? As far as I know, he didn't even do the U.S.O. bit."

"Not our Johnny!" sneered Knopff. "Hell, I saw Al Jolson on a stinking little coral atol singing his heart out to a handful of G.I.s that wouldn't have filled the orchestra pit at the Palace. Poor old guy died a few weeks later, too. Johnny Angel didn't even hand out free passes to his club at the Stage Door Canteen, and he was blowing to a full house every night a block off Broadway! You know how he dodged the draft?"

"No. Cue me in. I might want to miss the next war."

"A lundsman in the medical corps told me about it. Knowing Johnny, I believe him. You know, when you took your physical? The bit after they tap you on the knee to see if you got siph? The head shrinker takes you aside and asks you if you like girls?"

"Don't tell me," I said. "Johnny told them he liked boys."

"You are so right, Dad! And he had a couple of witnesses swear he'd been living with a colored fairy named Franky the Drum."

I said, "You know, that's pretty funny. Franky the Drum got his meat hook blown off in the South Pacific. He might have been in your outfit."

"Not if he was a spade. World War Two was Jim Crow, remember? Was he really queer?"

"Queer as they get. But I guess he thought he owed the country something. Franky was that kind of a guy. A pixie."

Marvin's girl said, "For God's sake, Bird Dog. Don't you men ever talk about anything but the goddam war? You act like it was a big deal or something."

Knopff shrugged. "Only to the cats who got killed, chick," he said. "And the poor jerks who'll spend from here on in a V.A. hospital because babes like you might get sick looking at them. It ain't important to nobody else. Now shuddup and listen to the pretty music. Ben's canary is going to chirp us a tune, right, Ben?"

I'd gotten so wrapped up in carving Johnny Angel I'd almost missed my cue. Ginger was looking at me from the wings and Freddy Zuber was making busy with spreading his maps on the music rack.

I got back on the stand and waved the idiot stick while Ginger stood in the center of a blue spot and made every woman in the room hate her. She rubbed that velvet voice all over the men in the joint until they were ready to beat their wives while I gritted my teeth and hung on.

Ginger was the first and only dame who'd made me look like a jerk since I was fifteen years old and madly in love with Irene Mooreheart, the sweetheart of Jefferson High. I wasn't going to jump through another hoop for Ginger if it killed me. And it looked like it just might do that.

Ginger did a couple of standards. One by Arlen and another by Johnny Mercer. Then she segued into a novelty we'd worked out one night at a session. Ginger'd made up most of the lyrics, with an assist from Tico, and we'd dug up a calypso beat that blended well with blue tonality and called the whole bit Run For The Jungle! The Dam Has Busted! It was pretty silly, but coming from Ginger, it swung. And the timing was right.

They called what we were blowing Cu-Bop. It didn't last. But nothing does in jazz. While it lasted, we had it made.

I latched onto Ginger right after the set and pointed at Knopff and his chick with my chin. "Come on, Ginger," I said. "I want you to smile pretty for a reptile." I cued her in on Knopff on the way to his table. I figured she might as well get in on the plug I expected for picking up his tab.

"That calypso was craaazy!" said Knopff. His babe said nothing. She froze solid as soon as she saw Ginger and didn't thaw out for the rest of the night.

Knopff said, "Like, Ben, you cut a side on that one yet? I'll spin it a couple of times for you."

I said, "No. I don't have any offers from the record companies. Far as I know they don't know I'm alive."

"Too bad, Dad." He shrugged. "Like, if you had an in with somebody who made platters, that thing might go."

A light went on in my empty head. I said, "Come to

think of it, I know one cat who makes discs, and he owes me some bread. I just might talk him into making a couple of sides."

"What are you waiting for, Dad? Unless the cat's stupid he knows Cu-Bop is going, and you cats Cu-Bop the most!"

"Yeah," I said. "But Flannery's pretty goddam stupid."

□   □   □

I didn't know how stupid George Flannery was until I tried to talk him into making the record for me. I knew better than to go over to Jersey empty handed. I'd had Ginger cut a demo on 42nd Street and took it with me. Flannery waited until the record was over and said,

"I don't know, Ben. Them lyrics ain't blue enough to sell to the stag party set."

I said, "Who the hell's talking about selling them under the counter? I got a D.J. lined up to plug them on the air. You got the machinery and the trucks and you must know *some* legit distributor."

"There ain't no legit distributor. The goddam geese! I take all the risk and they take all the dough. Jew bastards!"

"Yeah, but can't you get the sides out to the record shops?"

"Sure I can! Where in hell you think we sell the goddam things, candy stores? Our platters come in on the same truck. Only they go under the counter until somebody asks for them."

I said, "This disc can go right on top of the counter, George. You've got the wax and the machinery already sitting there. What have you got to lose?"

"Money," he growled. I was making him think and it irritated him.

"How in hell can you lose money on a hit record, George?" I asked. "With what you pay your help you can make money on a flop if it sells for nineteen cents on Sixth Avenue!"

He looked at his shoes for a while in uffish thought. The idea of putting out a record that couldn't get him thrown in jail must have struck his conservative nature a low blow. Finally he threw me a shrewd look and said, "What's in it for you, Ben?"

"Money," I said. "If it goes. Nothing if it doesn't. I'll blow the sound track for free. That's less than you usually pay. But not a hell of a lot. I never did collect for the last platter of smut we blew for you, George."

He smiled. Back on familiar ground. "I'm sweating out a check from the distributor, Ben," he said. "Things have been pretty rough."

"Yeah, I'll bet your yacht's leaking," I said. "How about it, George? Do you want to make a hunk of bread for a change or don't you?"

The mention of money must have softened his heart. He said, "I guess it won't hurt to run off a few hundred. What's the deal with the canary? You shacked up with her?"

I wanted to belt him, but he was an old man, and I'd already bent my lance on that windmill. I said, "That'll never happen, George. She don't like boys."

"A dike, huh? It figures. Nobody can sing as sexy as a dike."

I could see George felt better about it, as soon as the conversation got smutty. I wanted to belt him so bad I could taste it. But you don't get anywhere in this business playing Sir Galahad. If Johnny Angel could wind up with four headline bands and a penthouse on Central Park East by declaring himself a homosexual, the least I could do was swap dirty stories with a nasty old man.

So far, it looked like the world was going to the bastards. I was at a hell of a disadvantage. My mother and father were legally married for two years before I was born.

But maybe I could be a self appointed bastard long enough to get my foot in the door. And maybe open it a crack for the girl with the lavender eyes.

□   □   □

Run for the Jungle! The Dam Has Busted! Was cut a couple of weeks after Truman named MacArthur commander of the U.N. forces in Korea. I guess Mac thought he was going to make out a lot better than he did, too.

We had an old torch song from the Muscat days on the flip side just in case. Dixie will always sell well enough to pay for the wax. I sent a couple of platters to Knopff and every D.J. I knew of who might spin them for us. Then I sat by the radio and waited.

Couple of weeks went by and I was still waiting. A D.J. at a small local in the Midwest wrote that he'd spun it and gotten a mess of requests for it. But Bird Dog Knopff was playing it very nothing. I finally got him on the horn at his apartment and asked him what was wrong.

"Uh, this the first side you've sent around, Ben?" he asked.

I said, "Sure. You know that, Knopff. What's the pitch? First you twist my arm to send you the platter and then you cool it on me. I don't dig it, Dad."

He said, "Uh, look, Ben. Where are you now?"

"I'm at the hotel. We just finished rehearsals. Why?"

"Uh, Ben, you know that Mayflower doughnut shop on the Plaza? Could you meet me there in about half an hour? I don't like to talk business on the phone."

"Sure," I said. I couldn't figure it. That's how dumb I still was. A self-appointed bastard just can't think like the real thing.

Marvin Knopff wandered in a few minutes after I'd seated myself in a booth and ordered doughnuts and coffee. Later on, I realized why he'd picked the Mayflower. It was a little too public and the neighborhood was a little too classy for a fist fight.

After a little sparring around, Knopff got to the point. He said, "It's not my own idea, Ben. You know I'd be glad to do an old friend a favor. But it ain't up to me. There's at least a dozen cats got their hand out for bread between me and the turntable."

I felt a full head of steam building up in my boiler. I said, "Why didn't you tell me you expected grease, you bastard?"

"Hell, Ben, you don't have to get snotty about it. Everybody does it. Don't blow square with me, Ben. You been in this racket long enough to know nobody gets a free ride. You should be glad you own as much of yourself as you do, man. Half the top names belong to the mob and have to pay grease and income tax out of their own kicks after the agent and the Mafia get theirs!"

"So name a few!" I sneered. He did.

I said, "So how come I been beating my brains out to get ahead all these years without no help from the Union Sicilian? I could have used a few torpedoes to collect all the times I got stiffed."

"You're not big enough, Ben," Knopff said. "Soon as you get big enough you'll be hearing from the garlic bullet set."

"And for this I got to *pay?*"

"You'll pay, Ben. Everybody does. Or else."

"Or else what?"

"Or else nothing. You go right on playing small club dates until you're too old to hold up the doghouse any more. And then they bury you out in Brooklyn and nobody ever heard of you." He shook his head sadly. "Look, Ben," he said. "Don't glare at me that way. I didn't build this lousy world. I just got to live in it. Same as you. All I was trying to do was help you out and you act like I'm a heel."

"You're not a heel, Knopff," I said, getting up. "You're

what a heel steps in walking behind a policeman's horse."

"You don't want to play, Ben?"

"Not for pay, crumb," I said.

"You'll be sorry, Ben."

"I already am," I answered. I turned my back on Knopff and walked outside. It was a sticky summer day and I walked over to the lake in nearby Central Park and sat on a bench. I didn't know where else to go. I felt like the little boy with the little red wagon. I threw a lopsided grin at a gray squirrel coming across the asphalt walk for a handout and said, "Dod oh Dod, what do me do now?" It was a good question.

□ □ □

I didn't have the heart to tell the group what had happened. I didn't have to. They knew something was wrong and George Flannery kept calling me up at the ungodly hour of eleven in the morning to ask when Knopff was going to give us a plug. The platter had been out for weeks now, and with the low budget advertising Flannery had sprung for, it was just laying around waiting to be shipped to Sixth Avenue.

I'd been giving Ginger a miss since she'd gone to work for me. It's not good sense to mess with the vocalist anyways, and Ginger still made my fillings get radioactive every time I got near her. I tried to make that as seldom as possible.

One night—it was sometime after the First Cavalry rolled into Seoul, as I recall—Ginger followed me out the service entrance after the date. She must have been laying for me to time it so well. Out on the sidewalk she said, "Which way are you heading, Ben?"

"Over to Times Square, chick," I lied. "I got a date with a pony at the Latin Quarter."

"Mind dropping me off at my hotel, Ben? It's right near there."

"I'm walking," I said, pointedly.

"I don't mind, Ben. It's a nice cool night for a change. The fresh air will do us good."

What could I say?

Saint Pat's was open for late services because of the Korean mess. Across the street they'd put Radio City away for the night. The fountain was turned off and the big gold statue of Prometheus stared down at a guy washing down the sunken part of Rockefeller Plaza with a hose. I stopped and pointed at the statue.

"Now there's a cat you might go for, Ginger," I said. "He's been jumping through that same hoop since the depression."

Ginger said, "All right, Ben. Stop the world and I'll get off."

"Sorry," I said. "I promised myself I wasn't going to bring that up again. Will you tell me one thing, Ginger? On the level?"

"What is it, Ben?"

"The word's gone around that you're gay. Is it true?" Ginger laughed, that same damned skylark laugh. "Is that story still making the rounds, Ben?"

"Is it legit? Is that what's wrong with you?"

"I told you what was wrong, Ben," she sighed. "Con got that idea about my being a lez from that poor little sparrow I had for a lawyer on the coast. She looked pretty mannish, remember? I guess Con just couldn't take the blow to his ego when I turned him down."

"What did you turn him down with, a meat axe?"

"Please, Ben. I told you I was sorry. You did something to my adrenalin that night. I was friendly but firm with Con Conners. I didn't even have to slap his wrist. Con was a gentleman and... I didn't feel funny about him."

"Come on, kitten," I said.

"Where are we going?"

"Out on the street where it's light. I feel a rematch coming on and I'm not in training for dames that bite."

We walked over to Times Square and I said, "So where's the hotel?" Ginger pointed at the Tide sign that used to be on top of the building at 47th and Broadway. It had a bubble machine inside a big box of soap powder and kept puffing out clouds of bubbles. The kind kids make with those hoops they dip in jars of red goop.

"Go ahead and meet your pony," she said. "I've got to pick up some things in Whelan's and I want to watch those bubbles for a minute. They're so pretty."

I grinned and said, "There isn't any pony. I just made her up to get rid of you."

Ginger giggled like a school girl. A school girl with lavender eyes. "I made up the hotel to follow you over here, Ben," she laughed. "I'm staying with an old school chum over on Sutton Place."

"So where do we go from here?" I asked.

"Anyplace you like, Ben," she answered. I didn't think she meant that the way it sounded. I was so right.

It was nearly dawn. The one time in the day the Big Apple smells clean. There isn't a hell of a lot to do in New York after the clubs close at four. The town takes a short rest while the streetwalkers air their dogs, the street sweepers clean up what they can of the trash in the gutters, and the BMT gets ready for the morning saber dance.

"Ever ride the Staten Island Ferry?" I asked. It was the only thing open at that hour. Ginger said, "What's on Staten Island?"

"Nothing," I said. "But the ride across is pretty good for a nickel."

"Seems to me I've heard this line before, Ben. Is history repeating itself?"

"It better not," I said. "Or you'll have to swim back."

We grabbed a cab to the Battery and groped our way through the mess they were making of the old ferry building while they built the new one.

Considering how many tourist traps they have in the Big Apple, it's surprising more cats don't latch on to the five mile ride across the harbor you get for a nickel.

I walked Ginger up to the bow on the upper deck and pointed out the Statue of Liberty. The boat pulled away from the pier with a rumble of white water and Ginger leaned against me. I felt the palms of my hands going moist again and thought, "Here's where I get myself bit and cussed out again."

Ginger turned towards me as we were passing Governor's Island and said, "Benny, this is lovely! It's so cool and peaceful out here on the water."

I said, "Don't be so damned beautiful, Ginger. I'm a big hairy beast, remember?"

"I kind of like big hairy beasts, Ben, when I'm used to them."

I kissed her. She didn't stab me, so I kissed her again. Finally, I said, "Would it help if I gave you a whiff of chloroform?"

Her eyes were full of tears. "I'm sorry, Ben," she said "I *want* to respond to you, but something inside won't let me."

I took my arm away from her. I grabbed the rail. Hard. For a long time, neither of us had anything to say. The boat was passing the lady with the lamp and the lights of Staten Island pier winked at us across the black water. Off to the east, the sun was coming up over the narrows. Ginger said, "What happens now, Ben?"

I shrugged. "We'll be on the other side in a minute."

"What do we do when we get there?"

"Not a goddam thing, kitten," I answered. "There's nothing to do but take the next boat back where we came from."

□   □   □

The word around town was that Joe the Dishwasher

didn't take payola. Dope, yes, but no payola. Joe the Dishwasher broadcast from a small stage over a bar on the east side. When he wasn't at the bar lapping up sauce.

He'd mumble a few commercials from time to time, pile as many discs on the automatic turntable as he could, and see how much of his pay he could drink in trade.

I'd been staying out of Ginger's way since the cold and clammy act she'd pulled on me. But this was business. I grabbed a couple of sides of Run For The Jungle! The Dam Has Busted! and handed Ginger her coat.

"Come on, kitten," I said. "We got to smile pretty for a plug."

I knew Joe the Dishwasher occasionally threw in an interview for the peasants if some celebrity wandered into the joint. If Ginger could send a few bars of that sexy voice over the air late at night it might wake up the truck drivers and lobster shift workers who listened to the program.

When we got to the club, we found Joe the Dishwasher leaning on one end of the bar while the program sort of took care of itself. If there was a program engineer, we didn't see him. Up on the stage, the turntable was spinning away at a live mike while Joe got dead drunk. We sent him a card and sat down at a table.

He looked at the card and put it in his pocket. A warning light flashed on over the stage and he put the drink down and lurched up for the station break. "Hello, all you poor depraved victims of insomnia," he said, as soon as he was back on the air. "If you cats and kittens don't mind, old Joe's got to make some bread. So why don't you slobs turn to the Barry Gray program while I read some of these foolish commercials the agency sends me?"

He swallowed his drink, signalled for another, and read off what should have been enough commercials for two or three hours. I guess they were stacked up on him from all the time he goofed off.

Finally he wound up with a sage observation that a certain brand of weight reducing candy was the greatest, if you didn't mind the way it rotted all your teeth out, and went back to the bar and the blonde helping him hold it up.

I looked at Ginger and shrugged. "Wait here," I said. I went over to Joe the Dishwasher and said, "I'm Ben Parker."

He gave me the fish eye and said, "What do you want me to do about it? You've only got your mother to blame."

I laughed a standard stage laugh and said, "I'm a band leader, Joe. Maybe you've heard the record I just cut, Run For The Jungle! The Dam Has Busted!?"

"I'll just bet that's what you have in your grubby little fist."

"No bet, Dad. Me and the canary over there with the bedroom eyes and luscious lung tissue thought you'd like to do an interview and maybe spin it for us."

The Dishwasher cast a bleary eye in Ginger's direction. He said, "Does she put out?"

"You're a real nice guy, Joe," I said. "How'd you like to go home with a fat lip?"

"O.K. So she don't put out. I was just asking. Everybody gets so goddam physical these days. Must be the atom bomb. Whole human race is sick sick sick."

"How about the record?" I asked.

He shrugged and turned away to fondle the blonde's posterior. "I don't know," he said. "Send it through the agency, Dad. If it's any good I might spin it."

"Couldn't you spin it tonight?"

"Look, buddy. I got problems of my own. If your canary don't put out that's your problem. I'm having enough trouble making this one."

"That's not the deal, Joe. This is a good record."

"You deaf or something? I told you to send it through channels like the rest of the peasants. You got special dispensation from the Pope, maybe?"

I went back to the table and sat down with steam shooting out of my ears. Ginger said, "What's wrong, Ben?"

"The little twerp!" I fumed. "Look at him, Ginger! He comes to my belly button and can't stand up in a high wind. I could spit in his eye and drown him. And yet I got to crawl to cruds like that to get a lousy plug!"

"Is he going to play our record?" she asked.

"Quien sabe, kitten?" I growled. "You either got to pay grease or throw it over the transom with nine million other discs and hope somebody might break all the others by accident."

I'd already ordered another round of martinis and at what they were charging I wasn't going to leave them for the busboy to drink.

Ginger wandered off to the little girl's room and I polished her drink off and sat there glaring at the back of the D.J.'s head. Joe the Dishwasher was on cloud nine. He was drunk and on the make and hadn't turned his head in five minutes. I got a pixie idea.

Ginger was just coming back when I made my move. Heads had a way of turning when Ginger walked into a room. Joe the Dishwasher went on yakking at the blonde without the slightest show of interest in anything or anyone else in the room.

I slid the platter out of the manila folder and said, "Sit tight and keep your mouth shut, kitten. If I get clobbered with a bottle head for the door."

Before she could ask me what I was going to do, I was doing it. I strolled up on the stage like I owned it. If anyone noticed me, I was hoping they'd remember I'd been talking to the man with the power and think this was his idea.

Joe the Dishwasher was still staring down the front of the blonde's dress as I eased the other records to one side and waited for the platter he had cooking to stop spinning.

The second the disc was over I had ours on the turntable and picked up the mike. I made my voice sound as much like the D.J. as I could and said, "And now, for all you cats and kittens out there in radio land, the side you've all been waiting for. The new hit novelty that's been climbing right up to the top on juke boxes and record counters all over the Yoo-Ess of A; Benny Parker's hit rendition of Run For The Jungle! The Dam Has Busted! with Ginger Tracy on the vocal!"

Halfway through my spiel, Joe the Dishwasher hunched his shoulders like he'd been hit on the back of the neck with a blunt instrument and slowly turned around.

His jaw dropped open as he saw me up there in his chair. I grinned right in his face and wound up, "We've gotten a lot of mail on this one, gates. So all you hipsters write in and let us know what you think of little Ginger!"

The Dishwasher and a monster in soup and fish who was too big to be anything but the bouncer were headed my way as I got down off the stage. The record was going out loud and clear over five states and I figured it was worth a few bruises.

"It's all right, Gino," said the D.J. "What's the matter with you, Parker? You trying to get us both killed?" Then I noticed his eyes. He was scared skinny, and sober.

I said, "Sorry, Dad. I don't read you."

Joe the Dishwasher grabbed me by the elbow and steered me over to the bar. The blonde sauntered over. He said, "Get lost."

"But Joey."

"You heard me, chick. Wait in the car. Listen, Parker. Don't you know the score? This is a mob joint!"

"So?"

"So I got nothing to say about what I spin any more! There's a spaghetti bender up near the park decides whose discs spin and whose don't!"

"I heard you were a legit D.J.," I said.

"You heard wrong. This is going to cost you some bread to square things with the mob."

"Not me, mac. We didn't mention money and the platter's already plugged."

"Plugged hell. I wouldn't give that big a plug to Peggy Lee if she was my mother! The mob will be sure you greased me, Parker! If you don't spread the bread I'm gonna be in trouble."

"Like you said, Dad, what's so special about you? You got a dispensation from the Pope to stay out of trouble?"

I collected Ginger and walked out. I don't think anyone's seen Joe the Dishwasher that sober before or since.

□   □   □

You wouldn't think one plug would do as much as that one did. But a strategically placed puff can do a lot for a record. That's why people pay for them. At least a million listeners "out there in radio land" must have heard us that night. Only a small percentage thought enough of it to write in requests for a replay. But a small percentage of a million adds up to a few pieces of mail.

Joe the Dishwasher wasn't found in an alley so he must have paid the payola out of his own kick. My heart bled for him.

Once the network had seen all the mail he couldn't just drop the thing. He had to play it a few times a night or look fishy to some vice president who wasn't in on the take. All the D.J.s weren't taking payola. Not even most of them. Once Run For The Jungle had been given air time, some of the other D.J.s looked in the slush pile for it.

Every day the average disc jockey gets a fistful of new records sent out by the manufacturers. Even an honest D.J. hasn't the time to listen to half of them, let alone play them. Most of them are bad. A whole segment of the industry is based on turning out vanity platters. Records sprung for by the cat who wants to be on wax so bad he's willing to pay for it. Like me.

Small record plants press a few sides for the clam, send them out to the D.J.s, and forget them. Once in a blue moon somebody might take one off the top of the pile and play it just for the hell of it. If it's better than anything the established companies have out that week, they might even put it on the air. Like, once in fifty blue moons.

Our blue moon rose within a week after I'd pulled the switch on Joe the Dishwasher. Run For The Jungle! The Dam Has Busted! moved up from nowheres and started to climb. Before it was two weeks old even Marvin Knopff was spinning it. For free. And Ginger had her picture on the magazine stands.

The lavender eyes didn't come through the printer's ink the way they did a smoke filled room but the savages got the message, Dad.

Mel Davis was the first Hollywood producer to make her an offer. I told her to hold out for a bigger fish. Mel was a nice guy, but he paid off in cigar store coupons and Ginger was hot property. We didn't have anything between us on paper. We hadn't even shook hands on the split we'd agreed to if the disc went. I trusted Ginger like she was my wife as far as business went. Well, like a sister then. A guy kisses his wife once in a while.

So I could have put my foot down when Ginger got the offer from a bigger producer than Mel Davis. A cat named Uncle Sam.

"U.S.O. is for the birds, Ginger," I said. "You're just starting to fly. Stick around and make some loot."

"It's only a six month tour, Ben," she said. "We could use the publicity an overseas trip would give us."

"What do you mean, *we?*" I asked. "I had my war, Ginger. I like the American way of life almost as much as the French way of lovin', but how many times is a guy supposed to do the bit for democracy in one lifetime?"

Ginger nodded, "I know, Ben. You've done your share. But, you see, I didn't get asked the last time."

"So what? You don't owe the army nothing. They're all a bunch of hairy apes anyways. And I got news for you, kitten. Those G.I.s are going to get just as phallic as the rest of us Earth men."

"What can I say to make you forgive me, Ben?" she said. Those lavender eyes were getting misty again and felt like a heel. Ginger shook her head and said, "I told you I can't help the way I am. Do I have to go to bed with you? Is that what you want? Would that make you stop looking at me like I was something you found under a wet rock?"

"It's not nice to dangle a canteen in front of a thirsty man," I said.

"I'm not kidding, Ben," she said. "If I thought it would make you forgive me I'd tear off my clothes and lay down on the floor for you!"

"Sure you would," I sighed. "Until I reached for my belt buckle. And then you'd climb right up that wall and we'd have to call the fire department to get you down from the chandelier."

She suddenly smiled. "You're probably right, Ben. At the last minute I'd panic. A thirty two year old virgin is pretty silly."

"It's not only silly, it's unbelievable." I laughed. "So, when do we go to Korea?"

"Ben! You'll come with me?"

"Why not?" I shrugged. "Without you the band don't swing anyways. I'm staying near you until I get you to sign a contract. Maybe a few cups of army coffee will cure you of whatever ails you."

☐   ☐   ☐

It happened near a place called Mississippi Baker. A

code name for a rest camp just back of the lines on the In-
chon Road. We were on our way to play a date for some
cats from my old outfit, the 38th Infantry. Ginger was in
the back of the bus, getting a bit of shut eye. I was up
front sitting with Tico and watching the brown hills roll
by.

You know what Korea was like, Dad? Bleak! They cut
most of the trees down so long ago they make all the
houses out of mud and grass. You expect to see the three
little pigs come popping out of one of them, instead of the
almond eyed kids in white cotton pajamas that ran out to
stare at our bus.

I guess if this was a movie there'd have been a shot of a
grinning pilot in square goggles. The kind Baron Von
Richthofen wore in Hell's Angels. Remember? But this
wasn't a movie. So we never saw the goddam plane. For
all I know it was one of ours.

Freddy Zuber had just said something funny and we
were all laughing, when there was this woodpecker sound
from up in the sky and all hell broke loose.

Someone hit me across the back with a big initiation
paddle and it got kind of frantic as the bus went off the
road. When I untangled myself from Tico and the B-4
bag that had landed on top of me things were a mess. The
bus was laying on its side in a rice paddy. The right windows were now the floor and covered with two inches of
brown mud that looked and smelled like it belonged in a
toilet bowl.

"You O.K. Tico?" I said. He didn't answer. Just kept
staring up over my shoulder. He was still smiling at the
joke Freddy'd told him. Then I noticed the blue smoke
coming out of the front of his shirt. I'd seen that before.
It's what happens when a guy gets hit with a tracer bullet.

Outside on the road I heard the squeal of brakes as a
truck skidded to a stop. A rough voice said, "Oh, Jesus!
They strafed the U.S.O. bus! What a goddam fricassee!"

I started crawling along the windows above the seats towards the back of the bus. Towards Ginger.

It was pretty rugged. The bus was filling up with stinking mud and I had to climb over, under and through a clutter of instruments and people in various states of disrepair. The whole mess was spiced with blood and broken glass and a busted open can of scented talcum powder. I still get sick to my stomach whenever I smell that brand.

By the time I got to Ginger my knees were a mess. I could only hope the tetanus shots they'd made us take would slow down the little bugs in that paddy mud.

Usually, whenever I'd found myself in a tense situation, it had pepped me up. But getting to the rear of that bus was an awful drag. If it had been anyone but Ginger back there I'd have given it a miss.

The first thing I saw of her was her legs. They were sticking out from behind an overturned seat and I noticed she had a run in her stocking. Ginger was laying in the mud like a rag doll some careless kid had tossed under the bed. A trickle of blood was running out of the corner of her mouth. I picked up her head and wiped away some of the mud. I didn't know what else to do.

She opened her lavender eyes and said, "Hello, cousin. What happened?"

"We just lost an argument with a plane," I said. "How you making out? Anything busted?"

"I don't know, Ben," she said. "I feel kind of numb. It's so cold in here."

Outside, a voice said, "Anybody alive in there? Jeezus! What a mess!"

I called back and a worried looking G.I. stuck his head in the window at the rear of the bus. I asked him to send for the meat wagon. He said they already had. He looked at Ginger and said, "She hurt bad, sir? I got a first aid kit."

I shook my head. Ginger didn't need a first aid kit. I'd

already found the spot where the tracer had hit her. She looked up at me and asked, "How bad is it, Ben?" I forced a smile and said, "Flesh wound, kitten. You won't be able to wear a bikini now without swapping war stories."

"You're lying, Ben," she murmured. "You're trying to make it easy for me." I looked away. She dimpled and said, "This is so silly, Ben. Girls don't get killed in wars."

I didn't answer. After a while she said, "Ben. You're crying."

"It's just my nerves, kitten. Must be that time of the month."

"Don't play it light, Ben. We haven't time for witty dialogue. And, Ben, there's so much to say."

"Like beejum?"

"Like starkle. Like I love you and I'm sorry and all the things we never said because you were too proud and I was a frightened kook." Her eyes widened and she said, "Ben! I'm not frightened any more. It's getting colder and I'm not afraid. Kiss me, Ben. For the road?"

I kissed her. She wasn't frightened. She was warm and female and all the things her velvet voice and lavender eyes had promised. And then she was dead.

□   □   □

I don't remember blacking out, but I must have. It was night when I came to. I was laying flat on my face in bed. For one happy second I thought I'd dreamed the whole thing. Then I tried to roll over.

"Doctor, he's coming around," said a voice from the shadows. That's when I noticed I was strapped to the bed. My right arm was tied to the bedpost with gauze and there was a rubber tube running into my vein at the elbow joint. The kind they send plasma through.

"How you feeling, Parker?" said another voice. By twisting my neck I could see a cat in a white coat sitting on a stool by the bed. My back itched like I had on long winter underwear full of lice. I said, "I don't get it, Doc. I didn't get hit."

"Didn't you?" he grinned. "You're lucky to be breathing, Parker. You left a trail of blood a yard wide the whole length of the bus."

I remembered the slap on the back I'd felt just before the bus went off the road.

"Tracer?" I asked. He nodded.

"Fifty caliber, Parker. Went through the seat and key-holed through your lung. Should have knocked you out."

"I was busy," I muttered. There was a lump in my throat. "What happened to Ginger?"

"Miss Tracy? 'Fraid I've got bad news. Parker. She was dead when they lifted her from the bus. I'd let you see her but we can't move you."

"That's all right," I said. "I saw a body one time. Just wanted to make sure. How are the others?"

"Sanchez, Hererra, Vesta, and Golden are dead. Wilson and Pratt weren't hit. Lopez has a bullet in the hip and Zuber was scalped by flying glass. He'll be O.K. We pulled his forehead off the front of his face and sewed the top of his head back on. He'll be out of here before the rest of you."

"How long am I going to be laid up, Doc?" I was just making conversation. My mind was just getting over its numb feeling and I had to keep talking so I wouldn't scream.

"You're not going anywhere for the best part of six or seven months, Parker. You've got yourself a nasty wound there."

"I always do, Doc. Wars don't agree with me."

"I noticed the leg. You better swear off the stuff."

"I intend to, Doc. Soon as I get out of here I'm signing up with Soldiers Anonymous. These goddam wars are ruining my health."

The sawbones laughed. I guess he thought I was a big brave boy. Or maybe he didn't. I imagine he'd seen enough guys on the wrong end of the plasma tube to know I was just waiting for him to split so's I could bury my face in the mattress and howl.

□   □   □

As I'd already noticed, a guy's mail is in inverse ratio to how much time he has to read. Ginger's death made all the papers, natch. And for a couple of weeks I got a lot of wires and Flannery even sent a check. The record was selling like crazy. Getting blipped is great publicity but it can louse up a talent's future. Then the Rosenbergs were sentenced to death as atom spies and the world kind of forgot Ginger Tracy. It had never really gotten acquainted with me.

Alex and Martha sent me a couple of letters after we'd moved off page three and got lost. And Blanche Halloway remembered my birthday with a card and a couple of lines. The usual stuff. I kind of got the idea she'd written it in a hurry. But it made me get all misty for a minute.

Franky the Drum sent me back the half bill he'd borrowed and signed the letter Haji Ben Robinson. I didn't even know who in hell it was until I remembered Franky's last name was Robinson. Then I decoded the rest. I knew a lot of the Harlem cats were switching to Islam. Mohammedan cults were popping up in empty shops and rented pads across the country. I'd seen the spread in Life with pictures of Dizzy Gillespie Bowing to Mecca, and frantic types were starting to swear at the ofay in Arabic.

I don't know how many of them were sincere, and how many were just playing with a new toy now that it didn't look like Father Divine would make president. For what good Islam could do Franky, I wished the poor little pixie well. It might straighten him out. As I recalled, a good Moslem has a quartet of wives. Female, usually.

Another letter came that really surprised me. It was from Marvin Knopff. It read, "Sorry to hear, Ben. She blew a lovely torch."

I couldn't figure Knopff. In some ways he was as slimy as Johnny Angel, and in other ways, just as you had him pigeon holed with the guys in black sombreros, he'd pull something almost human. He bugged me. I didn't know where to put him in my stamp book.

The doctor had been optimistic as hell. General MacArthur got home before I did. And then they shoved me into Letterman General at the San Francisco Presidio the minute I hit the states. By the time I convinced them I could get along with all that scar tissue cluttering up my chest the Rosenbergs were dead and so was Cu-Bop.

A Memphis kid in a black leather jacket and pachuco sideburns started doing more bumps and grinds than a Galveston stripper as he sobbed out a mixture of field calls, ring shouts and hill ballads that brought the cats to their feet. His name was Presley and he called what he was blowing Rhythm And Blues. A lot of people called it something else. You either liked Elvis the Pelvis right off or he bugged you. Most cats liked him. Hippies, and just plain punks, all over the map stopped stripping hub caps, latched on to a second hand axe, and started imitating him.

It's a hell of a thing to say, but I thought the cat had talent. Rock and Roll was just plain old boogie woogie dressed up in a leather jacket with the axe doing most of the work and the eighty eights swapping places with it.

And boogie woogie was what I dug the most. So I couldn't see myself blowing bed pans any longer. The Presidio was an open post. A street car line runs right onto the military reservation and will get you to the railroad station south of the slot in twenty minutes.

Getting civilian clothes into the ward was no sweat. Once I had them on there wasn't much anybody could do to stop me. I wasn't a G.I. and all the sawbones could do was tell me I was lousing myself up with the V.A. if the wounds started acting up again.

"I'll send you a card to my funeral, Doc," I said, and latched on to some transportation. That night my chest hurt a little going over the mountains. But I didn't mind. I was on my way back to the Big Apple again.

□   □   □

First place I went after I walked out of Penn Station was over to see George Flannery. I had a bone to pick with that cat. Bone? Man, I had a skeleton!

"Benny, boy!" he said, as I breezed into his office. "It's good to see you back! You had us worried, Benny boy. We thought you'd be swinging in the big dark."

"Is that why you held back on my royalties, George?" I asked.

He looked hurt. "What are you talking about, Benny? You cashed every one of them checks I sent you!"

"Yeah, Dad. Only you didn't send as many as you was supposed to."

"Ben, you think I've been holding back bread on you?"

"I don't think it, Dad. I know it. As soon as I could sit up in bed I started writing letters to the distributor's office. I don't mind a guy dipping in my cigar box, George. But you took too damn many cigars."

"Distributors!" he growled. "Bunch of goddam Jews! Who you gonna believe, Ben, me or them?"

"Them. They got no axe to grind by lying to me, George. One record's not enough for them to juggle their books for. According to the figures they gave me, Ginger's record sold like rice in a Chinese famine. Not counting the extra sides you pressed on the quiet and peddled to the pirates. That disc sold Oh-You-Tee, Dad. Run for The Jungle is a collector's item today."

Flannery looked like a small boy of sixty five who'd

been caught in the cookie jar. He grinned sheepishly and said, "Yeah, it did sort of move, Ben. But you got your share."

"The hell I did. The boys swung for what I paid them and Ginger got a percentage she never collected. Figuring on what we agreed on, you owe me about eighteen more grand than you paid me."

"You're nuts. I ain't got that much in the till, Ben."

"You better dig for it then, Dad. You owe me the bread and I got papers to prove it."

George shook his head sadly and said, "I don't know what gets in to you guys, Ben. I take you out of the gutter and give you a job and this is the thanks I get."

"You'll get your thanks, George. Just as soon as I see the loot."

"You can't get blood out of a stone, Ben." He smiled smugly. "All you'll get out of suing me is the judge's sympathy. Hotsi-Totsi is a corporation, Ben. I'm covered." I knew he was lying. I'd checked that angle.

"Who said anything about suing?" I laughed. "I'm taking this to the D.A. They got a law in this town against stealing."

Flannery looked pained. "I don't think you're in any position to bring criminal charges, Ben," he said. "Do you remember all those blue sides we cut a few years back? As I recall, you didn't report them on your income tax, did you, Ben?"

I had to smile at the look of certainty on his little crooked face. I let him enjoy his moment of triumph and said, "My dear old dad gave me a sage bit of advice before he passed on, George. It was all he had to leave me but an empty bottle of muscatel. He told me never to cheat on my income tax. It ain't worth it."

Flannery's eyes widened and for the first time he looked worried. "Everybody cheats on their income tax!" he stammered. I think he believed it. Admitting you pay your income tax is unheard of in certain circles. Like admitting you watch Howdy Doody.

"Let this be a lesson, George," I grinned. "I declared every dime you ever paid me, Dad. One reason was that I saw the day when we might be having this little conversation. So get up the bread, man. The bank closes at three and the D.A. hangs around until four-thirty. I'm going one place or the other when I leave here."

"You've got to give me time, Ben," said Flannery. His face was getting pasty. Things were happening a little fast for old George. He looked like a wolf that had just been bitten by a sheep and hadn't figured what he was going to do about it yet.

"You've had time, you crud," I snarled. "I've been waiting for a check for two years in a hospital ward. I'm not waiting another goddam day!"

Flannery sighed and walked over to his wall safe, the place he usually went when he handed out bread. This time he had something else in mind. He took out a fistful of envelopes, leafed through them until he came to my name, and handed me a set of glossy photo prints.

"I hate to use these methods, Ben," he whined. "But a guy in my racket has to protect hisself. You're forcing me to use my ace in the hole."

I looked at the photos and felt my face getting red while a cold ball of hate formed in the pit of my guts.

"I've got negatives in case you want to tear those up, Ben," he said. I handed them back to him and asked, "Did Bunny know you were taking these, George?"

He grinned as he looked fondly at the pictures. "Nope. I didn't want to bother her with sordid details. A shamus I know took them through a hole in your closet door with infra red film, Ben. I'll bet you thought the lights was out."

"I wouldn't have been in that silly position if they hadn't been," I said. "Mind if I use your phone?"

"What? Sure, Ben, go right ahead." I guess he thought I wanted to call my lawyer. In a way, I did. I dialed the D.A.'s office and asked for his nibs as Flannery made a frantic grab for the phone wire.

"Touch that outlet and I'll break your goddam arm," I snarled.

"Ben! My God, you gone nuts?" he whimpered.

I got a wheel on the phone and said, "I'm calling from Hotsi-Totsi Records on Summit Avenue. There's a man here who's threatening me with blackmail. If you send a prowl car over here you'll find a whole wall safe full of dirty pictures." Then I hung up and got my back to the safe.

"What about these?" yelled Flannery. "You want the cops to see what you was doing to Bunny that night?"

I said, "For eighteen thousand dollars, George, I don't give a good goddam if they print it on the front page of the Sunday Times!"

George made a noise that sounded like "Gleep," and ran out into the plant. I figured he'd be back. I was right.

He brought company. Two muscular types who unloaded trucks full of record wax out back. That stuff comes in fifty pound boxes. It had done wonders for those boys' biceps.

"Throw that bastard out!" yelled Flannery "And hurry!"

I reached in my pocket and pulled out a switchblade. It snicked open with a wicked snap and the boys in the doorway looked worried.

"You cats better stay out of this," I said, making like Humphrey Bogart. "I killed thirty-seven Krauts who never said boo to me and you guys are giving me a reason."

George Flannery was hopping up and down like a flea on a hot plate. "Hurry up!" he screamed. He was hoping it would take a lot longer for the cops to get here than I was.

A couple of frightened looking girls from the outer office

looked in at us. One of them screamed, "He's got a knife!"
I could have kissed her.

One of the workmen said, "I don't know, Mr. Flannery.
You better wait till the cops get here."

"You sonofabitch! You do what I tell you!" yelled Flannery.

"Not for no seventy five cents an hour," grunted the
biggest one. The other nodded in agreement and the two
of them went away.

George slammed the door of the office shut and said, "I
got friends in City Hall, Ben. I can have you put in jail for
this."

"That's nice, George." I laughed. "I'll be able to play
chess with you on long winter evenings."

His shoulders sagged. "Look, Ben," he whimpered.
"Isn't there some way to square this?"

"Sure, George. Just write me out a check for eighteen
thousand dollars and you'll never see me again. Unless
the check bounces."

Flannery mopped at his brow. "Ben, the whole goddam
business isn't worth eighteen thousand skins. Maybe I did
dip into the till, Ben. The dough was rolling in and I
sprung for some other legit records. I should have stuck
to dirty ones. I lost every dime I put into your kind. I'm
broke, Ben. I haven't got a pot."

"You got this plant."

"Like I said, Ben. I couldn't raise that much cold cash
on the whole joint. The building's falling down and the
machinery is from the fall of the Roman Empire. We got
a press out back they say is haunted by Bessie Smith."

"O.K.," I said. "You got yourself a deal."

"I don't get you."

"You sign Hotsi-Totsi Records over to me and I'll hand
you a quit claim on the eighteen Gs."

"What? Sign over my business to you for a lousy eighteen
grand?"

"That's more than you just said it was worth, Flannery. The cops will be here pretty fast and they say it's rough on an old man to draw a five year rap. That's what you get for blackmail."

Sure, I was being rough on old George. But by now you can see where being a nice guy had gotten me. Besides, I never stomped a cat's toes unless he stomped mine first.

Flannery's mean little face looked like there was a rat inside his skull running around and around, looking for a way out. Outside there was a sound of police sirens. It wasn't the prowl car I'd called, but it jarred his computer loose.

The color came back into his cheeks and he sighed, "You win, Ben. I'll call Mike Stark and have him draw up the papers tonight."

"Uh uh," I said. "Right now."

"We need witnesses, Ben."

"We got them. Call them chicks in from the outer office and dictate a bill of sale on that Underwood. The pug uglies you were pointing at me awhile ago can be our witnesses too."

George stalled. But not for long. He didn't have that much time.

For "one dollar and other considerations" he signed the record pressing plant on Summit Avenue over to yours truly and I dictated a paper saying George was my best buddy, next to my mother, and that I would never sue him for any reason he might have given me prior to this here like day. As soon as he landed me the bill of sale I stuffed it in my pocket and said, "Now get out of here, you creep. This is a respectable house and we don't allow no crumbs."

He shrugged and walked out murmuring dark gypsy curses. Last I heard of George he was in Florida, raising the biggest passion flower vine in the state.

Five minutes after George had left, one of the girls

showed a pair of prowl car boys in. I told them it was all some sort of a gag, as nobody around Hotsi-Totsi Records had called the law. The hired help nodded helpfully and I told one of the chicks to give the cops a couple of free samples of our smut. As soon as the gendarmes cut out I called together the handful of cats Flannery had working for him and told them to take the rest of the day off.

All but the two cats Flannery had sicked on me. I called them back as the rest were leaving. I guess they expected to be canned. They didn't look too happy until I told them what I wanted.

"Take down that goddam sign from the front of the building," I said. "Hotsi-Totsi Records is a pretty pedestrian name for a high class establishment like this. In fact, it makes me urpy."

"Sure... boss," grinned the larger of the two. I later learned his name was Peterson. "Never liked the silly thing anyways. What you gonna call this joint now?"

It was a good question. I said I'd have to think about it.

□   □   □

By payday I knew why Flannery gave up so easy. Making the payroll just about cleaned me. All but two of the office staff were harem girls posing as secretaries. I let them go. They could make more on the turf than they could with me. That still left me fourteen salaries to meet every week.

I got Alex over from Manhattan along with a couple of C.P.A.s and a lawyer to see what in hell I'd bought for eighteen grand. It wasn't much.

I had a few hundred pounds of the cheap compound Flannery was still using to press records with. It came in the form of dirty looking black slabs, about the size of a king sized Hershey bar. It was dusty and cracked up a bit, but Alex said it would press out all right. I made up my mind to spring for some colored vinyl first chance I got. Maybe the cats Flannery had been shooting at didn't mind their platters cracking after they'd been spun a few times, but I wasn't looking for their trade.

There were four hand operated presses out back. They looked like a cross between a high school printing press and a wane iron. There was a hot plate built onto the left hand side of each press. The girls would put one or two slabs of the compound on the plate and after a while it would stop looking like pressed coal dust and slump down into a puddle of tar that smelled like shellac.

The impressions for the disc were on the inside surfaces of the big waffle iron that formed the top of the machine. The girls would take two labels out of the box below the hot plate, put one label face down over a hole in the center of the bottom die, fit the other one the same way over a stud on the top die, and scoop a gob of melted goo off the hot plate with her putty knife. She'd toss the glob between the jaws of the press and pull the handle. The jaws would close and the steam running inside the two king sized waffle irons cooked the glug until the chick thought she'd see what was in there. Half the times it was a record.

The platters came out of the machine like waffles and the babes stacked them on another wing on their right side. A cat named Lester, the smaller of the two goons Flannery had sicked on me, was supposed to keep the girls supplied with wax and take the stacked discs over to the shipping department where Peterson packed them.

There was a little room next to the shipping department where one of the chicks I hadn't fired spot checked the plates on a low-fi turntable.

If the labels didn't fall off, the only thing she had to worry about was that the dirty words came through. Poor Peterson packed records in a constant din of the same dreary sides, over and over again. It's amazing what some guys will do for seventy five cents an hour.

I intended to drop the smut. But it wasn't that easy.

Hotsi-Totsi wasn't over the door any more, but we still had a lot of orders to fill. After I got rid of the harem and plugged a couple of other leaks in the dike George Flannery had been too clever to see, the distributor's checks started to balance the payroll and I started putting my ASCAP checks in my own kick again.

Alex and Martha put in a few bills and we formed a new corporation with Hotsi-Totsi as a subsidiary company. Martha was the one who suggested the new name. I gave Peterson's nephew twenty five bucks to paint a new sign over the entrance and sprung for some printed bill heads. We called ourselves Summit Records. So you could think of a better name for a plant on Summit Avenue? I wasn't figuring on selling sides on the name, anyway. I was going to put music on them.

I let Alex handle the unfilled orders and went across the river to scout up some talent. There isn't as much of it around as a lot of cats think.

Elvis wasn't blowing for what I was ready to pay, so I went looking for the next best thing. There was a kid from Bushwick High over near Ridgewood. His father was a rabbi and wanted him to be a cantor. The kid wanted to make like Elvis. Neither of them got their own way. When he tried to field holler it got mixed up with the oriental sob of the synagogue. Not that I had any complaints. With a bass and guitar behind him that cat swung. It was our first big one.

So it wasn't as big as all that. Maybe you never heard the side. It never made the top ten but it moved. I'd put Ginger on the other side. The side that hadn't been played too much when Run For The Jungle was big.

It wasn't just sentiment. Ginger was good. The greatest. Better than anything else I had to put on the back of the disc, and I kind of wanted some of the cats who'd missed her first time out to latch on to the girl with the lavender eyes.

The ancient Greeks had an idea about that. They had one about everything else, so it figured. They said nobody was really and truly dead until they'd been forgotten. Down deep inside I guess I figured if enough cats believed in Ginger it would bring her back. Like Tinker Bell. I know that sitting inside my office with Ginger's voice spinning off the check sides in the sound room made her seem like she wasn't as far out in the big dark.

A funny thing happened with that record. I got a plug where I least expected it. I'd been out to a party on the Island, and coming home on the parkway I caught Ginger on the car radio. I'd been flipping across the dial for some music to drive by when her voice reached out from under the dashboard and I said, "Hello, cousin," and sat back to listen.

I rode about a mile with Ginger and the old bunch blowing to me from nowheres. Most of the people on that disc were dead. But I didn't feel spooked. I thought of poor Tico and the joke he never got over laughing at. It was as good a way to go as any. Smiling.

The disc faded out and I braced myself for the commercial. The voice of Marvin Knopff came on instead.

"Man," he said in a stagey nostalgic voice. "Wasn't that the greatest? The late Ginger Tracy in a new release by Summit on her big hit of a few years back. Alas, poor Ginger. I knew her, Horatio. A real doll and a beautiful hunk of woman." His voice sank to a lower key. "It was a lousy break for a gal just making it." Then he shut up for the station break. It was damned good theatre. It brought a lump to *my* throat and I *knew* Knopff. At least I thought I knew him. But this was an angle I couldn't figure.

It was almost time for the Bird Dog to sign off and I wasn't in the mood to hit the sack any more. I needed bright lights and noise, and some answers.

Knopff spotted me in the entrance as he walked out of

the studio. He'd grown a really frantic beard since I'd seen him last. His hairline was receding and he'd let the wig grow into a fringe of wild looking mop.

"Benny boy!" he said. Somehow, I knew he would. I slipped him a civil amount of skin and we went across the street to an all night greasy spoon and ordered a mug of joe.

"So what's with the plug?" I asked.

Knopff looked like I'd caught him robbing the poor box in Saint Pat's. He sipped at his coffee a couple of times and shrugged. "There any law against me giving you cats a boost?" he asked belligerently.

"For free?" I grinned. "What will the rest of the crowd think? I didn't even send you that side. You must have sprung for it."

"So I sprung for it. And you act like I made a pass at your sister instead of doing you a favor."

"You don't give plugs like that for the cats who pay you, Knopff," I said. "What's the angle?"

Knopff looked puzzled. "Beats the hell out of me, Parker. I must be losing my marbles." He grinned and looked around like he was afraid he'd be overheard. "It was a whim, I guess. Up to a few months ago I never had whims. Couldn't afford to. I was too busy brown nosing the bastards who run this lousy world." He shook his head and laughed. A bitter sort of laugh. Like a guy on a scaffold might get out of noticing the executioner's fly was unzipped. He said, "I've been watching you beat your goddam head against a brick wall for years, Ben. I think you're nuts. I think you'll lose. But it's been nice watching you."

"That why you gave us a plug?"

"Why not, Ben? I'm big now. It's cost me my soul but I'm about the biggest D.J. around. I've even got a foot in T.V. A Saturday stomp with the switchblade set. And it don't cost me a thing."

"You're a funny cat, Marvin."

"Coming from you that's the everloving end. I'm like nine million other cats clawing up the big greased pole to nowheres. You're the screwball, Ben."

"How so?"

"You don't play the game, man. You act like the world was run by God. You act like you really think you can make it clean, without the mob, without the payola. You act like all you need is talent and a good men's deodorant. I can't figure how you got this far."

"Neither can I," I said, getting up. "Thanks anyways, Marvin."

"Forget it. The next one will cost you some bread. I just got carried away tonight, and it was like a good record."

I threw four bits on the counter and headed for the door. Knopff said, "Hey Ben?"

"Yeah?"

"You know what? I hope you make it. I don't think you will, but if you did it would be nice. Like finding out there really is a Santa Claus."

□   □   □

Knopff's plug didn't put us on the Hit Parade, but it didn't hurt us, either. A few honest D.J.s were impressed enough with the great man to spin us a few times and the mail took care of the crooks.

They don't take payola on everything they spin, by any means. Once a side has had a little exposure they get requests. And the fan still decides the final issue. Payola just gets you over the first hump. But, man, that first hump is a lulu!

We didn't get many calls to record the boys who'd hit the street. (By that I mean 52nd Street in the Big Apple. Until a cat's blown on 52nd, he ain't blown nowheres.) But there were a lot of good lads around who still blew old fashioned gut bucket jazz, and that's what I'd been trying to make a buck at ever since Big Charlie Green died of malnutrition on a Harlem doorstep and the wise money said Chicago style was finished. Most of the old-timers were getting a little thick around the middle and I had to look for them in the warehouses and shoeshine stands they'd been hiding out in, but I was gambling there'd be enough jazz lovers out of a hundred and fifty million Americans to justify an album or two.

Covering all bets, I made a few Race records to pay the rent. Race records are cut strictly for the spade trade. It's hard to define what it takes to make a record Race. It's not dirty stuff. The bluest side we put out was one called, I Used To Love You, But Oh God Damn You Now! and it certainly isn't Hotter or even Cooler than the commercial sides.

Negroes, a segment of them anyways, are annoyed at any hint of what they call Uncle Tom in another colored cat. If you remember Uncle Tom, good old servile grinning watermelon eating Tom, you don't have to have the resentment explained. At the same time, they have pride in their own music and traditions, and aping a white man's taste doesn't satisfy them either. I guess the best way to explain Race records is to say they are played by negroes, for negroes, and bought by negroes. As soon as a swinging cat starts selling to the ofay he's automatically Uncle Tom. It's hard to figure.

Not too many of our legit sides really got out there and moved. Marvin Knopff wasn't just woofing when he said the next plug would cost me bread. I sent him a dozen releases and he didn't spin a one.

But the word got around. Summit Records wasn't going to make the stock holders in Columbia lose any sleep, but the oldtimers who'd heard the real thing, and a lot of crew cuts from the Ivy League who hadn't but wanted to, started sending in for our discs.

I got better compound, had the machinery tuned up,

and told the girls to slow down a bit. Flannery had been paying them on a piecework basis and they'd been batting them out like pancakes. Most of them didn't sound much better on the turntable, either.

The hi-fi trend was coming in and we picked up a few sales by cutting discs that let the boys play around with the woofers and tweeters they'd paid all that bread for.

□   □   □

It's too bad old Alex didn't stick around. We were just starting to see a steady column of black ink in the books for a change when he stopped breathing. I guess he figured it wasn't worth hanging around any more, now that Jimmy Dean was dead.

Martha called me in the middle of the night. She was pretty frantic. I never woke up to find the person next to me stiff, but I can imagine it was a lousy feeling. She'd called the M.D. and the law and everybody she knew who might be interested, and then she'd sat alone in the living room waiting for someone to come and hold her hand and keep the big black spider from crawling out of the broom closet at her.

They'd just taken Alex away when I got there. Martha was huddled up in one of his oversized bathrobes with paper curlers in her hair and red rims around her eyes.

"Do you want something to eat, Ben?" she asked as soon as I got inside. I didn't, but I said I did. The little mouse just wanted to do something to keep from screaming, and feeding men was one of her hobbies.

Martha fluttered around in the kitchen making an omelet. "I knew it would happen, Ben," she said. "Alex was a lot older than me, you know. And he'd had this cardiac thing for some time."

"Really? He never mentioned it."

"That's why he had to stop drinking. He had an attack one night on the subway and spent the rest of the year in

Bellevue."

I mumbled something inane about it being just as well
this way. Alex had had a few good years off the sauce and
wasn't it better to go while you were happy and all that
gas. It was pure crap. It's never better to go. A live busboy
is having more kicks than a dead movie star and everybody
knows it. But I had to say something inspired and there
isn't a damn thing you can say to somebody who's lost a
loved one but "Wake up. It didn't happen."

Martha wasn't listening anyways. She was making little
bird chirps of agreement and building a seven dollar omelet
like her sanity depended on it.

Soon as I'd polished it off, she was making another. I let
her go right on busting eggs. It was better than having her
sob all over the front of my white on white shirt.

I told Martha not to worry. She was still a partner in
Summit and I'd take care of the funeral arrangements. It
was nearly dawn. The grey light was coming through the
lacework of the Queensborough Bridge. I told her to get
some shut eye.

"Don't leave me here alone, Ben!" she cried. And that's
when I got the mascara all over my shirt. She insisted on
coming out to the plant with me. There wasn't a damn
thing for her to do out there, but I got the message. I put
her in the sound booth I'd had built to spare Peterson's
ears and told her to check records.

I told Lester to keep her supplied with plenty of hot and
brassy music and turned the volume high. With the music
blaring out and the booth double insulated, she could
scream all she wanted and see the people working in the
plant at the same time. I don't know if it was good therapy
or not, but by noon she wandered into my office and
said, "Thanks, Ben. I'll be O.K. now."

I took her to lunch across the street. I usually had it sent
but I wanted to change the scenery around for Martha. It
was a noisy joint, full of factory workers and drivers, but

no memories.

"Was it like this with Ginger, Ben?" she asked.

I nodded. "Worse. I was in a hospital ward and couldn't get drunk."

"I wish I could get drunk," she sighed. "But the taste of the stuff nauseates me." I guessed I must have raised an eyebrow.

"I know," she smiled. "Alex told you he met me at A.A. He did, Ben. I used to go there with my first husband. He was a terrible alcoholic. He died about a year before I met Alex."

"Let me get the picture, Martha," I said. "You mean you were never on the sauce? So why did you keep going back there?"

She smiled at her coffee cup. "You'd be surprised how many lonely people go to A.A. meetings, Ben. There are lights and food and conversation. The people are witty and clever and so much nicer than the ones you meet in the lonely hearts clubs."

I threw back my head and laughed. "You little crook! Pretending to be carrying a cross all this time just to meet a guy."

"Not pretending, Ben," she said. "There are worse crosses than alcohol. New York is no place for a shy person, Ben."

"New York is no place for Earth people," I said. "A screaming extrovert can live ten years in the same building without meeting the folks in the next apartment."

"I know, Ben. It's frightening. I used to walk up Fifth Avenue at night when the crowds had gone home and all I had for company was the echo of my heels on the tall buildings. It was eerie. I always expected to meet a troll or a werewolf."

"All the trolls hang out in the Holland Tunnel after midnight," I said. "And the last werewolf I saw was getting tossed out of the Savoy for not having a tie on.

Don't let the Big Apple bug you, kid. Everybody over there's just as scared as you are."

"Nobody's scared as I am, Ben. Not now," she said. She looked out at the sunlit street. A big red truck was rumbling by and the building shook. She shuddered and said, "It's all right now, Ben. But in just six or seven hours it will start getting dark."

It was like finding a stray pup. Once Martha had latched on to me I couldn't shake her. She hung around the plant all day and when I was ready to split I had to take her with me. I'd intended to go to a cocktail party uptown with one of the guys who recorded with us. I was supposed to pick up the chick I was working on and meet him and his wife at their apartment.

I told this to Martha and she just kept agreeing with me while she tried not to cry with her big brown eyes. I said, "Oh hell. I'll call my date and tell her the deal's off. I got to go to this party. Some big mucky muck from a TV station is blowing it. Why don't you come with me? It won't be much fun, but it'll be noisy."

Martha said, "In this dress?" Just like a dame. I had to admit she had a point. This basic black bit is O.K. but Martha was overdoing it. The rag she was wearing looked like it came out of the bargain basement, and I don't mean Bloomingdale's.

"So I'll run you home and you can change," I said.

"Oh Ben! I can't go back to that apartment. Not yet."

"So go the way you are. Nobody at a cocktail party pays any attention to anyone but themselves anyway."

"Oh Ben. I couldn't. People would think you picked me up in the Village."

"So what? It'll give me color," I said.

As it turned out, the problem was solved at Claude's apartment.

Musicians' wives come in two sizes. Bitches and dolls. Claude's was a doll. She dragged Martha into the bedroom and fixed her hair, put some eyebrows on her, and loaned her a hundred and fifty dollars worth of blue dress and a mink stole. Martha Bodanoff wasn't going to steal Prince Rainier away from Grace just yet, but it was a hell of an improvement.

I didn't know who was giving the party until we'd been there for half an hour. By then Martha was twinkling pretty with a glass of bubble juice in her hand and I didn't have the heart to cut out. Besides I didn't know where to take her, and I wouldn't leave a Times Square streetwalker in Johnny Angel's pad unescorted.

The years had been good to the creep. Angel had filled out a little and lost the punky look he'd had. He was a good looking bastard in his middle thirties and aware of the fact.

He'd sprouted a pointed blond beard and cultivated a Vincent Price voice since I'd seen him last. He looked like a Nordic Mephistopheles. Angel was a funny name for him.

"Benny." He smiled as he spotted me trying to hide behind a large columnist. "It was so good of you to come."

"I didn't know who was giving the brawl," I growled. "Claude told me it was a studio vice president. I didn't know they gave the job to reptiles."

Angel chuckled fondly. "Still got the old chip on the shoulder, Ben?" he laughed.

"For you, old buddy? Always. Care to step out in the hall and knock it off?"

Angel shook his head and strolled away to refill his glass.

"Some day, Ben," he muttered, "I'm going to have to have you killed."

That's one thing I liked about Angel. He was so goddam subtle. I went looking for Martha and ran into another beard. A black one. Marvin Knopff was smiling out at me from behind it. He said, "Benny boy! I didn't expect to find you here."

"Neither did I," I said. "But you don't surprise me in the least. You and Angel look like Trade and Mark. What's with him and the beard bit anyways?"

"I guess he thinks it's expected of him now that he's an author."

"Did you say author or adder? He isn't harmless enough to be an adder. I've always figured the cat for a pit viper or a cobra."

"So he's a cobra. But the book's going like water pistols at a Legion convention. It's about the history of jazz."

"I'd like to see that book," I growled. "I'll bet it's full of bull."

"Who said it isn't, Ben? This is the age of the common bull. Nobody wants to read the truth. The truth is too damned dull. The aficionados want to carve the squares with how much they know about the relative humidity in New Orleans the night Red Bird first sang the blues."

"I'll bite. Who in hell was Red Bird? Never caught his sound."

"See, Ben? You're square. You didn't know that Miss Red Bird, a Dahomey slave who belonged to a cat named Culpepper, was the first jazz singer who ever got her name in print. An English writer touring the South caught her act in 1812. He said she wore a gris-gris bag around her neck and had tribal markings on her cheek, but that didn't stop old Culpepper from having six kids by her. Now don't you wish you'd read the book before you came here tonight? You could have impressed hell out of that broad in the gold dress."

He pointed his beard at a chick in a gold lame evening dress and shocking pink hair. Not bad. I would have estimated her at a two hundred dollar campaign, but I was too tired to find out. I hadn't slept since three in the morning and it was catching up with me. I told Knopff I'd see him around and split. Martha was still yakking with the green turban. She was talking too loud and her eyes were too bright. I wondered if it was better to let her have fun or get her out of here before she started screaming.

When I saw the statue in the alcove, it jarred hell out of me. It was in a wall niche just off the hall to the john. Angel had set it up like the little shrines you see in Spanish Catholic homes. Only I don't think the Church would have approved of this shrine.

The statue was bronze. Green with age. Real age. Not the phony verdigris they brush on with carbolic acid. I'm not much on art but I knew this wasn't something Johnny picked up in a junk shop. It was early medieval, or maybe Roman. Something whipped up during dark ages by a cat with a lot of talent and a twisted mind.

It was evil. I don't mean just plain bad. It was Evil with a capital E. The statue was about a foot high. Naked and nicely proportioned in the classical style. But the body was that of an hermaphrodite. The sex organs, male and female, were a little out of proportion for good taste, and the face, a handsome homosexual face, was twisted into a perverted leer, as if the statue were dreaming up unusual things to do with its obscene body and thought the whole idea was funny as hell. On either side of the statue, black candles burned in silver Florentine holders. The flickering light made the evil little bronze face look like it was alive.

At my shoulder a voice said, "Like it, Ben? It's old Angra Manyu, my patron saint."

Something Alex had said one time came back to me. I said, "He's a good choice for you, Angel."

Angel looked disappointed. He was used to having folks ask who Angra Manyu was. He said, "You know about him, Ben?"

I said, "Sure. Angra Manyu was what the ancient Persians called the devil. A cat named Zoraster told us all to watch out for him twenty five hundred years ago."

Angel raised a satanic eyebrow and grinned. "Why, Ben.

You read!" he laughed.

I wanted to gather Martha and split. But I knew I wasn't going to get any sleep unless I tied up some loose ends. Angel had the same effect on me as dirty pictures. You remember the blackmail photos Flannery'd had in his safe? Sure, I burned them. It was the only thing a decent cat could do. But I looked at them first. (Wouldn't you have? Who are we kidding?)

I said, "O.K. So what's with his nibs, Johnny? You on a Zoroastic kick? What's wrong with Zen Buddhism? I understand that's all the rage with the beards this season."

Angel looked sharply at me, the little wheels going around in his ferret eyes. Something dropped in a slot inside his head and he nodded. "Why not?" he laughed. "I think it's too late to save you, Ben. But it's such a goddam waste to see you on the losing side."

"What are you selling?" I asked, "The C.P. or religion?"

Angel chuckled. "You might call it a religion, Ben," he said. "Come out here on the terrace with me."

"I don't know, John," I grinned. "I'm not that kind of a boy. I heard how you ducked the draft."

Angel opened the French doors leading out onto the roof garden and said, "You heard about that, huh, Ben? You know a better way to stay out of a war?" I had to admit he had a point.

"I guess I'm bashful," I said. "But looking a head shrinker straight in the eye and telling him I'm a fairy would embarrass hell out of me."

Johnny shrugged. "It did," he said. "But so what? I never saw the cat again. You poor slobs marched off to save the world while I made bread blowing for the free spending swing shift."

Angel led the way to the parapet and waved his hand out over the lights of New York winking up at us through twenty stories of exhaust fumes.

"I wouldn't have this layout if I'd gone with you, Ben,"

he said. "I'd be down there on the dirty streets with the rest of the insects tonight instead of sitting up here above the Big Apple. I might even be under a few feet of dirt or sitting in a goddam wheel chair like my old man. That's where he wound up. He went off to a war one time. Back in '17. He was a goddam hero, my old man. And you know what being a hero got him, Ben? Poverty! The rest of his stinking life in a wheel chair and his kids growing up on potato peel soup!"

Angel glared down at New York and New York glared back. The neon signs from the shops below threw a red glow on his face, like he was looking into a witch's cauldron.

He said, "I know about war, Ben. I was raised on one. My father couldn't wait for America to get into it. He left the wife he had, a couple of months pregnant, and went up to Canada to join the Royal Flying Corps. They gave him about six weeks training and put him in a De Havilland-5. You know anything about De Havillands, Ben?

"The only De Havilland I ever saw was Olivia. I liked her in Robin Hood. The only trouble was Errol Flynn got her. I was rooting for the Sheriff of Nottingham."

"Very funny. You must go over big at a Kiwanis convention. Who writes your material, Ben?"

"O.K. I was reaching. So what kind of a De Havilland are we talking about?"

"A De Havilland-5. It was a plane. A lousy collection of cedar and doped linen that went up like a torch if you rubbed a boy scout against it. It had two seats and they put my old man in the rear one with a Lewis gun so the pilot wouldn't get lonesome while he burned to death."

Angel wasn't talking to me any more. He was telling it to the lights shining up from the streets below. I shut up and listened in. There had to be an answer to Angel and maybe this was it.

"The old man was pretty hot with that Lewis gun," he

said. "He knocked down a couple of Hun planes that got too close and then he and his pilot ran into the Checkerboard Squadron. Ever hear of them?"

I nodded. I'd read about all that stuff in the pulps you used to pick up in the bus stations. The ones with garish red and black Fokkers on the covers and the little "tripes" with checkerboard designs on their three stubby wings. It was hard to believe that men had really killed each other in those flimsy little planes with their bright armorial colors in the same gray sky I'd seen full of B-17s a few years back.

"The old man lived through it," said Johnny. "The pilot was a lot luckier. He burned to death. My old man just made it halfways. Then some sonofabitch of a German infantryman pulled him out of the wreck with his hair and clothes all full of burning white gas and castor oil."

He shuddered. It was the first time I'd ever seen Angel show that much human emotion. He said, "I never saw my father's face. He lived for twenty years more, but I never saw what he looked like. He wore a black mask over the bottom of his face, like Lon Chaney in The Phantom of the Opera. All you could see were his eyes. He had no hair or eyebrows left and in the half light of evening he looked like a goddam skull wearing a mask. It creeped me. My mother must have been nuts. She had six kids by the damned mess. It was all he could do. Make babies. And I'm damned if I can see how he did that. His legs were off at the hips.

"My mother took in washing. Don't that sound like a goddam soap opera? But it's true. The only other woman on the block who done washing was a nigger woman who'd been left by her man. When I was old enough to shine shoes I started shining them. I had to whip eight nigger kids to hang on to my corner. Then the depression came along and I had to stomp white kids. A big Bohunk named Walter Skeletky finally wound up with the corner.

He was five years older than me and bigger than the cop on the beat.

"I sold Liberty Magazines with a white canvas bag over my shoulder for a while. So did a million other kids. There were more kids selling Liberty on the streets of Springfield those years than there were people who had the nickel to buy one."

"Springfield Mo or Springfield Mass, Johnny?"

"Never mind. I left home as soon as I was able to walk. Me and my kid brother Al. I'd read Little Orphan Annie and figured if a dopey girl with no pupils in her eyes could make it on her own so could me and Al. I'll bet Orphan Annie never hit the same jungles we did, Ben. The bos would have raped her and ate Sandy."

He didn't have to draw me a picture. I'd ridden the rails during the depression. That's where I acquired the habit of carrying a switchblade.

Johnny said, "It was a cold night in '38. Coming over the Donner Pass on a long freight. It gets cold in the Sierras at night, man. And we were riding the blinds. Me and Al and a kid named Smokey. You ever ride the blinds, Ben?"

"Once," I said. I knew about riding the blinds. The space between freight cars. A dangerous way to get where you're going. A bo stands with a foot on each of the narrow ledges along the bottoms of the two cars and his crotch across the empty air between him and the wheels. He hangs on by the grab irons or the brake rods between the reefers. He'd better. If you let go, a mile of freight train rolls over you before anybody's liable to notice.

Johnny said, "Smokey was the first to go. Me and Al never seen him lose his grip. It was colder than a well digger's ass, and the wind was howling like a banshee over the rumble of the big iron wheels below us. If Smokey screamed we never heard it. As soon as I noticed he was gone, I put my mouth next to Al's ear and yelled, 'Keep

moving around, kid. Don't let yourself fall asleep.' Al
nodded. He was scared. But the next time I looked at him
I could see his eyes were dopey. We'd been riding the
blinds for six or seven hours and we hadn't been getting
too much sleep before that. With the goddam cold an' all,
Al was having a time staying awake.

"I knew we were nowheres near the end of the line. We
had a good four, five hours ahead of us before there was
a prayer of the train slowing down. We were highballing
down the western grade, doing sixty miles an hour with a
cowboy in the engine. I thought of jumping, but a look
out the side of the blinds cured me of the idea. The pon-
derosa trees were going past like propeller blades and we
had a choice of going off the mountain on the one side
and smack against the wall of the cut on the other. We
had to stay awake and hang on. Al's lips were moving
and I put my ear next to his mouth. The dopey kid was
praying to Jesus.

"You know what, Ben? I gave it a try. I already knew
better but I gave it a try. Ain't it a comical picture? Two
half frozen kids hanging over the clickety clacking wheels
of a highballing freight and sending up smoke signals to
the great white father in the sky."

I said, "Someone must have heard you, Angel. You're
still breathing."

"Yeah, Dad. But it wasn't anybody up there in space,"
he sneered. "Al kept praying to Jesus and Mary to put a
little strength in his fingers. Not much. Just enough to
keep a hundred and ten pounds of scared kid hanging on
to that cold cold grabiron. I guess they didn't hear him. I
guess they were too busy with the holy joes who go to
church every Sunday and throw a nickel in the plate to
save their souls.

"I saw Al let go and I grabbed him by the sweater. I had
one hand on a brake rod so cold it burned and the other
buried in that old red sweater a Salvation Army cat gave

him in Reno. You know what? I was a hell of a lot stronger than that sweater. Al hung down with his feet just over the track. He was yelling and making swimming motions with his arms, like he thought he could fly back up to me through the cold air. The jerk should have grabbed my arm and thrown a leg over the coupling. I yelled at him to, but the wind tore the words out of my mouth and he just kept swimming there on the end of my arm while the sweater... sort of unraveled."

Johnny looked down across the Big Apple towards the southwest, like he could still see it happening. He said, "So there I was, Ben. Hanging on to my kid brother while his life slipped through my fingers. I prayed. I prayed so loud they should have heard me on Mars. I swore I'd be the nicest little boy since George Washington. I swore I'd never lie or cheat or steal or diddle little girls in the bushes. And then there was this funny snap and Al was gone. I damned near went with him. I lost my balance and the next thing I knew I was hanging on to the brake rod by both hands with the wheels snapping at my dangling feet. I got a knee on the coupler and hung there crying like a damned fool.

"After a while I stopped crying and the cold didn't bother me any more and that's when I knew I was falling asleep. I forced myself up that goddam brake rod like a nigger climbing a coconut tree. Crying and praying all the way. I don't know just when I stopped praying to Jesus and switched to the devil but it seemed like a hell of a good idea at the time. I hung there in the dark and swore a promise, Ben. I swore I'd be on Angra Manyu's team. I didn't know his name in those days. But I promised to be a bad boy. It was the same thing."

I said, "You've sure kept that promise, Angel. You're, like, the baddest boy *I* ever met. What did Satan do then, reach out and hand you an electric blanket?"

"Better than that, Ben. He stopped the train."

"You're kidding."

"The hell I am. I'd no sooner prayed to the devil than the train slowed down and braked to a stop within a mile. The reefer ahead had a hot box and the brakeman had spotted it just in time. If that bearing hadn't overheated I'd have fallen for sure in half an hour or less. And if the brakeman hadn't seen it the reefer might have jumped the track when the bearing froze and dumped us all in the canyon. You can't say Angra Manyu didn't time it right."

"Horse turds, Angel," I laughed. "Do you really believe all that? Do you really think there's a big black demon with horns and a tail down there under the ground? The devil is just another name for the boogie man."

"No more than God is another name for Santa Claus, Ben. You've seen enough of this world. Which makes more sense to you, a nice old guy with whiskers handing out pie in the sky, or a sonafabitch with a pitchfork handing out grief?"

"Maybe there's nobody at either end." I shrugged. "What good does it do to be on the devil's side, anyways? From what I hear, that cat plays with loaded dice."

"Propaganda, Ben," said Angel. "The devil takes care of his own. I know. I've kept my promise, Ben. I've busted every one of the rules and any others I could think of. I've gotten away with everything but treason and incest. Mainly because the Commies ain't approached me yet and my mother's dead. I've even gotten away with murder, Ben."

"Anybody I know?" I asked.

"Wouldn't you like to get *that* on me, Ben?" he grinned. "Doesn't it bug you? Here I am telling you I committed cold blooded, premeditated murder, and there isn't a damn thing you can do about it because you don't know who it was or when it happened! Murder and arson are the two easiest crimes to get away with. Did you know that, Ben? I used to burn houses for kicks and I know."

He was enjoying himself, the bastard! I said, "My heart bleeds for you, Angel, or whatever your name is. You use the depression and a rough childhood as an excuse to be a rat and I'm supposed to feel sorry for you. You think you're the only cat who had it rough in those days? I swiped coal for the grate a few times, Dad, but I didn't parley a couple of missed meals into open season on the human race."

"That's because you're stupid!" Angel snarled. "Look where you've gotten being such a good hearted slob. A little record company I can buy and stuff in my hip pocket any time it looks like a good investment."

"O.K. I ain't a vice president. Big deal," I said.

"You think that's all I've got, you jerk?" He laughed. "Hell, I've got seven bands out under my name. I own a booking agency that takes a third of what half the cats who blow on my network make. I own a voting share in sixteen record companies that make yours look sick, and I get a cutback on every goddam record spun or cut in certain parts of the country which shall remain nameless."

His voice sank half an octave and got dirty. "That's not all, Ben," he confided. "If a vocalist is worth looking at I don't have to twist any arms for bedroom privileges."

"Well, goody for you. Do you like the girl vocalists or the boy vocalists best?"

Angel's mouth tightened. "I take what I want. I don't want the male vocalists. But don't think the bastards wouldn't jump if I told them to! I own them, Ben. I own every goddam one of them. I'm the guy who says if they get a booking and I'm the boy they see if they want to cut a side. Angel pockets the kickback the talents pay the recording company, and Angel pockets the payola they give to have it aired. I'm going to wind up owning the whole goddam industry yet, Ben. What do you think of that?"

"You're, like, an angel!" I said. "So if you're so goddam big why are you bending my ear? I'm just a poor stupid slob who thinks the world is run by the guys in the white hats. Why tell me your plans to conquer the universe?"

"I can use you," he said. "You and guys like you. I'm spreading out too fast, Ben. It's getting so my right hand don't know what the left one's doing any more."

"So what's wrong with Marvin Knopff? All you have to do is whistle and you can get a battalion of stooges."

"I don't want stooges, Ben. The woods are full of creeps like Knopff. One hand out for grease and the other one holding a stiletto. Knopffs make good corporals but I need lieutenants. Give me ten guys who think like I do, Ben, and wind up owning this whole goddam town." He spread his hand expansively across the view of the Big Apple below.

I said, "Give you ten guys who think like you, Angel, and you'll be dead. Did you ever hear what happens to the leader of a wolf pack when he loses his footing?"

Angel smiled. "I don't intend to lose my footing," he said, "How about it? Are you ready to sell your soul?"

His eyes were kind of funny looking in the red light from the neons below. I said, "I'll think about it, Johnny. But don't call me, I'll call you." I started to walk back inside for a breath of fresh air. Behind me Angel purred, "Have you ever seen a guy get hit with a garlic bullet, Ben?"

I turned and said, "I don't know, Angel. I never sniffed at no bullet holes. What's the point?"

Angel chuckled like a big cat with a nasty secret. He said, "The minestrone set go in for them, Ben. They cut an X on the point of a soft nosed bullet and smear it with crushed garlic. I've heard it's a nasty thing to get hit in the guts with."

"Must play hell with a guy's breath," I said. "Remind me not to step in front of a garlic bullet."

"That's just what I am doing, Ben."

"Meaning?"

"Meaning anybody who isn't with me is *against* me!
Do I make myself clear?"

I stood looking at him for a second and said, "Angel,
you take yourself too goddam serious. What do you do
for kicks, stand in front of the mirror all night making
faces? You're so goddam scary you're funny! Drop the
act, Angel. Ming the Merciless was even meaner looking
than you and you know what happened to him? Flash
Gordon got him with a zip gun."

I turned away and went back inside. Knopff was talking
to Martha and the cat in the green turban. I walked over
and said, "Grab your mink, Dale. You and me is pushing
off for Earth."

Martha went to find the borrowed stole and Knopff
said, "Angel give you the recruiting speech, Dad?"

"Yeah. I told him to shove it."

"Not smart, Ben. Angel has a lot of suction. He can put
in a bad word for you here and there around town."

"Hell hath no fury like an Angel scorned, huh?" I said.
"Do me a favor, will you, Marv?"

"Depends. What is it, Ben?"

"Sooner or later that heel's going to slip, Knopff. When
you and the boys do the third act of Julius Caesar... stab
him once for me?"

I couldn't get Martha to go back to her pad so I brought
her to mine. We didn't need a chaperone. We were too
beat.

Martha took the bedroom and I camped out on the studio couch, which is conventional as all hell but not fair.
That little mouse hardly filled half my bed, while I over-
flowed at both ends of the couch. But what are you going
to do? The guy always gets the couch.

The next day went pretty much in the same groove as
the one before. Martha followed me to the plant and spun

records when she wasn't making coffee for us in the kitchenette of my office. There was only one thing missing. I didn't have a cocktail party to take her to that night. I stuck around until the help went home and there was Martha, hanging around like a lost kitten. I took her to Laurent's for dinner and sat through The King And I with her, hoping she'd get tired.

She didn't. Just cried all through Hello, Young Lovers and had to put on fresh mascara. We went to Lindy's for cheesecake and joe while I tried to talk her out of the blues. It was no go. I suggested it was about time she went home, or to a hotel if the place creeped her too bad, and Martha said, "Couldn't I come home with you tonight, Ben? I'll go out a window if you leave me alone."

"Look, Miss Mouse," I said, "you're not talking to Sir Galahad. I can go this couch bit one night for an old friend, but you know damned well what's going to happen if you keep hanging around my pad."

She dropped her eyes and flustered. "I know, Ben. I'm human too. And we're supposed to wait until after the funeral. But I'm hurting, Ben. I don't want to be alone."

I didn't say anything. She waited to see how her bombs were landing and then sighed, "I suppose you think I'm terrible? It's not sex, Ben. It's the lousy feeling you get in the middle of the night when you wake up to find an empty pillow staring at you in the dark. You've been through all this, Ben. Can't you kind of understand?"

I said, "You know you'll never mean anything to me, Miss Mouse? I mean... nothing *special*?"

"I know, Ben. But couldn't we sort of keep each other company?"

I smiled at her. The kind of smile you reserve for lost mice, and said, "Hell, I can't let you jump out a window. What's your favorite color?"

"I don't know. Green, I think. Dark green. Why?"

"Just wanted to know what kind of paint to pick up,

Miss Mouse. The first thing I have any girl of mine do is paint my apartment."

I don't know just when Angel started to work on me. Not right away. Angel was too busy taking over the network to spend time dreaming up ways to put Summit Records out of business. But a year or so after that little talk, our sales started taking a real slide. The business is seasonal so it didn't worry me at first. But when we didn't break even on Christmas platters, I knew something was wrong.

I had a sentimental snow and jinglebell number Con had written, and every year that standard brought the cash in like the swallows of Capistrano. When that platter didn't sell I knew we were in trouble.

It was Peterson who located the sides, where they weren't supposed to be. I'd promoted Peterson. He had a brain under that dumb Swedish face, and I'd put him in Alex's place, looking after distribution and the Race and stag records.

He came in a couple of days before Christmas and said, "Boss, we got troubles."

"So what else is new?" I said. I'd been out checking record shops. They didn't have our platter in stock.

Peterson said, "I found a hundred and fifty sides of that Conners disc over on Sixth Avenue, boss. On the nineteen cent counter of a used record shop."

"Used records! For Chrissake, we ain't even sold the damned things. How can they be used?"

"That's what I asked the guy, boss. He said where he got his sides was none of my goddam business."

I got up and put on my top coat. "Come on," I said. "We're making it our business."

Peterson hadn't counted right. There were more than a hundred and fifty of our sides in the shop on Sixth Avenue.

A stack of eighty he hadn't noticed was on another counter. I picked one up and walked over to the manager. "Where'd you latch on to these sides, Dad?" I asked.

He recognized Peterson and shot me a bored, here we go again look. He looked at the record like he'd never seen it before and said, "How should I know, mac? The cats bring them in here by the boxful for eating money. They're like used, Dad."

"Bull. These sides are still warm from the presses, Dad. I ought to know. I'm the guy that pressed them. Now how about it? You want to talk to me or do I call a cop?"

"Look, Dad. Don't make no trouble. I got like connections, see?"

I said, "Peterson, run out on the street and get the law. There's usually a couple having coffee in Hadley's at this hour."

The shop owner looked bored. He said, "Look, wise guy. You're only asking for trouble, see? I'm covered."

I said, "We'll see." And took up a station near the piled records. The manager went in back and got very busy on the phone. I didn't think he was calling his wife.

Peterson came back in a few minutes with a harassed looking cop. The law nodded to the manager and said, "What's this all about, mac?"

I said, "This guy here is fencing hot records, officer."

"How do you like that?" the manager laughed. "I'm getting rich on international crime, selling lousy used sides at nineteen cents a throw!"

I ignored him and said, "He's got over two hundred records put out by my company in this store, officer. The label numbers show they were pressed less than a week ago and they've never been played. According to Mr. Peterson here, this particular shipment of records was supposed to be sent to St. Louis. I want to know what they're doing here."

The manager grinned and said, "Look, mac. I got troubles of my own. I paid good gelt for these sides from a cat who said he got them legit. If he stole them from you, it ain't my problem. I didn't steal them."

The cop looked thoughtful and said, "So who was the guy you bought them from, mac?"

"How the hell should I know? We got guys coming in all day with used platters. Just a guy type guy."

I said, "Not good enough, Dad. I want names and addresses or I press charges."

"So press charges. Like I said, I'm covered. I'll be home before you are, and suing you for false arrest."

The cop said, "I don't know, mister. This is getting over my head. Maybe you better wait and see the D.A. in the morning."

"Nuts," I said. "That'll give this creep all night to ditch the records. I'm pressing charges, and I'm pressing them now. I'm accusing this cat of stealing my records, officer. At a buck and a half a throw it comes to grand larceny. Now, do you make the pinch or do I have to take your badge number?"

The cop looked pained and said, "Let's not get our bowels hot. I never said I wouldn't make the pinch." He turned to the manager and said, "How about it, mac? You want to give me the gory details or do I gotta call the wagon?"

The manager licked his lips and said, "Look, I just work here. I don't want no trouble. I told you I don't know where the platters come from. What more can I say?"

"You'll have to do better than that," sighed the cop.

The manager shrugged his shoulders and said, "What the hell, I got nothing to hide. They told me the deal was greased. They told me there wouldn't be no trouble because if anybody makes a bitch they're liable to lose their distribution. I guess they told me wrong, huh?"

"They sure as hell did, Dad," I said. "Who slipped you my discs?"

"No trouble if I tell you? You drop the whole thing?"

"Just tell me who swiped my sides and pay the freight to Jersey and we part friends, Dad."

Wryly relieved, he wrote down a name and address in the garment district and handed it to me. I told the cop I was happy and sent him back to finish his hamburger.

Peterson and me drove downtown to the address we'd been given. It was closed but we didn't mind. The puzzle was falling into place fast. The address was the Manhattan warehouse of our distributor.

"You ever have any experience as a second story man?" I asked Peterson.

He grinned. "Only thing I ever stole was a box of Black Crows off a candy store counter. My old man caught me and whipped my behind. We going in, boss?"

"We're going to try. First I got to make a phone call." I parked the car near an all night diner and dialed an old army buddy. A nice quiet guy uptown who owned a pizza joint and sent his kids to a nice private school. A few years back, he ran with Dutch Schultz.

When he came to the phone I said, "Harry, I need a couple of boys for a little job down in the garment district. Can do?"

"Sure, Benny. Light work or heavy?"

Heavy work means beating a guy up or knocking him off, so I said, "Light, Harry. I want a couple of doors unlocked for me."

"Dammit, Ben," sighed Harry. "Ain't you never heard of phone taps?"

"Sorry, Harry, I haven't been reading Dick Tracy lately. Can you send me the right lads?"

"I ain't saying I can and I ain't saying I can't. Where in hell are you, Ben?"

"You know the old Serbian church on 26th Street? I'll be waiting on the stoop of the brownstone across the street. C.P. Headquarters."

Harry the Glove hung up and I went to wait with Peterson. In a little while a couple of cats in white stevedore hats strolled over to us.

"You Parker?" one of them asked.

I nodded and said, "You boys know how to get in a warehouse without setting off the alarm?"

"Would we be here if we didn't? Where is the joint?"

I led them down the street to the deserted building and we walked through the parking lot to a side entrance. The two safe-and-loft boys Harry had sent looked annoyed.

"You call us all the way over here to crack this cheese box, Parker?" one of them laughed. "Hell, my little brother could short that lousy alarm. You've been neglecting your education, Parker. Them old tinfoil strips date back to the Hudson Duster days." He reached in his pea jacket for a length of jump wire and a screw driver. It took him thirty seconds to open the door with a pair of tire irons after he'd shorted the alarm.

If you go in for crime, the experience was very educational. By the time the night was over I knew the rudiments of breaking and entering. That wasn't all I knew. Peterson found our whole shipment of Christmas records in the basement. No wonder we weren't making any profit on them this year. They were rotting on the damp floor instead of being on the record counters I was paying to have them shipped to. I sure as hell wanted to know why.

I paid a call on a cat named Eddy Barclay the next morning. He looked kind of like a chipmunk, and even talked like one when he was excited. When he wasn't robbing blind men, he was my distributor.

He was the picture of innocence as I told him about the bit with the hot records on Sixth Avenue. I didn't mention the fact that I'd burglarized his warehouse the night before. He didn't look like he'd understand.

"You've got to expect a certain amount of pilfering, Benny," he chirped merrily. "The boys on the truck sort of figure a box or two of records ever now and then is fair game."

"When I was working for a living, Ed, guys got fired for stealing."

Barclay nodded in agreement. "It's the goddam unions, Ben. Half the guys they send us got police records as long as your arm. If we fire a guy for a little pilfering they send us another one just as bad. I can't keep firing them. You want I should have a strike?"

I said, "If it means they get to steal my wax, Ed, you're damned right I want a strike. For God's sake, I been all over town looking for our Christmas sides. The only ones I've found are in used record shops. What in hell's going on?"

Barclay looked sour. "Aren't you happy with your distribution, Ben?" he asked. I ignored the veiled threat. I had a couple of my own I'd been saving.

I said, "I'm not only unhappy, Ed. I'm steamed. For all I know those sides never left your warehouse."

I thought he was going to swallow his cigar. He caught himself and went dead pan. "Maybe you better find yourself another distributor, Ben," he said coldly. "You act like you don't trust me."

I said, "Suits me, Ed. Just write out the check for my sides and I'll start looking around."

"What are you talking about, Ben? Your check ain't due until after the first of the year. We don't know how the sides sold yet. How can we settle up?"

"Why, Ed, I figure we must have sold out."

His voice got cagy. "How in hell do you figure that, Ben?"

"Well, Ed, if you put those records on the trucks like your contract read they must have been shipped out to the stores, right?"

"So?"

"So if they ain't there now, they've either been sold or stolen. Either way, you're responsible for them until they've either been sold or returned to yours truly, right?"

Barclay was looking like he wanted me to go away and leave him alone with his phone. I grinned and said, "Of course, there's one other thing that might have happened, but I don't think you'd pull a dumb stunt like that."

"Like what, Ben?"

"Like maybe you never put them on the trucks at all? Like maybe they're rotting in your waterlogged warehouse right now?"

Barclay's face turned a lovely shade of green. He said, "Now what in hell would I do that for, Ben? Neither one of us would make any gold out of your discs if I didn't distribute them. It just don't make sense."

"That's just what I told my lawyer, Ed."

"Your lawyer?" Barclay looked like he wanted to vomit.

"Yeah," I said, reaching in my breast pocket. "He seems to think you might have it in for me. Or be in cahoots with somebody else who wants to put Summit out of business. I think they call that sort of thing criminal conspiracy in this state, Ed."

I handed him the paper across the desk. He looked blankly at the legal type and chirped, "What's this, Ben?"

"An injunction, Ed. From magistrate's court. It says you can't move any records out of the Manhattan warehouse until my lawyer and a couple of lads from the D.A.'s office have gone over your books."

Have you ever faced an enraged chipmunk? Barclay jumped to his feet and came around the desk at me with blood in his eye. Then he thought better of it and went over and kicked his filing cabinet.

"Listen, Ben," he chirped. "Maybe we got a few sides we ain't put out on the street yet, but how we gonna do right by you if we can't move nothing in our trucks? You trying to put me out of business?"

I shrugged. "If it's got to be me or you, Ed, it'll be you. You and Johnny Angel sure as hell haven't been trying to do me no favors."

Talk about a shot in the dark! That one hit Barclay where he lived. He turned beet red and started to sweat. "Who's been putting bugs in your ear, Ben? I'm your pal. You and me got nothing to fight about."

I said, "We'll see about that when the D.A. goes over your books, Ed. I'd better leave now so you can call your boy. When you find out Angel's going to throw you to the wolves, maybe we can make a deal."

I walked out. Behind me, Barclay was dialing like mad. I knew he'd call me up at the plant as soon as he found out my lawyer had slammed another injunction on his bank account.

Nat Sassower, my lawyer, maintains a plush office on Madison Avenue, looks like Melvin Douglas, and drinks nothing but imported scotch. He has an LL.D. from Harvard and is a pillar of the Westchester Country Club set and he fights as dirty as a garment district shyster. That's why he's my lawyer. Any other kind is a waste of time and money.

Ed Barclay had called me twice before I got across the river. As soon as he got me on the horn he shouted, "You sonofabitch! What's the idea of freezing my bank account?"

I said, "It's my lawyer's idea, Ed. He seems to think you might skip town. We just want to make sure Summit gets the money you owe us, Eddy boy."

He hissed, "You stupid bastard! I'll blacklist you! You'll never get another distributor to touch you. I'll see to that, Parker. This ain't the way the game is played, Ben. The boys in the field don't go for guys who fink to the D.A. You're going to find yourself all alone, Parker. When we get through with you, the only way you'll hear one of your records is on your own hi-fi."

I said, "And you'll find yourself walking, chum. I've got one of my boys out looking for your car. We've got an injunction on that, too." Then I hung up.

I walked out into the plant to see if Lester was keeping the girls supplied with wax. I'd given him a raise but it didn't look like it had done much good. I found him in the john reading a science fiction magazine and asked him if he would be good enough to inform me when he was through, as two of the presses were sitting idle.

I was watching a new girl we were breaking in when Martha came out from the office and said there was someone to see me. I thought it was somebody from Barclay but it turned out to be a chick. A little doll about the size of Martha. A Latin type with long black hair and eyes that bugged me. She reminded me of someone I'd seen before, but I couldn't place her.

She said her name was Lila Murillo and she'd brought a record she wanted me to hear. The disc was one of those low-fi sides they cut for you on Sixth Avenue for a buck. After you've played them about twenty times, you might as well throw them away.

Martha looked at me over the girl's shoulder and begged me with her eyes. Miss Mouse was the sympathetic kind. She didn't have to twist my arm. I remembered a scared kid a million years ago who'd waited all afternoon outside a South Side stage door to see if a god named Bix would let him sit in just once. That kid had pounded too many pavements in his time to brush a talent without at least listening to its sound. The little Latin number was looking at me with that mixture of hope and desperation you get used to seeing on their faces. Peterson stuck his head out of the door and yelled, "Boss, you're wanted on the phone." And Lila Murillo died a little.

I said, "Tell Barclay I'm busy, Pete. I got a record I want to hear."

The girl shot me a surprised, grateful look. Damn those eyes. They did something funny to me. They were big and sad and velvety brown with little flecks of green when the light hit them. It was like when you hear a melody and can't remember the name of the tune.

I dropped the cobra on the disc and turned the volume up. For the kid's sake I hoped the record wouldn't be as bad as most of them were. It wasn't.

It was a cha cha with a tricky beat. The piano blowing in back of the voice was from hunger and the maracas sounded like maracas. That's all they ever sound like. The voice on the side was like Craaaazy.

I looked at Miss Mouse and grinned. Martha had an I Told You So smile on her face. Lila Murillo had a voice. Period. You could make a lot of sage pronouncements about it. You could say it swung. You could say it made you want to laugh and cry at the same time. You could say anything you wanted about it. But unless you've heard one of Lila's platters you don't know what I'm talking about. It was like Solid.

The kid was watching my face like I was about to announce the second coming of the savior. I must have a poker face. She looked worried. I listened to the record and sized her up. She wasn't hard to figure, except for the haunting eyes.

Her face was just a face face. Pretty. Sort of exotic in fact. A blend of all of the south of the border races melted into what the Hawaiians are supposed to look like, but don't. And she was green as hell. Had on one of those organdy dresses with fuchia blossoms sewed to the hip.

I waited until the side had run down and said, "It's good, Miss Murillo. You've got a talent. Now what can I do for you?"

She looked confused. She said, "Well, I heard you were a good company to work for, Mr. Parker. I mean, like if I was cutting a record for you."

"You got an agent, kid?"

"No."

"No agent? You got your union card paid up?"

"I got to be in a union?"

"You sure as hell do, honey. You got any connections? Know any musicians? I mean anybody who might give you a job?"

Her eyes welled up and she looked frightened and very young. Most of them do. The fan magazines don't tell you about union dues. Every Greyhound that rolls into the Big Apple has at least one kid aboard who thinks all they have to do is stand on 42nd and Broadway and wait to be discovered. It doesn't work just that way. But they keep coming.

I said, "Where you from, Lila?"

"L.A.," she answered.

I said, "And you came all the way to New York? The last time I was out in Levittown on the Pacific, it was right next to Hollywood. Don't they still make discs out there?"

She wrinkled her nose and said, "All they wanted to make was me, Mr. Parker. I heard you was a right guy. I heard Summit was one of the only companies where a dame didn't have to... you know? To cut a side."

I didn't know if I should be complimented or insulted. I'm not that old yet. I led the way back to the office. I parked Lila Murillo across the desk from me while Martha poured coffee and we tried to fill her in on the field. It wasn't easy.

Lila came from so far east of the L.A. switchyards that the Coca Cola signs are printed in Spanish. She was one of those little wetbacks who never speak English until they get dragged to school by the truant officer. The neighborhood she came from was tough. The toughest. The only reason she was still a good girl, if she was one, was that the pachucos in that part of town are too busy slamming girls with garrison belts to rape them.

Yet you got the idea she was a decent kid. Dumb and green but decent. Something in her eyes brought out the big brother in me. And she had a voice.

I said, "Look, chick. I'll level with you. Summit is fighting for its life right now. Even if we put out a side together, you'll have to wait for your gold. You may never see it, in fact."

She sat forward in her chair and her eyes blazed. "I don't care, Mr. Parker!" she said. "I don't care if I make a dime on the first record. If only I get one side published..."

"Hold it!" I cut in. "It won't mean a goddam thing. Remember that. All it will mean is that you've cut a side. Period. The next side will be just as hard to sell. Keep that in mind, Lila. You kids think all you've got to do is hit the air once and then your only worry is which network to sign up with. It don't work that way, Lila. For every hit there's a thousand flops. And even a hit don't mean as much as people think. A lot of people make one big record. And spend the rest of their lives trying to repeat. I know a cat in the Village who's got a gold record framed on the wall of his cold water flat. You know what a gold record is, Lila?"

"The one they give you when you've sold a million copies."

"Right. This cat cut a side a few years ago that went like cotton candy in an orphanage. He's working today as a counterman in a beanery. Still dreaming of one more big hit. It's worse than heroin."

The phone rang. I picked it up. It was Barclay. He wasn't mad any more. He was scared. He must have talked to his lawyer. He said, "Look, Benny. You and me is old friends. Can't we drop all this bull and lay our cards on the table?"

"I said, "No problem, Ed. Just send me a check the size of the one we got last Christmas and I'll call off the hounds."

He muttered under his breath and said, "Goddam, you're a hard guy to talk sense to. This is a holdup and you know it, Ben."

"That's what happens to boys who play with matches, Ed. They get burned. How are you and old Angra Manyu coming along these days?"

There was a hiss of indrawn breath at the other end and Barclay snapped. "Him and his goddam statues! He told me you weren't going to make any trouble. Said you were a schnook. Some schnook."

His voice got cozy as he said, "Look, Ben. I wasn't supposed to get caught in the middle like this. I'll level with you. A certain competitor of yours is putting the shaft to you and I'll admit it. It wasn't my idea, but he pulls a lot of weight around town and I had to go along. Now I'll tell you what, Ben. I'm sending you a check for the sides that was lifted and we'll get the others out on the street just as soon as you take that silly injunction off my neck. I'm on your side now, Ben."

"Please don't do me no favors. It's two days before Christmas and this year's sales are shot to hell. So I'm going to tell *you* what you're going to do. You're going to send me the same check you sent me last year. And then I'm going to get another distributor. I don't need you to cue me in on Johnny Angel. I've known the lad longer than you have. So I'll cue *you* in, Ed. Get as far away from him as you can. He snaps. Only, send me a check before he steals all your money."

I hung up and turned to a more pleasant subject. Lila Murillo. The Mexicali Rose. I grinned and said, "O.K. What are you going to do for eating money while we wait for union clearance and line up a band for you?"

Lila said, "I guess I better get a job."

"I guess you better," I said. "Come on." I led the way out to the plant and took her over to Maria Vargas. I said, "Show this chick how you work one of these monsters, will you, Maria?" To Lila, I said, "Don't look so sad, kid. You wanted to be in the record business, didn't you? Well, you're in it. You've got to have bread while you're waiting for some sucker to cut a spec record with you."

"A spec record?"

"Spec for speculation, doll. Meaning no dough if no go. On account of that's the only way we can afford to do it right now. Summit's a shoestring outfit, and somebody's trying to cut our shoestring."

Later on, because of what happened, a lot of people got the wrong idea about Lila and me. So this is as good a place to fill you in on how I felt about the chick as any.

Sure. I'd have gone to bed with her if she'd asked me to. But she never did, and I was old enough to be her father. By then, Dad, I was just about old enough to be anybody's father.

It wasn't sex that made me feel the kid was something kind of special. I'd heard a lot of talent in my time so that wasn't it. I guess Lila was kid sister special.

She sort of adopted Martha and me during the time she worked for us. Mostly Martha. I never heard her mention her family, if she had one. I guess Miss Mouse and me were the closest thing to a real family she ever had.

She wanted to make the scene so bad it was frightening. It must have been hell for Lila to stand over that press all day and bake the sides with other talent's voices grooved on them. But she never bitched. Once in a while she'd throw me a look with those familiar eyes and I'd know she was dying to ask about when we were going to cut her big dream. I played it cool. I wasn't ready yet.

Sure, I could have dragged her over to Tin Pan Alley and thrown her to the wolves. Any one of a dozen agents

I knew would have been happy to book her into a club date. After they'd spent a week end with her. She was kind of country. And it showed.

So I waited. I waited until Mike Cornado blew in from the hills with his redheaded wife and maracas. Mike was a right guy. Older than me, if that's possible, and his wife watches him like a hawk.

Mike owed me a favor. I'd pulled him out of a scrape one time by advancing him a few bills on an unsold record. Once he'd heard Lila belt out Granada he didn't have to be sold on cutting a side.

They cut the tape of Lila's record the same night Harry the Glove called me up. At least, it was Harry's voice. He said he was calling from a booth and one call was all I was going to get.

"Benny," he said, "you got troubles."

"Who hasn't?" I answered. "What's up, Harry?"

"Skip the names, Ben. I shouldn't even be calling, and if you say it was me I'll call you a liar. You dig me?"

"Loud and clear, Dad. What's the scoop?"

"Ben, the word's out on you. I mean it looks like you made trouble for somebody in the mob."

A little furry ball of fear started doing flips on my ulcers. I didn't even know anybody in the mob except Harry, and that was a good turn left over from the war. Harry and me had spent the longest night of our lives in the same fox hole during the Ardennes push. You get to know a cat pretty well in a spot like that.

I said, "Harry, as far as I know the mob's got no reason to know I'm alive."

"They know it now, Ben," he answered. "And somebody don't like the idea too much. You stepped on somebody's toes, Ben. Somebody big."

"How hard they going to lean on me, Harry?" I asked.

I could almost see him shrug at the other end of the line. He said, "Can't say, Ben. The word's out that your records are Oh-You-Tee with the jukebox boys. No mob joint will let one of your sides through the door. That's supposed to be a warning. If you don't take the hint and square it with the boys you'll start having union trouble. It could even get like physical."

I said, "Look, Harry. I don't even know who in hell I'm supposed to have crossed up! Can't you even find out who's leaning on me?"

Harry's voice became carefully blasé. He said, "Look, Benny. I done all I can. I've stuck my neck way out already. I must be nuts." His voice rose an octave as he almost shouted, "An' don't ask me to do nothing else, Ben! I don't buck the mob, see? Dutch did and you know what happened to him! Face down in a puddle of slime with a row of slugs up his spine! I tipped you off, Ben. That squares us for the day you dragged me in out of the street that time in Aachen, you damn fool. You could have got blipped."

I didn't answer. After a while he said, "Well don't it, Ben? Don't it square things?"

I said, "Sure, Harry. It squares things."

He hung up without another word. I looked at the receiver and said, "Have a nice life, Harry." Then I walked over and pulled down the blinds. It looked a lot darker outside than it had a while ago.

But then Martha came in with Mike and Lila and Mike's wife Dolores, and I forgot about the warning. Mike had a portable tape recorder. He'd taped the date and wanted me to hear it.

Lila had been a little hurt that I'd given her big night a miss. Funny thing is, I can't explain why I didn't want to be there. The studio was the same one where Ginger and me cut our big side but I'd been there a dozen times since and it hadn't creeped me. But Lila was haunted. I'd told Martha to sit in for me and pretended I had some book-keeping to catch up on.

Mike played the tape back and it swung. I've been wrong on a few sides, but not often, and halfway through Flamingo Beach I knew we had a winner. Lila had it. The spark. The whatever it is that separates the real talents from the poor pedestrians who never make it.

I nodded at Martha and said, "Well, Miss Mouse, they'll spin this one without payola. Even Johnny Angel can't keep this one off..." And then I froze.

Martha said, "What's the matter, honey? You look like you've seen a ghost."

I said, "I just turned over a wet rock, doll, and guess who crawled out?"

Mike Cornado looked at me and said, "Man, I've heard bop talk but you cats lost me right after Martha said ghost."

I filled Mike and his wife in on Angel while Martha made sandwiches and Lila mixed drinks. I didn't mention the bit with the mob. I'd just figured the way out of that one.

Mike had heard of Angel. Who hadn't? But I filled him in on some of the heel's latest escapades and Mike knew a couple of stories about Johnny I hadn't heard. The creep was becoming a legend. A Paul Bunyan of the music field. If you can imagine Paul Bunyan as a bastard.

I waited until the hootch was low and told Martha I was going out for more. Naturally Mike insisted on going with me, but I managed to get him to leave me alone in the phone booth. He thought I was calling up another babe. I let him. One reason Miss Mouse is still around is that she's not jealous. At least not dumb enough to show it if she is.

I wasn't calling a babe. I was calling an Angel: Johnny didn't seem surprised to hear from me. I said, "Skipping all the crap, Angel, I got a message for you. You and the boys."

"I don't know what you're talking about, Ben," his

voice gloated.

"I mean like cut it," I said. "I'm not scared. Go make faces at somebody else. You dig me, daddio?"

"Are you drunk, Ben?"

"Like a fox, Dad," I snarled. "Like I've written a few lines down on a piece of paper and stashed it where the law will find it, just in case I get hit by a truck."

"Really, Ben," he sneered. "You're pretty corny. They don't even use that bit in English movies any more. What's on the paper, Ben? A list of my foolish mistakes? You're pretty funny."

His voice didn't sound like he was amused. It didn't sound worried either, but Angel was too smooth to let you know if he was worried. Before he could pump me any further, I hung up. It was good terrorist psychology, and all I'd wanted him to know was that I was on to him.

Angel was too smooth a lad to fool with the big black chair up at Ossining. The trouble was, so was I. I'd checked this move, I hoped, but you don't win chess on the defensive, and Angel was starting to play a very nasty game of chess.

I was right about the record. Flamingo Beach slept for a few weeks and then an honest D.J. in Cincinnati put it on the air and got a few pieces of mail. By the end of the week the platter was moving up fast and even Marvin Knopff and Joe the Dishwasher were spinning it for the shook set.

Lila had her picture in Life and was booked on a couple of TV shows. Mike Cornado dragged her down to the studio and cut an album while the trend was hot. I had to farm out some of the pressing to a firm on Long Island. Even before the album was released we had more orders for it than Summit could have turned out.

Marvin Knopff invited Lila to appear on his afternoon

show and I let her go. Knopff was going big and he was paying the chick in real green gelt. All I insisted on was that Martha go along.

Lila also got her picture on the cover of a fan magazine that told all the little boys and girls how their Lila, after working her way up from the slums of Mexico City (where she sold violets, no doubt) was still the same sweet unspoiled simple and charming beast her friends and family knew when.

I've got news for whoever wrote that story. It didn't quite work out that way. I couldn't tell Lila a damned thing after she'd been on TV the first time. After Marvin Knopff took her to the Stork Club, Martha couldn't tell her anything either. By the time the album was out, Mike Cornado was being cued in on how to blow Latin music. Lila had arrived, and the whole goddam world was going to know about it.

I didn't say anything until Knopff bought her the sable wrap. Then I felt it was my everlovin' duty to stick my nose in. I called up Knopff and said, "Marvin, I got a question to ask you."

"Shoot, Dad. It's your dime."

"Do you know how young Lila Murillo is?" I asked, feeling like a goddam idiot.

Knopff digested my question and answered, "I don't read you, man." It was a lie, but the same answer I'd have given.

I said, "Look, Marv. The chick is pretty young."

"So what? You her father?"

"Let's say I'm her big brother."

Knopff chuckled. "You want to know my intentions towards little Nel, Dad?" It even sounded silly to me.

I said, "I just wanted to let you know she was jail-bait, pal. You don't mess with anything that young unless you're on the level."

Knopff didn't answer for a moment. Then he said, "Ben,

what would you say if I told you I was on the level?"

"I'd say you were nuts. She's a snotty little kid and she's at least twenty years younger than you are."

"That's what I thought you'd say," he chuckled. "By any chance am I cutting in on you, Dad?"

"Goddammit, Knopff. I'm crowding fifty."

"So what are you lousing my act up for, Ben?"

"I just don't want the kid to get hurt," I said. "She's a brat and she ought to get a good spanking. But... I don't want her hurt."

Marvin said, "Don't worry, Ben. She won't be."

"She'd better not be," I said, and wondered what in hell I'd do if Knopff loused her up. What the hell, I wasn't anything to her. If I wanted to cuddle a pretty little bowl of Spanish rice all I had to do was stroll over to Eighth Avenue. There's a Lila Murillo in every other bar over there. What the hell did I care?

I think it was the eyes. Somehow, I knew just how those eyes would look if Lila got hurt. And I didn't want to see that look in them. Not ever.

It was a good thing the album sold. We were losing our shirts on the others. Peterson told me we were having trouble with our stag sides. Shipments were being grabbed by the local law across the land of the free and the home of the blue law. We had to go the bail of a record shop proprietor when the gendarmes latched on to him.

I knew the cops would never bother with that sort of thing unless some cat put in a complaint. I had a pretty good idea who was blowing the whistle but there wasn't much I could do to make him stop. I sent Nat Sassower up to New England to get the store owner off the hook. Then I had Pete discontinue the damned things. I never liked them in the first place and sales had fallen off since we'd dropped the dirtier sides from the catalogue.

The Race records held their own. I guess the mob hadn't made any Harlem connections yet. But we were really bleeding from the beating we were taking on the jukeboxes. It wasn't just the loss of trade. Jukeboxes buy a lot of sides, but that was nothing to what it did to our ratings. To sell across the counter at the five and dime, a side has to be rated high with the disc jockeys, and the D.J.s base their ratings on how many times a side gets spun on the jukebox circuit. Do I have to draw you a picture? The mob doesn't own every jukebox in the country, but it owns one hell of a lot of them. So I was more than a little surprised when Flamingo Beach kept climbing in spite of its low jukebox sales. It didn't figure.

Then Lila's album got a big play. Bigger than we'd hoped. Mike Cornado suddenly found himself in demand. For some reason, he blamed me for all this. Lila didn't. Lila seemed to think it was just about time the slobs sat up and noticed she'd made the scene. The kid had gotten so impossible even Martha was snapping back. I'd never seen Miss Mouse annoyed at anyone.

So I didn't try to stop Lila when she announced she was going over to a certain large company to cut a few sides. Like Knopff had said, I wasn't her father. I wasn't even her big brother, really.

Mike dug up a chick from Dallas with bleached hair and a mouth full of hominy grits. Her name was Florida Burns and all she could do was wiggle her bazoom as she shook a maraca and sang about love under a tropical sky. She could carry a tune. Just. And that's about all you can say for Florida Burns, except that the side she made with Mike Cornado went like shovels at a forest fire.

It was weird. Mike had blackjacked me into the damned record in the first place, and I hadn't liked it as much after he cut it as I'd thought I would. But it went.

Then someone got a Race record we'd made, with Cutter MacDonald on the eighty eights and Shoo Shoo Vernon

on the vocal. It was a low down torch blown twelve to
the bar. Not a bad side, but not any better than the stuff
Cutter and Shoo Shoo had been making for years.

Then suddenly Shoo Shoo's sexy contralto started popping out of radios all over town and the esoteric spade set
didn't talk to her any more. Shoo Shoo was like commercial. Not that it seemed to hurt her too much to have the
ofay buying her records. There are, as Cutter philosophi-
cally observed, ten times as many of them cats.

A punky type in dirty dungarees wandered in with an
axe under his arm and announced he was God's answer
to Elvis. If vulgarity was what he was shooting for, he
really made the scene. He sure as hell couldn't sing. This
cat's name was Reb Johnson. He said it proudly, like I
should have heard of him. Said he'd cut a couple of sides
down south with a company I'd never heard of and had
to leave town because of professional rivals who accused
him of knocking up somebody's daughter.

Peterson was set to throw him out but I had a hunch. I
got him to take a bath and called up a few of the boys I
knew who were out of work. The kid had written a song,
he said. It was a direct steal on a steal on Fire on the
Mountain which was stolen in the first place, so I figured
we were in the clear with public domain. It was like bad.

Peterson said, "Boss, have you flipped? That punk is so
god awful he almost comes around the other way and
sounds good. You're not really going to put that thing
out, are you?"

I grinned. "Like Alice said to the white rabbit, Pete,
things are getting curiouser and curiouser. This disc is an
experiment. If I can sell Reb Johnson I can sell anybody."

I guess I can sell anybody. I pressed a few sides, put
them out and waited for the dull thud. The D.J.s spun the
wax off them. Reb Johnson got so big he wouldn't even
spit at me. Gave me a couple of bills to let him off his
contract and went to another company. The last I heard

he was selling magazine subscriptions in Brooklyn. He never had another successful side after he left Summit.

Like I said, it was curious....

It was like the time, when I was maybe seven, and my old man took me to a fair out on the edge of town. They had a ferris wheel a mile high and this big steam powered merry-go-round that went around at fifty or sixty miles an hour. I remember my Dad putting me on a big dapple gray horse and telling me about the gold ring.

There was a green metal chute full of rings off to one side of the whirling horses and if you could reach out over the awful empty gulf of spinning gray nothing below the horses and grab the gold ring you got a free ride. I still don't know how I got up the nerve, but I did, just as the ride was slowing down. I'd been watching the big boys grab at the rings as they went by, and some of them missed and some of them caught the iron rings that didn't count, and then I leaned out and the next thing I knew I was sitting on the big gray horse staring at the gold ring in my fingers and trying not to cry. I wonder what Freud would make out of *that?* Anyway, the sudden luck we were having with Summit's releases had the same effect on me. Sort of a bittersweet taste in the heart, like I was glad it finally happened, but sad because it took so goddam long. A little of this luck a few years back would have saved a lot of grief for a lot of people.

There was poor Con Conners. The stuff he'd written was mostly standard now, and Con's music will be around when all of us are gone. But the poor guy died thinking he was in a concentration camp. Angel was still making a buck on the music he'd stolen from Con. Con and Daddy Halloway.

Angel's Flight had become a classic, like Stardust. But Daddy's daughter was living in a slum with a guy that beat her. Up to now, God had been handing everyone but Johnny a lousy script. And all at once I seemed to have grabbed the gold ring out of nowheres. It bugged me.

The mystery of the Midas touch cleared up a few months later, when a D.J. from Tacoma blew in to the Big Apple. He was one of the cats who was giving Summit a big play, so Martha and me took him and his frau out to see the sights.

Turned out it was the kid's honeymoon. He'd just married the cutest chick from Walla Walla U. Her name was Ruthie and she thought her husband was the biggest D.J. who'd ever spun a platter.

I didn't try to disappoint her. I got the kids tickets to a couple of shows over by Shubert's Alley and arranged a radio interview for Chuck. That was the cat's name. It was the standard treatment we gave visiting firemen. Well maybe a little more than usual. The kids were kind of cute. But I wasn't expecting anything from the deal but a big bill at the end of the month. Then Chuck let the cat out of the bag.

It was in the cocktail lounge at Laurent's. Chuck and I had been over by Radio City to see if we couldn't get him on Jack Paar's night show. It might let the cats in Tacoma know their boy had made the Apple. The CBS wheel I knew wasn't in, so we wandered over to Park Avenue to kill time and I sprung for a round of brews.

Laurent's is one of those intimate type places. Not flashy but quiet and classy. A joint where you can talk over the problems of the universe without having the maître de giving you the fish eye to order another round. Chuck seemed impressed. There were a couple of names across the lounge and the bartender knew my brand. On such things, Dad, rests Benny Parker's claim to fame.

Anyway, about the second drink, Chuck started blubbering about what a hell of a swell cat I was to treat him and Ruthie so jazzy, me being a New York big shot and all that crap.

I said, "Look, Chuck. You guys out there in radio land keep me in bread. When one of the few lads who plug our discs hits town the least I can do is buy him a drink. I can't afford payola."

This seemed to strike Chuck as the funniest thing he'd heard since Jack Benny was selling Jello. I let him guffaw until a few heads were turning to see what all the yaks were about, and then I said, "So what did I say? If it's that funny I'll send it to Earl Wilson."

"You putting out for payola!" laughed Chuck. "Ben Parker, of all people."

I said, "O.K. I'm cheap. So what's this all about, Chuck?"

"Hell Ben," he said, "you know what you and Summit stand for in the industry. You're the white hope of the few honest cats left."

I looked across the table at him. He didn't *look* like he was ribbing me. I said, "When did all this happen? I didn't read the papers that day. All I've been doing, Chuck, is trying to make an everloving buck."

"O.K. Dad," he smiled. "Play it modest. Play it tough. But you're not kidding anybody, Ben. I've been watching you for a while. Me and a lot of other cats. I started buying your sides when I was still at Walla Walla. Remember the remake you made on that old Fletcher Henderson classic? So I knew who you were when I went to work. And one of the first things the wise money boys told me at the station was that you were washed up.

"They told me you were a fink. A jerk. An honest john who thought he could buck the system. Ben Parker was held up to all us aspiring young D.J.s as the horrible example to watch. They told me to watch you and see what happens to clams who try it the Horatio Alger way."

"When was all this?" I asked. I couldn't believe anyone had heard of me all the way out in Tacoma. Chuck grinned sheepishly and answered, "O.K. It wasn't very long. I guess you know I'm pretty wet behind the ears."

"We all are, Chuck. By the time we get dry we start to fall apart. Keep talking. A picture is starting to form in my feeble brain."

He said, "Well, I've watched. I've watched for the big fall the wise money boys have been predicting for you. And you know what? Summit keeps getting bigger."

He picked at the tray of cashew nuts between us as if he was trying to make up his mind about something. Then he said, "You know what, Ben? They almost had me convinced. I've known for a long time this old globe isn't run the way they say it is. The meek may inherit the earth, but the loudmouths have it now. I've even taken my share of the old payola. Not any cash, yet. But presents I never could have bought Ruthie on my salary. I've held out on the cash, Ben. I've been waiting."

"Waiting for what, Chuck?"

"Waiting to see who's right. There's a lot of talk going the rounds. You've heard about the way the quiz shows are being rigged? The deal where the contestants get the answers and then kick back part of the take to the producer? One cat's even known to be making all the good looking heads who apply for the show. And they don't all get on, either."

I said, "Chuck, you mean to tell me that nice old Italian shoemaker is sleeping with his producer?"

"O.K. Ben, laugh it off," he said. "I'm not saying every show is rigged. Just most of them. Like the payola deal. Every D.J. isn't standing there with his hand out, but a hell of a lot of them are and you know it. It's getting so bad a guy hates to admit he's legit. Saying you don't ask for payola is like admitting virginity at a fraternity bull session. We still run in packs and the lone wolf has to fight like a bastard just to stay alive."

I said, "O.K. But how did I get to be Joan of Arc? All I

want is to put out a disc now and then. I'm not on any goddam crusade."

"Sure you are, Ben," he said. "You're sort of a... well, symbol. The fact that you can put out that disc once in a while without greasing the wise guys proves it can be done. You bug them, Ben. You bug them just by getting away with being on the level. All over the industry there are little guys who've been told you got to play the game a certain way. The smart money set's way. And while the wise cats are flapping their mouths us little guys are watching Ben Parker, a nothing guy with no connections and a little record plant in Jersey. A guy who don't ask for favors or spread the grease. A guy who just can't make the scene, according to the way the smart cats blow it.

"So there you stand. With your hands in your pockets and a cigarette pasted to your lower lip. And every time they drop the roof on your head we wait to see what's going to happen. And then when the dust clears away you're still standing there. It makes the smart money boys sweat. You're lousing up all their sophisticated logic and making their bow ties feel tight around the neck. With this quiz show business about to blow open, you're really a thorn in their sides."

"I don't get you, Chuck. I've got no fingers in that pie."

He laughed. "Haven't you? Hell, man. Do you think it's going to stop at quiz shows? The whole rotten mess is about to blow wide open. The New York D.A. has had a couple of contestants on the carpet already, and the word's going around that the Senate may investigate the whole industry. Don't you see what that'll mean?"

"Nope. I'm in the record business, Chuck."

"The smart money set is running scared. Heads will roll if anybody really turns over the rotten log and looks at what's been crawling around under it. The only chance they have of squashing the whole thing is to keep the cats in the industry from talking. God knows we got enough to say, Ben. We don't owe the bastards nothing, and cleaning out the scum would leave a lot of room for the lads with clean shirts."

"So what's stopping you?" I asked.

"Fear. Plain fear. We are all standing alone in the dark while we wait for someone to turn the lights on."

"So I'm the cat who's supposed to climb on a white horse and lead the charge?"

"That's about the size of it. You've got a reputation for thinking on your feet. You fight clean, but you fight hard and tough. If you ever do decide to start a march on the Bastille, I'm just one of the guys who's willing to carry a torch in your parade."

What was I supposed to say? Cats like Chuck had been plugging my sides all over the map just to shaft guys like Angel. But that didn't mean I wanted to make like Joan of Arc. In the first place she was a broad, and in the second place I remembered what happened to the chick for climbing up on her white horse. She was barbecued by a bunch of cats who weren't particularly interested in eating her.

I picked up the tab and told Chuck I'd think about it. A fence is a lousy place to sit without a parachute, and I didn't like the jump in either direction.

Chuck didn't bring it up again until Martha and me were loading them on the plane out at Idlewild. As we shook hands for the last time, he winked and said, "I'll expect you on that white horse, Ben. And I'll be right behind you."

"Don't walk too close," I grinned. "You might step in something."

I didn't climb on the white horse. I was shoved. I started getting mail from all over, asking me to hold the fort and all that jazz. Franky the Drum wrote from Tulsa and I even got a letter from a jazz fan in Denmark. Seems a Danish newspaper had written an article on the payola situation and I was being held up as a sterling example of the red blooded American boy. Martha said it made her very proud. All it made me was worried. I hadn't asked anyone to appoint me chief bottle washer and target for tonight. Harry the Glove had made my nights a little darker.

Then I got the summons from the grand jury. Someone wanted me to blow them a tune about Johnny Angel. I didn't know if I wanted to sing for them or not. Angel had been in my hair for years. He'd loused up half the people I knew and he'd tried to push my head under every time he got near me. But grand juries make me nervous.

But, as Nat pointed out, you don't cancel a date with the grand jury because you have stage fright. The song festival was set for less than a week and they tell me the D.A. frowns on people not showing up after they've been asked real nice.

I had Nat check to see who I owed my good fortune to. It turned out to be Marvin Knopff. I called Knopff and asked him why he'd been so good to me. In a little while he came over to our apartment. I noticed he had a packed suitcase with him. Martha was out and there wasn't anything good on TV so I let him come in and even poured him a beer. I'm a democratic type.

Knopff studied his can of beer for a while and said, "I hope you don't mind, Ben. The bit with the grand jury, I mean."

"Keep talking, Knopff. Were you the cat who got me subpoenaed?"

He nodded. "I've got another one just like it in my pocket, Ben. That's why I'm cutting out for Mexico. The booze is cheap down there and the dames all look like Lila. You heard what happened to my job?"

I'd heard. Knopff was one of the lads who'd been told

to resign for the good of the industry. The patsy.

I said, "So you were the fall guy on the Angel's team. What reason is that to sick the D.A. on Summit? We're clean and you know it."

Knopff said, "That's just it, Ben. You're clean as a goddam whistle. They'll listen to you. Remember the time you asked me to knife Angel once for you, Ben? Well, I'm handing you the shiv. I'm in too deep. I sold my soul a long time ago. Back when I found out I couldn't blow a piano like Thornhill. You know what I am, Ben? A mediocre talent."

"Let's not brag, Marv. You're not that good."

"O.K. Have your fun, Ben. I'm washed up. I wanted in. I wanted in so bad I played on the wrong team. And now the game's being called on account of rain and I'm headed for the showers. But I got a score to settle with Johnny Angel. The bastard knows I can't testify against him. I'm as bad as he is, on paper. So I called up the D.A. the other day. The same day I made my plane reservations. And I spilled my guts.

"I told them about Angel. I told them everything I knew. Halfway through the conversation I started hearing the beep beep beep of a recorder, but I kept right on talking. And then I told them about you. I told them you knew almost as much about Angel as me, and that you were one hairpin who wasn't afraid of the bastard. I told them to ask you about the creep. I know the way the bastard has everybody scared but you. I figured if you go in there next week and lay it on the line for those cats all the guys and gals he's loused up will come crawling out of the woodwork like termites. Once a shark is bleeding, even a little bit, the other sharks rip his liver out. But somebody has to take that first bite. Some cat with castiron guts."

I looked at Knopff and curled my upper lip. "Thanks a lot," I sneered. "Mamma's boy got caught in the cookie jar and now he wants me to spank the kid that helped him."

Knopff looked startled. "You think it's because I lost my job?" he snapped. "Don't you know about Lila?"

I felt a cold ball of ice in my belly. "What about Lila?" I said.

Knopff looked like he was ready to cry. He gripped his beer can so hard it buckled, as he said, "I should have known, Ben. I should have known the bastard would move in on her. He never wants nothing unless some other cat has it first."

"Keep talking, Knopff."

"I never touched her, Ben," he said. "Honest to God. I was on the level with the chick. Can you beat that? The only dame besides my mother that I ever leveled with. I guess that's why she thought I was such a poor schtunk."

"What happened?" I snapped. Knopff's self pity made me want to throw up. He sounded like a couple of SS men I'd guarded after the war.

"What in hell do you think happened?" he snarled. And his face wasn't very pretty as he said, "The sonafabitch moved right in on me. That's what happened. He's a good looking creep, you know, and he can be charming as hell when he's on the make. I never had a chance with Lila, I guess. But I'd have liked to play the bit all the way to the finale. Johnny didn't give me the chance. He stomped all over my lines and waltzed her out from under me like I was a pile of nothing."

"Where's Lila now?" I asked. The picture of that green kid in Angel's bed made steam come out of both my ears.

"Praying to his goddam statues with the bastard, I guess," sighed Knopff. "You know about his devil worshipping cult? Him and a bunch of society cats from Sutton Place get together once a week to pitch a black mass in front of that bronze idol. How about that?"

"Some guys collect stamps. Some chase dames. I guess devil worship is as good a hobby as any for a growing boy. Does Johnny know the kid is jail bait?"

"I told him, Ben. He just laughed. Said it had been a couple of months since they'd sacrificed a virgin to Angra Manyu. He said he was going to make her right on the rug in front of the idol. According to Johnny it really sends a girl to be sacrificed."

My beer didn't taste so good any more. I went out in the kitchen and poured it down the sink. Then I got out a bottle of Old Crow I'd been saving for an occasion. If this wasn't an occasion, I didn't know when I'd ever see one. I poured Knopff a stiff one. He looked like he needed it. Then I hoisted my own glass and looked at the bead in the bourbon.

"To Ahura Mazda," I said, and downed my booze. Knopff drank his, wiped his mouth on the back of his hand and asked, "Who dat?"

"Ahura Mazda, Dad," I said, "is the other one. Old Johnny forgot about Ahura Mazda when he got on this Zoroastic kick. He's been so busy praying to the prince of darkness he forgot there's another side. Ahura Mazda is the other god in Zoroaster's book. The cat in charge of the angels. And I don't mean Johnny's kind. The ones with white nightshirts and wings. Old Zoroaster said the world was a sort of battleground between good and evil. All his life a cat has to choose between right and wrong, and when he dies the angels and the demons fight over his soul."

Knopff nodded and held out his glass while I poured another round for him. He said, "It makes more sense than any of the jive they blew in schul, Ben. Fits the facts better than anything the Christians or Jews have about one good old feller god who loves hell out of everybody and lets kids get run over by trucks. What you say that cat's name was? The one with the wings?"

"Ahura Mazda. Like in light bulbs."

"Oh. hell, I'll never remember it anyway. But here's to

the old basser and I hope you and him win. I got to catch my goddam plane."

They came the next night. Two of them. I should have been expecting them, but I hadn't known the word had gotten around the Big Apple so fast. Peterson and me were closing the plant down for the night. The girls had gone home. I looked up from the pile of records I was checking and there they were, standing in the service entrance. I didn't think they'd come to ask me for a job.

They wore trench coats, even though it hadn't rained in days. They walked towards us in step. Both of them weighed at least two hundred pounds and had that tilted look across the shoulders you get from wearing a shoulder holster.

"Which one of you is Parker?" asked the darker of the two goons. I noticed he had a little blue cross tattooed on the web of his thumb. I'd always wondered what pachucos did when they grew up. Now I knew.

Peterson looked sick. He didn't want to point his finger but he sure as hell didn't want them thinking he was me.

I took a deep breath, let half of it out so my voice wouldn't crack, and said, "I'm Parker. What's on your minds?"

Blue Cross ignored me and said to his pal, "You hear what the man say? He wants to know what's on our minds."

"Yeah, man, tell the rat what's on our minds," grinned the other one, a red faced beefy type with a drinker's nose and the insolent look a guy gets from bullying people all his life. He looked at Peterson with a sudden sneering smile and said, "What you hanging around for, Bo? You waiting for sumpin?"

Peterson's face went carefully blank. The spades ain't the only cats who can play Uncle Tom. That boy looked like the dumbest Swede who ever lived as he said, "Who me? I just work here, man."

Red Face grunted in satisfied curiosity. He'd filed Peterson in his harmless stooge drawer. He gave the Swede a hard look and said, "Then what in hell you hanging around for?"

"I was just going," said Peterson. He didn't look at me as he turned and headed for the door. You could feel his shoulders bracing for a bullet between them all the way from where I stood.

Blue Cross snapped, "Hey, stupid!"

Peterson turned. His face was lizard belly white. He said, "Yeah?"

"If anybody asks what you seen here tonight, mac, what you gonna tell 'em?"

"Man, I ain't seen nothing. What's to see?"

"See that you remember that, mac. You never seen us at all, you read me, jerk face?"

Peterson licked his lips and uttered the war cry of the mid century American. "Look, I don't want no trouble, buddy. I never seen you cats before and I don't aim to see you later. I just don't want to get involved, O.K.?"

Blue Cross chuckled. "How 'bout it, Red? Do we let him slide?"

Red Face sneered, "Sure, let him slide. We can always come back if he gets gabby."

Peterson didn't wait to be told to leave. He took off like a shot. So there I was. All alone in the deserted plant with the two goons the mob had sent to see me. It was like cozy.

Nobody said anything for a little while. The script called for me to try and crawl out from under a beating. I wasn't going to play it that way. If they wanted to work me over they had to work themselves up to it. I wasn't going to feed them straight lines.

Blue Cross looked at me for a long time. His dark eyes were hard and cold as black glass. The kind of eyes you see on a blown up picture of a spider. I was beginning to know how a fly must feel.

He sighed and said, "Man, this guy's cool. You know that, Red? He's cool as ice. I bet he thinks he can do wonders and eat cucumbers."

Red Face said, "Yeah, I bet he thinks he can go downtown and fink on his pals to the law. That what you think, pal?"

I said, "O.K. Get it over with. I'm late for supper."

Blue Cross looked hurt. "You hear that, Red? He don't like our company. What makes you think you gonna eat supper, mac, ever?"

I grinned and tried to look like they didn't have me as scared as I was. I said, "You let the Swede go, and you talk too much for a heavy piece of work. Johnny Angel sent you cats down here to rough me up so I'll be too scared to talk to the grand jury."

For a minute I thought I had them. Goons are not picked for a high I.Q. They start out bullying the other kids on the block and then they get up the nerve to scare protection out of candy store owners. It doesn't take much nerve. Most people are cowards, anyway, and it sure as hell don't take brains. When a goon runs into a guy who won't buy his bluff it throws him into a funk. He either has to run or bulge a muscle. I was unlucky enough to pick on the muscle bulging types.

Man, you would have enjoyed that fight if it had been on TV. The three of us had the whole empty plant for a ring and we went round and round. By the time they cornered me against one of the presses the joint was a mess and so was I. Red Face had my arms pinned and Blue Cross was working me over with a cold controlled anger. I knew why they wore trench coats now. It kept the blood off their suits.

Not that there was too much of it. These boys were pros. Blue Cross avoided my face and worked on my guts

with hard stabbing jabs of his fist. Waves of pain shot
through my belly and all of a sudden I felt a warm trickle
down my leg.

They worked me over until I was almost unconscious,
but they didn't want to let me off that easy. Blue Cross
stepped back and grinned at me.

"You still feel brave, Parker?" he laughed. "Ain't you
just a little bit scared of us?"

I gasped in a lungful of air and wheezed, "So I'm scared."

"You hear that, Red?" laughed Blue Cross. "The man
says he's scared."

Red Face grunted, "He don't look scared enough to
me."

Blue Cross nodded. "Yeah. I think you're right. I don't
think we scared him enough yet."

His spider eyes flickered around and came to rest on the
jaws of the press. He grinned and said, "Put his hand in
that waffle iron, Red. I know something that'll *really* scare
him!"

I fought. I fought as hard as I could. But I was weak as
a kitten from the beating and Red Face had wrists made
of solid oak. He twisted my left hand halfways off at the
elbow and slammed it palm up on the bottom die of
Flamingo Beach.

Blue Cross studied the press a moment. Mechanics
wasn't his line. But a moron could see how pulling the big
lever would bring the top jaw down to within a sixteenth
of an inch from the bottom. I didn't think my hand would
quite fit in the space left.

Blue Cross picked a label up and put it on my hand. He
grinned and said, "We're gonna make us a side, Parker.
We're gonna stamp Flamingo Beach on your south paw
and see how it comes out."

Red Face grinned and said, "Yeah, maybe it'll play pretty
music when he scratches his itchy palm." He shook me
like a terrier shakes a rat and slammed my hand down

hard on the grooved die. "That what you want, big mouth? You wanna hear all them little bones go crunch crunch crunch?"

I didn't say anything. If I'd opened my mouth I'd have screamed for mercy and that's what the bastards wanted to hear. They weren't going to give me any but they wanted me to crawl for it anyways.

Blue Cross lowered the jaw down until it pressed tight against my hand. My fingers spread out under the metal and I could feel the grooves of the record die with my finger tips. Then it started getting kind of rough. Blue Cross put pressure on the handle and all I felt was pain.

I was biting my lip not to scream when a strange voice said, "What's going on in here?" The pressure let up and I almost fainted from relief. Red Face pulled me up from the press and said, "Nothing, officer. We was just horsing around with our pal Parker."

I looked across the room and there was Peterson with two prowl car cops. He looked pretty scared and the cops must have been impressed by what he told them. One of them had drawn his revolver and the other had his hand in a very suggestive position on the butt of his holstered gun.

The cop with the rod out said, "We heard you were having trouble here, Mr. Parker. What's all this about?"

Blue Cross smiled. "You heard wrong, officer. We just dropped in on our old school chum here and I guess we got to fooling around. Ben used to play left tackle and we were kidding him about how soft he's gotten around the middle. That right, Ben?"

Blue Cross had something round and firm and fully packed pressed against the small of my back. All I could do was nod. I hadn't gotten my breath back yet.

Red Face was looking accusingly at Peterson, "Guys shouldn't jump to conclusions," he grinned. It wasn't a friendly grin. "A guy can make a lot of trouble for himself jumping to conclusions."

Peterson looked bewildered and scared. I remembered the time George Flannery had told him and Lester to throw me out and he'd said George didn't pay him enough. I was paying him more, but not that much more. Peterson was as big a jerk as I was.

All I had to do was keep my mouth shut. All I had to do was tell the cops it was all a mistake and I was in the clear. Like all I had to do with the grand jury was say Johnny Angel was a living doll who'd never even drawn mustaches on the Spearmint girl as a kid.

What the hell? Johnny was going to win. He always did. He had every angle covered and no matter how hard I tried to pull the rug out from under him next week he was going to land on his feet with his claws showing. All I was going to get out of bucking him was a garlic bullet. If not tonight, another night. And there was poor stupid loyal Peterson and his five towheaded Swedish kids to think about. I was asking for a couple of bullets in Peterson's thick skull, and maybe a one way trip to view the river for Miss Mouse. That was something to think about.

Miss Mouse and I never had what Ginger and me would have had. At least, I don't think we did. But we ... kept each other company. I didn't like to think of her on the bottom of the harbor with the crabs crawling around through her ribs.

The cops were getting an annoyed look. Peterson had called them in out of a warm squad car and made them miss the race results for nothing. The younger cop started to holster his rod.

I thought about all the things I'd heard about the mob. How they'd get you no matter how far you ran. I remembered how the Jersey City cops are supposed to be run by the syndicate. How a smart money boy with mob connections can get away with murder in Jersey. Then I took a deep breath and said, "Officer."

The cop stopped putting his gun away and the rod in Blue Cross's hand jabbed hard against my spine. I licked my lips and said, "Watch the one in back of me. He's got a gun aimed at you. Right through me."

Blue Cross hissed, "You gone psycho, Parker? You wanna get killed?"

The cop's gun swung up level. The other one had his out so fast he should have been on Gunsmoke. The younger cop said, "Let's everybody put their hands where I can see them."

Blue Cross dropped his heater. It clunked on the floor between my feet and I kicked it out towards the cops. The older cop said, "Over against the wall, mac. You know the routine by now."

Red Face and Blue Cross put their hands over their heads against the wall while the younger cop frisked them. He took a German P-38 from Red Face's coat and said, "Shame on you."

The other cop said, "I don't think you boys have been telling us the truth and that kind of hurts. Care to tell us what really happened, Mr. Parker?"

I filled them in on my date with the grand jury and they got the pitch. As they were slapping the cuffs on Blue Cross, he sneered, "Big deal. You dumb cops think you can hold us? We'll be out on a writ in no time and you'll wind up pounding a beat in the Jersey Meadows. We got connections."

"You scare me," said the older cop. "For a pair of smart operators, you and your buddy sure pulled a boo boo. Think your connections will be able to fix a federal rap?"

"Whatcha talking about? Since when is roughing a cat up a federal rap? The most you can book us on is simple assault."

"You want to bet?" laughed the cop as they frog-marched the two goons out to the prowl car. "You tried to intimidate a witness for the New York grand jury. Not smart, punk."

"Dumb," said the other cop. "You beat him up in Jersey. That means you crossed a state line to do it. You know anybody who can grease the F.B.I., mac? You're going to need him in a hurry. I imagine the Hoover boys will want to hear about this little caper. And I'm making sure they find out as soon as we hit headquarters. I don't like the Jersey Meadows. Too many mosquitos."

I suddenly felt a lot better. I hadn't even thought about that angle. I was too hot for the mob to mess with now. It sort of makes a torpedo nervous to shoot a cat with a G man looking over his shoulder. I knew Miss Mouse and Pete were in the clear too. Angel was going to be sort of unpopular with the mob for sicking the boys on me without telling them I bit back.

The last I saw of my two playmates, they were being booked on every charge but leprosy. The cops wouldn't let me go until I'd signed a statement and let an interne from the Medical Center wrap a mile of tape around my middle. Even then, I had to promise to see a doctor in the morning. You'd think I was something delicate.

I dropped Peterson off in Union City on my way home. As he got out I said, "Thanks, Pete. For a little while there, I thought you were going to play it smart."

"I lost my head." He grinned.

For a minute we just looked at each other. Then Peterson did a funny thing. He threw me a G.I. salute and walked away. It was hard to figure. I'd never made it past tech sergeant.

By the time I got home, it only hurt when I breathed. The old adrenalin glands were starting to simmer down and all I had left was the bruises. Those last few steps up to the apartment felt like the summit of the Matterhorn, and mountain climbing was never my idea of a way to spend Saturday night.

I pasted a smile on my face as I walked in. There wasn't

much I could do about the green color. Martha took one look and forgot all about the program she was watching on TV.

"My God, darling," she gasped. "What happened? You look like you've been in a fight."

"I was tied up with a couple of Karate students and the lesson got a little rugged," I said. "I'll be O.K. as soon as I wrap myself around a drink." I threw my coat over a chair and eased down onto the couch. Martha went out in the kitchen for my drink while Betty Furness tried to sell me a refrigerator on the TV.

Then things got sort of fuzzy for a while and I was staring up at the overhead light in our bedroom and Jerry Graham was holding my hand. This didn't puzzle me half as much as how I'd gotten from the living room to the bed. Jerry was a brand new M.D. who lived down the hall in 4-B. He'd just finished his internship at St. Vincent's and hung up his shingle. I figured he could use the business and I sure as hell could use a doctor.

"How do you feel, Ben?" he asked as I swam back up for a breath of air. I felt like death warmed over, but Martha was sitting on the foot of the bed and she looked like she was going to cry.

I said, "I'm all right, Jerry. I must have blacked out for a minute."

Jerry wasn't listening. He had a little flashlight and he kept flicking it off and on in front of my eyes. Finally, he said, "You've had a slight concussion. What happened, get hit by a bus?"

"Two of them," I said. Then I had to tell him and Martha about the goons. I went light on the fight, and stressed the fact that they were out of circulation. Martha still looked pretty sick about it.

Jerry gave me a couple of pills and told me to stay in bed for the rest of the week. I didn't go into the grand jury bit. As he turned to go I said, "Thanks for dragging me in off the floor, Jerry."

"I didn't," he said. "You were in bed when I got here."

When he'd gone, I looked at Martha and said, "You kooky little dame. You might have ruptured yourself."

She dimpled and flustered. "Girls don't rupture themselves. I don't think."

"You want to bet? Come here."

And then she was all over me like a puppy dog. Crying. I let it go for a while and then I said, "Look, Martha. We got sort of a problem."

"What is it, hon?"

I said, "Look, I don't want to dramatize this grand jury bit, but the Angel is running scared. I'm sending you upstate until this deal blows over."

Martha looked me right in the eye and said, "Go to hell!"

I blinked a couple of times and said, "Madam, would you care to repeat that last statement under oath?"

Martha said, "You heard me, Ben. I'm not going anyplace because of Johnny Angel. Unless it's downtown with you to listen to you hand him his head in front of the grand jury!"

"Hey, what happened to my scared mouse?"

"Still scared, Ben. But I'm not running away when you need me."

I started to say, "So who needs you?" and then I thought about it, and put my arm around her waist instead. I looked at my mouse, the girl who wasn't pretty until she smiled, and I said, "Remember the first time I ever kissed you, Martha? The time I told you you'd never mean anything special to me?"

For a long time she didn't answer. Finally she said, "I remember."

I said, "Well, I was wrong. I mean like maybe you are sort of special."

She didn't answer. Just sat there looking blank for a

minute while her eyes got all misty, and then ran out of the room. I never *did* get my drink that night. But it's a funny thing, ever since then she puts an olive in my glass.

The night Lila Murillo came down to our place must have been just a day or so before the grand jury investigation was set for. I'm a little hazy on the date because the hearing had to be put off after what Lila had done. Later there was a hell of a stink and all the papers made a big deal about it, but I'm getting ahead of the story.

It must have been right after dinner. We'd had a sort of creole thing that Martha makes out of black beans and rice piled over chicken. I was watching I've Got a Secret, trying to decide between Martha and Faye Emerson once and for all, when the doorbell started up and didn't stop. It sounded like some kids had put a pin in it.

It was Lila. She was a mess. She'd cried mascara all over her face and one eyebrow was rubbed off. She'd chewed off her lipstick and she didn't look like a glamour puss any more. She looked like a frightened kid who'd just looked through a doorway to Hell.

She said, "I'm sorry to bother you, Ben. But I don't know where else to turn. My mother told me if I ever got in a jam to look you up. She said you were the only right ofay she ever met."

I said, "Your mother said this, kitten? Did I know her?"

Lila nodded and said, "I'm colored, Ben. Did you know that? I can pass for white. Mexican white anyways, but my mother was a spade."

I knew I'd seen those eyes before. I said, "You're Blanche Halloway's daughter."

Lila nodded. "Blanche Murillo, by courtesy of common law and a Mexican sign painter. I figured you'd get the connection as soon as I said my mother was a nigger. How do you feel about that, Martha? How's it feel to have a nigger in your house?"

Martha said, "Cut that crap out, Lila. You know us better than that."

I said, "Your mother was a lady, Lila. That's more than I can say for the way you're acting. Suppose you tell us what the score is. I'm tired of doing penance for Simon Legree. My granddaddy was a Yankee. The one that was over here then. The others hadn't made the boat yet. Now what's this all about? You didn't come down here to get us to join the N.A.A.C.P."

Lila's eyes welled up and suddenly she buried her head in my shirt.

"He knew it, Ben!" she sobbed. "I could have forgiven him if he hadn't known. It would have been awful but I could have forgiven him. When I found out about it he just laughed. He said all he needed now was treason to complete the list. What in hell do you suppose that meant, Ben?"

I felt sick. I said, "What year were you born, Lila?"

She sighed and stepped back. "You don't have to count on your fingers, Ben. The bastard's my old man. My mother told me about him. When she was on the bottle she didn't talk about anything else. She told me about the good looking ofay who knocked her up, and about the right guy named Ben Parker who slammed hell out of him in a Frisco parking lot. But she never told me his name. I didn't know until a couple of days ago that Johnny Angel was my father."

Martha looked at me and her face went green. "My God!" she said. "And you've been…. Oh, you poor little schnook!"

I said, "I'm going to kill the bastard." I meant it. Lila tittered hysterically. "You don't have to, Ben. I've already done it."

"You've done what?"

"Killed the bastard. Just before I came here. I tried to

break away when I found out who he really was, but he wouldn't let me go. And tonight he wanted to do something nasty. Something a man don't ask a decent whore to do. Right in front of his statue. That's when I killed him."

I said, "Martha, get Nat on the horn and tell him to get up here fast. Look, Lila, are you sure you killed him?"

"I killed him. The bastard," she said, and her face went Indian. She might be Negro and Northern European by birth, but there was a lot of Sonora squaw in her makeup. Growing up as a Mexican had rubbed off on her. Her eyes glowed with satisfaction as she said, "I put six bullets in the cabrone. Right in front of his goddam idol. Bang bang bang. Just like that. He said, 'You little bitch,' and fell down. There was one bullet left in the gun. I aimed it at his head."

I said, "Martha, you keep her here until I get back. Tell Nat to meet me at Angel's penthouse. You know where it is."

"Ben, you're not going up there?"

I nodded. "Lila could be wrong," I said. "And even if she isn't, we might be able to dope something out if the law hasn't found him yet." Then I went down the hall and pounded on Jerry's door.

Angel's apartment door was unlocked. It was nearly dark inside and the flickering light from all the candles threw an eerie light on the body near the altar. Angel lay face down in a puddle of blood. He was stark naked. In the flickering light you couldn't tell if he was breathing or not.

I flicked on my cigarette lighter and found a floor lamp. Jerry and me both felt a lot better with it on. I'd been expecting Boris Karloff to step out from behind the drapery and tell us to get lost. I spotted the gun a few feet from

Angel's naked feet. It was laying near a black leather coach whip.

"The lad's been getting his kicks with whips already," I sighed. It figured. That's the trouble with pure sensualists. Without a little mutual respect, sex has to get dirtier and dirtier to give you a real thrill. And Angel didn't have respect for anyone or anything. I felt kind of sorry for the poor jerk. With all his effort, he hadn't gotten as much out of it as a soda jerk on his honeymoon with the fat little neighborhood chick he loves.

"Hey, he's still alive," said Jerry. "But I have to report this, Ben. You can't mess around with gun shot wounds."

"Later," I said. "Right now I want to know what the damage is."

"Like I said, Ben. He's alive. Just. He's got four slugs in him. One of them's through the spine. I think he's had it."

"He's going to croak? Can't you do something?"

"I can call the ambulance if you'll just shut up and let me. He's a mess. Ten years ago he'd have died for sure. But they'll be able to patch that perforated stomach and colon up. It's his spine I'm worried about. I think it's finished."

"Paralyzed?" I asked. My mouth felt brassy and the hairs on the back of my neck rose. I remembered what Johnny had said about his old man and knew a better Hell couldn't be invented for Angel than a wheel chair. It made you feel like somebody, or something, was writing the script after all.

Jerry nodded and said, "Let's cut the yakking and get the meat wagon up here. I'll phone Knickerbocker. You'd better throw something over him. He's in shock and we've got to keep him warm." I went into the bedroom and got a satin bed spread. I knelt down and covered Johnny with the expensive gold brocade. I got a little blood on it, but it didn't seem important.

Angel's eyelids flickered at the touch and he muttered,

"Somebody get me a drink."

I looked at Jerry. He looked up from the phone and shook his head. "Not with abdominal wounds, Ben."

"I'm thirsty," whined Angel.

I said, "Take it easy, Johnny. We've sent for the ambulance. You'll get a drink in the hospital."

He opened his eyes and looked at me in surprise. "That you, Ben? What in hell you doing here?"

"Lila came to me after she plugged you. For Chrissake, Johnny, couldn't you have even left your own daughter alone?"

Angel's eyes flickered with a trace of his old sardonic humor. He said, "So she told you about it, huh? The little snip! What in hell was wrong with what I done? The Egyptians married their own mothers and sisters and it didn't stop them from building the pyramids."

"Yeah verily, Pharaoh," I said. "But Lila ain't no Egyptian. That chick was raised Spanish Catholic. And, Johnny, you just don't get more Catholic than that."

He sighed. "I figured all the angles, Ben. I had all the loop holes plugged. There wasn't nothing between me and the top of the apple. Nothing I couldn't knock out of the way. And then this little chippy flicks her finger seven times and louses up my whole act." He winced as he tried to move. "My legs feel cold, Ben. I can't move them. I feel like I'm all mush inside. Like my insides are melting. Like I was the wicked Witch of the West. Remember her? The wicked Witch of the West? She had all bets covered, just like me. She had magic spells and an army of purple monkeys and green faced candy soldiers. And then this snotty little girl with a ribbon in her hair throws a bucket of water on her and the poor old witch melted away. I think she was made out of green candy too."

I said, "Listen, Johnny. We haven't much time and I want to cue you in on a few things before the meat wagon gets here. You're going to have to tell the cops you were cleaning the gun and it went off. It'll sound fishy as hell but they'll have to buy it if you stick to it."

Johnny said, "You're nuts. That little bitch is going to burn for this. I'm just hanging on long enough to make a statement that'll put her in the chair."

"The hell you are," I said. "It'll all come out. The whole bit about you and Blanche. With a grand jury investigation hanging over you I don't think you'll want people to know you're the kind of louse who'd take his own daughter. You've got enough to answer for as it is."

"What the hell do I care what people think of me when I'm gone? They can say anything they want about me after I'm dead."

"Relax, Camille," I said. "You're not going to die."

Angel's eyes opened and for the first time since I'd known him there was a flicker of fear in his eyes as he said, "On the level, Ben? I'm going to live?"

I nodded. His frightened eyes searched my face until he knew I was telling him the truth. He licked his lips and muttered, "Jesus, that sort of complicates things, don't it?"

THE END

Lou Cameron was born in San Francisco on June 20, 1924 to a vaudeville comedian and his vocalist wife. After serving in the army during WWII, Cameron found work illustrating comics before turning to fiction writing in the late 1950s. He wrote a number of movie and TV novelizations, and in the late 1970s created the adult western hero, Longarm, which he wrote under the name "Tabor Evans." He also penned the Renegade western series as "Ramsay Thorne" and the Stringer series under his own name, eventually winning the Golden Spur award for his western novel, *The Spirit Horses*. Cameron wrote an estimate of over 300 novels before he passed away in New York City on November 25, 2010. *Angel's Flight* was his first published novel.

Lou Cameron Bibliography (1924-2010)

Novels

Angel's Flight (1960)

The Empty Quarter (1962)

The Sky Divers (1962)

None But the Brave (movie tie-in, 1965)

The Block Busters (1966)

Iron Men with Wooden Wings (1967)

The Bastard's Name Is War (1968)

The Good Guy (1968)

Green Fields of Hell (1968)

Mistress of Bayou LaBelle (1968)

Ashanti (1969)

Big Red Ball (1969)

The Black Camp (1969)

The Dirty War of Sergeant Slade (1969)

The Dragon's Spine (1969)

File on a Missing Redhead (1969)

Hannibal Brooks (movie tie-in, 1969)

The Mud War (1969)

The Outsider (TV tie-in, 1969)

Amphora Pirates (1970)

Before It's Too Late (1970)

Spurhead (1971)

The Tipping Point (1971)

Zulu Warrior (1971)

Behind the Scarlet Door (1972)

The Girl with the Dynamite Bangs (1973)

Cybernia (1973)

California Split (movie tie-in, 1974)

North to Cheyenne (1975)

Barca (1975)

Closing Circle (1975)

Guns of Durango (1976)

The Spirit Horses (1976)

Tancredi (1976)

Drop into Hell (1976)

Dekker (1976)

Sky Riders (movie tie-in, 1976)

Code Seven (1977)

How the West Was Won (miniseries tie-in, 1977)

The Big Lonely (1978)

The Cascade Ghost (1978)

The Subway Stalker (1980)

The Hot Car (1981)

Grass of Goodnight (1987)

The Buntline Special (1988)

Crooked Lance (1989)
Yellow Iron (1990)
Eagle Chief (1990)
The First Blood (1992)

Making of America series
1. The Wilderness Seekers (1979)

Stringer series
1. Stringer (1987)
2. On Dead Man's Range (1987)
3. Stringer On the Assassin's Trail (1987)
4. Stringer and the Hangman's Rodeo (1988)
5. Stringer and the Wild Bunch (1988)
6. Stringer and the Hanging Judge (1988)
7. In Tombstone (1988)
8. Stringer and the Deadly Flood (1988)
9. Stringer and the Lost Tribe (1988)
10. Stringer and the Oil Well Indians (1989)
11. Stringer and the Border War (1989)
12. Stringer On the Mojave (1989)
13. Stringer On Pikes Peak (1989)
14. Stringer and the Hell Bound Herd (1989)
15. Stringer in a Texas Shoot-Out (1989)

As Justin Adams
Chains (1977)

As Julie Cameron
The Darklings (1975)
Devil in the Pines (1975)

As Dagmar
The Spy with the Blue Kazoo (1967)
The Spy Who Came In from the Copa (1967)

As Tabor Evans
Longarm series
1. Longarm (1978)
4. Longarm and the Wendigo (1979)
7. Longarm and the High Graders (1979)
10. Longarm and the Molly Maguires (1979)
13. Longarm in the Sand Hills (1979)
16. Longarm and the Mounties (1980)
19. Longarm in the Four Corners (1980)
22. Longarm and the Ghost Dancers (1980)

25. Longarm On the Old Mission Trail (1980)

29. Longarm On the Big Muddy (1981)

33. Longarm and the Laredo Loop (1981)

37. Longarm and the Stalking Corpse (1981)

41. Longarm On the Barbary Coast (1982)

45. Longarm in Deadwood (1982)

49. Longarm and the Eastern Dudes (1982)

52. Longarm On the Great Divide (1983)

96. Longarm and the Bone Skinners (1986)

100. Longarm On Death Mountain (1987)

104. On the Overland Trail (1987)

107. Longarm in the Bighorn Basin (1987)

110. Longarm and the Hangman's Vengeance (1988)

112. Longarm and the Utah Killers (1988)

230. Longarm and the Wyoming Wildwomen (1998)

235. Longarm and the Wicked Schoolmarm (1998)

236. Longarm and the River Pirates (1998)

238. Longarm and the Blossom Rock Banshee (1998)

257. Longarm and the Nevada Belly Dancer (2000)

260. Longarm and the Church Ladies (2000)

262. Longarm and the Sins of Sister Simone (2000)

265. Longarm and the Mad Bomber's Bride (2000)

270. Longarm and the Lady Bandit (2001)

274. Longarm and the Gunshot Gang (2001)

278. Longarm and the Sidesaddle Assassin (2001)

284. Longarm and the Haunted Whorehouse (2002)

288. Longarm and the Amorous Amazon (2002)

292. Longarm and the Lady Hustlers (2003)

296. Longarm and the Bad Girls of Rio Blanco (2003)

297. Longarm and Town-Taming Tess (2003)
300. Longarm and the Dead Man's Tale (2003)
304. Longarm and the Great Milk Train Robbery (2004)
310. Longarm Sets the Stage (2004)
313. Longarm and the Boys in the Back Room (2004)
316. Longarm and the Unwelcome Woolies (2005)
319. Longarm and the Sidekick from Hell (2005)
327. Longarm and the Ungrateful Gun (2006)

Longarm Giant series
17. Longarm and the Calgary Kid (1998)
20. Longarm and the Hangman's Daughter (2001)
21. Longarm and the Contrary Cowgirls (2002)
22. Longarm and the Deadly Dead Man (2003)
23. Longarm and the Bartered Brides (2004)

As John Wesley Howard
Easy Company and the Suicide Boys (1981)

As Howard Lee
Kung Fu #4: A Praying Mantis Kills (TV tie-in, 1974)

As Mary Manning
The Last Chronicles of Ballyfungus (1978)
This Fever in My Blood (1980)

As Ramsay Thorne
Renegade series
1. Renegade (1979)
2. Blood Runner (1980)
3. The Fear Merchant (1980)
4. Death Hunter (1980)
5. Macumba Killer (1980)
6. Panama Gunner (1980)
7. Death in High Places (1981)
8. Over the Andes to Hell (1981)
9. Hell Raider (1981)
10. The Great Game (1981)
11. Citadel of Death (1981)
12. The Badlands Brigade (1982)

13. The Mahogany Pirates (1982)

14. Harvest of Death (1982)

15. Terror Trail (1982)

16. Mexican Marauder (1983)

17. Slaughter in Sinaloa (1983)

18. Cavern of Doom (1983)

19. Hellfire in Honduras (1983)

20. Shots at Sunrise (1983)

21. River of Revenge (1983)

22. Payoff in Panama (1984)

23. Volcano of Violence (1984)

24. Guatemala Gunman (1984)

25. High Sea Showdown (1984)

26. Blood On the Border (1984)

27. Savage Safari (1984)

28. The Slave Raiders (1985)

29. Peril in Progreso (1985)

30. Mayhem At Mission Bay (1985)

31. Shootout in Segovia (1985)

32. Death Over Darien (1985)

33. Costa Rican Carnage (1985)

34. Golden Express (1986)

35. Standoff in the Sky (1986)

36. Guns for Garcia (1986)

Black Gat Books

Black Gat Books is a new line of mass market paperbacks introduced in 2015 by Stark House Press. New titles appear every three months, featuring the best in crime fiction reprints. Each book is sized to 4.25" x 7", just like they used to be. Collect them all!

Haven for the Damned
by Harry Whittington
978-1-933586-75-5 $9.99

Eddie's World
by Charlie Stella
978-1-933586-76-2 $9.99

Stranger at Home
by Leigh Brackett writing
as George Sanders
978-1-933586-78-6 $9.99

The Persian Cat
by John Flagg
978-1933586-90-8 $9.99

Only the Wicked
by Gary Phillips
978-1-933586-93-9 $9.99

Felony Tank
by Malcolm Braly
978-1-933586-91-5 $9.99

The Girl on the Bestseller
List by Vin Packer
978-1-933586-98-4 $9.99

She Got What She Wanted
by Orrie Hitt
978-1-944520-04-5 $9.99

The Woman on the Roof
by Helen Nielsen
978-1-944520-13-7 $9.99

Stark House Press

1315 H Street, Eureka, CA 95501 707-498-3135
griffinskye3@sbcglobal.net www.starkhousepress.com

Available from your local bookstore or direct from the publisher.

CPSIA information can be obtained
at www.ICGtesting.com
Printed in the USA
LVOW10s2303200317
527896LV00007B/45/P